Books by Frances and Richard Lockridge

Hanged for a Sheep

Murder Out of Turn

The Norths Meet Murder

A Pinch of Poison

H·A·N·G·E·D
FOR A SHEEP

FRANCES & RICHARD
LOCKRIDGE

HarperPerennial
A Division of HarperCollinsPublishers

Originally published in hardcover in 1942 by J. B. Lippincott Company.

HarperCollins books may be purchased for educational, business, or sales promotional use. For information, please write: Special Markets Department, Harper-Collins Publishers, Inc., 10 East 53rd Street, New York, NY 10022.

First HarperPerennial edition published 1994.

Designed by R. Caitlin Daniels

Library of Congress Cataloging-in-Publication Data
Lockridge, Frances Louise Davis.
    Hanged for a sheep / by Frances and Richard Lockridge. — 1st HarperPerennial ed.
        p. cm.
    "A Mr. and Mrs. North mystery."
    ISBN 0-06-092488-8
    1. North, Jerry (Fictitious character)—Fiction. 2. North, Pam (Fictitious character)—Fiction. 3. Private investigators—United States—Fiction. 4. Women detectives—United States—Fiction. I. Lockridge, Richard, 1898–. II. Title.
PS3523.0243H36   1994
813'.54—dc20   93-38614

94 95 96 97 98 ❖/RRD 10 9 8 7 6 5 4 3 2 1

"As good be hanged for a sheep as a lamb."
—Old Proverb

H·A·N·G·E·D
FOR A SHEEP

• 1 •

TUESDAY, JANUARY 21
3:15 P.M. TO 4 P.M.

Pamela North got out of the cab and leaned against the wind. It was a furious wind, banging through the street and full of street dust; as she stood with her back to it, the wind rounded her skirt against her legs and tugged at the cab door as she held it open. The cab driver, peering out at her, knocked his flag down and, with a little shrug, climbed out on the other side and came around. He said it was windy.

"Because New York's on the bias," Pam North told him. "If it weren't, the wind couldn't blow through it this way, because northwest would be up that way."

Pam pointed. The taxi driver looked at her with some doubt, said "Yeh, maybe you got something there, lady," and took the tugging door from her. He hauled two bags from the interior of the cab and reached for a black box with a mansard roof. The box, on being jiggled, yowled. The taxi driver let go of it and looked at Mrs. North reproachfully.

"Cats," she said. He said, "Yeh!"

"Look, lady," he said. "I don't like 'em. Creeps. You know how it is."

"Of course," Pam said. "Lots of people are that way. I'll carry them."

1

Gingerly, he handed out the black case with the mansard roof. It yowled on two tones. The taxi driver looked puzzled.

"Two of them," Mrs. North explained. "But quite small, really. Will you carry the bags up for me?"

He nodded and carried the bags across the walk and up the gritty stone steps to the door of the house. Pam, carrying the cats, followed him and stood just inside the doorway, looking very new against the old house. Sand opened the door while she searched her purse and said, "Good afternoon, Mrs. North." The taxi driver took his money, skirted the black case, which had ceased to yowl, and went away. Back in the cab, he leaned across and looked at Mrs. North and the black case and shook his head doubtfully. Then he drove off. Sand carried the bags inside and Mrs. North lifted the black case over the threshold. It yowled on one note.

"One of them's getting tired," she told Sand. "They've both been yelling all the way, nearly. Is my aunt—?"

"Yes, Mrs. North," Sand said. He looked frail to be carrying the bags, she thought, but there was nothing to do about it. He followed her into the foyer and put the bags down by a small table which held a silver tray and a vase which sprayed daffodils.

"In the drawing room, Mrs. North," Sand said. "Shall I tell madam that you—?"

"No," Pam said. "Don't bother, Sand. If you'll just take care of the bags, please?"

Sand thanked her for the opportunity, started toward the stairs which spiraled grandly upward from the hall, stopped and turned. His face had a slightly different expression, as if he had become momentarily, and within proper bounds, a slightly different person.

"She's Mrs. Buddie again, Miss Pam," he said. "I thought you ought to know." He paused a second. "Since this morning," he added.

Pam said, "Oh." Then she smiled at Sand.

"I should think you'd rather like it, really," she said. "It must be—well, homey? I mean, there's nothing as comfortable as an old name, is there, George?"

Sand really smiled. It was an affectionate smile.

"Well worn, Miss Pam," he said. "A well worn name. It is—more comfortable." Then he became, to a reasonable degree, a butler again. "Thank you, Miss Pam," he said. He carried the bags up the spiraling stairs. Pam watched him a moment, smiling. Then she straightened herself, took a deep breath, and advanced toward the drawing room and Aunt Flora.

"Maybe *this* time I'll really believe in her," Pam thought, stepping into the room which opened off the hall, the box banging softly against her right calf and yowling quietly; the arching feather which rose from the back of her hat and peered out over her face bobbed briskly. "Maybe——." But Pam knew that she was whistling in the dark, because she had not seen Aunt Flora for weeks and because, after even one day's separation, Aunt Flora always drew from her niece an astonished, inward gasp of disbelief. There was, Pam realized anew, never going to be any getting used to Aunt Flora.

Aunt Flora occupied a chair by the fire as few can occupy chairs anywhere. She turned her head as Pam advanced across the room and spoke.

"Hello, dearie," said Aunt Flora deeply. "A new cat?"

Pam's inward gasp interfered with immediate answer. Aunt Flora's wig, which Aunt Flora fondly believed to resemble hair, was as yellow as always. Her face was, as always, immobilized behind its uncrackable facade—unwrinkled because it could not wrinkle, fadeless because it was put on afresh each morning.

"Or," Pam thought suddenly, "maybe once a week. And just *left*."

Aunt Flora's wig was undulant with immaculate curls. Above the waist, Aunt Flora expanded dramatically; Aunt Flora's head sat atop Aunt Flora without the punctuation of a neck.

"I know," Pam thought. "She's built like a snowman. That's it."

Aunt Flora was dressed in a red silk dress, and ruffles fluttered on her bosom. Pam advanced toward Aunt Flora, and, circling, came to a pause before her. Aunt Flora had on red shoes.

"Look at me, dearie," Aunt Flora commanded, deeply. "Did you ever see the like? I said, a new cat?"

"You look—lovely, Aunt Flora," Pam said, her voice hardly weak at all. "Yes—only it's two. Do you want to see them?"

"Sly," Aunt Flora said. "That's what cats are. Of course I want to see them, Pamela. Why two?"

"Because one gets lonely," Pam said. "Everybody advises two." She opened the black box and looked in. "Come on, babies," she said. "Come on, Toughy. Come on, Ruffy." The cats yowled. "They're part Siamese," Pamela North explained. "It makes them yell. They're brother and sister." She paused and looked down doubtfully. "So far," she added.

Aunt Flora laughed. Her laughter was deep and her blue eyes were bright and alive and merrily wise.

"You'd better say 'so far,'" Aunt Flora advised. Her advice was a chortle.

"I know," Pam said. "Jerry says—." She paused, wondering whether to report what Jerry said.

"I'll bet he does," Aunt Flora told her. "Where *is* that man of yours?"

This was characteristic of Aunt Flora. Because she knew where Jerry North was; Jerry North's absence in Texas, where he pursued an author, was part of the complex which had brought Pam North to the home of her Aunt Flora, the family legend.

"Listen, darling," Pam said. "You know perfectly well where Jerry is. I told you all about it on the telephone. There's this man who's written a big book, something like 'Gone With the Wind,' Jerry hopes, and they want to publish it—Jerry and the firm, that is. And there are a lot of other publishers after it, because they all think maybe it's another 'Gone With the Wind.' On account of it's about the South, I guess. So Jerry had to go to Houston, which is where it lives and now he's got to stay there and read it right away, because of all the other publishers. And it's very long. That's why they think it's another 'Gone With the Wind,' really—that and the South. Jerry says he thinks it is even *longer* than 'Gone With the Wind.'"

"God!" said Aunt Flora simply. "About Oklahoma, you say?"

"Texas," Pam said. Aunt Flora said "Oh."

"I never thought much of Texas," she said, dismissing it. "Not a patch on Oklahoma. The Indian Territory. I can remember—."

"Yes, darling," Pam said. "I know you can."

Aunt Flora laughed. It was the hearty laugh of one amused.

"All right, dearie," she said, shaking throughout. "All *right,* dearie."

The cats came out of the box cautiously. They were gray cats. One was a curious dark gray from nose to tail. The other was lighter and had a white collar of fur.

"Ruffy," Pam explained, pointing. "Because of the ruff. But either spelling. And Toughy"—she pointed now at the all gray cat—"because it fits. And—."

Toughy looked at Aunt Flora with growing consternation. Then he yowled, went across the room in a streak and vanished under a sofa. Ruffy, with rather the air of one who performs what is expected, streaked also, squirming under a chair.

"She wasn't afraid," Pam pointed out. "She's the she, by the way. She just didn't want to let him down. Make him feel foolish."

"Naturally," Aunt Flora said. "Why don't you sit down, dearie? They'll come out."

Pam sat down in a deep chair on the other side of the fireplace.

"D'you want a drink?" Aunt Flora said. "I do. Cold weather always makes me thirsty."

A small, rectangular box housed a button on the arm of Aunt Flora's chair. She pressed it.

"I don't know," Pam said. "Isn't it early? But—."

"It's after noon, isn't it?" Aunt Flora demanded. "Well after. What are you talking about?"

Sand came in and said, "Yes, madam?" Aunt Flora looked at Pam.

"Oh," Pam said. "Well—a martini, I guess. Dry please, Sand."

"I'll have the usual sher—" Aunt Flora began. Then she stopped, and an odd expression made its way hesitantly along her jovially painted face. "I'll have a martini too, Sand," she said. "And bring them in a small shaker."

"Yes, madam," Sand said. He turned.

"Remember," Aunt Flora Buddie said, and there was a curious insistence in her voice, "remember, Sand—*in a small shaker.* Don't pour them out!"

"Certainly, madam," Sand said. "Thank you."

There was a somehow nervous silence for a moment after Sand left. Then Aunt Flora spoke.

"You may as well know," she said. "It's one reason I wanted you here, really—one reason I insisted, I mean. You see, dearie, some-body's trying to poison me."

She broke off and stared commandingly at Pam North.

"I won't have it," she said. She said it with finality. Then she wait-ed, having passed the conversational turn to Pam. It came over Pam, disconcertingly, that this was by no means one of Aunt Flora's little jokes.

"But—" Pam began. Aunt Flora seemed to feel that this finished her niece's turn.

"Surprises you, doesn't it?" she enquired. "Surprised me, too, I can tell you. Arsenic, they say. I had the—that is—there was an analysis." She looked at Pam defiantly. "I threw up," she said. "Naturally. And they say it was arsenic. I might be dead."

"Yes," Pam said, "I can see you might."

"Except," Aunt Flora went on, "somebody miscalculated. There wasn't enough. Except just to make me sick as a horse." She paused, reflectively. "Why a horse?" she enquired. "They never were in the old days."

"Than a dog," Pam substituted. She paused in turn. "Cats too," she added, "particularly when they eat grass. They seem to enjoy it."

"Sly," Aunt Flora said, apparently of the cats. "Where are they, do you suppose?"

"Under things," Pam said. "They'll come out. But for heaven's sake, darling—*arsenic!*"

"Think I'm crazy, don't you?" Aunt Flora enquired, in a tone more of detached interest than disclaimer. "Maybe. Your mother always thought so, Pamela. Still does, I shouldn't wonder. It's the husbands—she wouldn't understand about the husbands."

"Listen, darling," Pam said. "Let's get back—you're—you're worse than Jerry says I am. When it's merely that he can't follow, really. But you—" Pam paused, thwarted. "You said somebody tried to poison you. Who?"

Aunt Flora shook her head.

"Any of them, dearie," she said. "They're all here. For my money, of course—the major's money. Because I've hung on to it, Pamela.

And to the house and—by the way, I'm Mrs. Buddie again. I decided this morning. Stephen's gone, you know. The whipper-snapper. He's the only one it couldn't be, because it was after he left. But there was no reason to go on being Mrs. Stephen Anthony, was there dearie?" She paused a moment. "Silly name," she added. "I think myself he made it up."

"But, then, why—" Pam started to say. Aunt Flora shook her head. It involved shaking most of her torso, also, but Aunt Flora was up to it.

"Don't ask me, Pamela," she said. "You'd never understand, any-way—you and your Jerry. But—well, take the cats, dearie. The little cats of yours. One cat gets lonely."

"Of course, darling," Pam said. "I didn't mean that. And I think you're probably too hard on Stephen, really. But—" Pam pulled herself back to the business at hand. "You really believe—" she began. But Aunt Flora signalled with her eyes, as Sand brought cocktails, still in their shaker.

"Just put them down, Sand," Aunt Flora directed, pointing toward a coffee table by the side of her chair. "We'll pour them."

Sand put them down and learned there was nothing else and went out. Aunt Flora picked up the glasses in turn and examined them; with a piece of paper tissue she polished their bowls. Then, and only then, did she pour from the shaker and before she drank she sniffed doubtful-ly at the cocktail. Pam sniffed too.

"Smell all right, don't they?" Aunt Flora enquired. Pam nodded, not happily.

"Well," Aunt Flora said, reasonably, "we can't live forever, dearie. Here's to us."

She drank. Pam wished briefly that Jerry were not so far away. Then she drank too. After the first sip both women waited, as if for an expected noise. Nothing happened. They drank again, with increased confidence.

"Well," said Aunt Flora. "One more bridge crossed. And now, Pamela—I want you to find him. That's really why I insisted on your coming. From all I've heard, it's right up your alley. Pamela North, the Lady Detective."

"That's nonsense," Pam said. "Of course I'll help, if I can. But it's Bill you want—Bill Weigand. Lieutenant William Weigand. He's the detective."

Aunt Flora shook her head and body emphatically.

"No," she said. "Not your policeman, Pam. Not yet anyway, dearie. For now, anyway, we'll just keep it in the family. Because it's already in the family, you know. Just a little arsenic among relatives, dearie."

• 2 •

TUESDAY
5:15 P.M. TO 7:30 P.M.

Pam carried a squirming cat under each arm and dumped both on the bed. Then, before she did anything else, she went to one of the two windows at the end of the room and looked out into the street. She tried to look up toward Fifth Avenue, but the projecting corner of the apartment house next door cut off her view. The projecting corner of the apartment house on the east cut off her view toward Madison Avenue. Directly across the street, which was the only way left to look, another apartment house rose haughtily. The view, Pam decided, was not inspiring. She wondered absently why her first inclination on entering any room was to look out of it and decided that she would have to ask Jerry. He, she was sure, would have a theory.

"He always has theories," she told the cats, which sat on the bed and stared at her, turning their heads in unison. "I wish Jerry were here. Particularly if there's going to be arsenic." She paused and shook her head at the cats. "Not for him, sillies," she told them. Ruffy talked back, cat fashion, in an affectionate growl. Toughy jumped on Ruffy's head, evidently intending to smother her. Ruffy hissed and wiggled, emerged and instantly regained calm. She began to wash behind her right shoulder. Toughy looked at her in surprise, got the idea and began to wash his tail. Ruffy jumped down, landing on the carpet with a soft plunk, and began to smell the room. It was, Pam thought, going to take Ruffy a long time if she did it all. It was interesting to discover that houses still had such large rooms.

But when you thought of it, as Pam idly did, it was odd that people should still be living in New York in such houses as the old Buddie house, which could hardly have been really a new house when Major Alden Buddie was a small boy and neither a major nor, by any reasonable stretch of the imagination, a prospective husband for so different and—well, remarkable—a woman as Flora Pickering, who was then an even smaller girl and living on a farm in Upstate New York. The house was older than any of them and, even considering Aunt Flora herself, more unexpected. More unexpected, certainly, as a final home for Flora Pickering, afterward Flora Buddie, afterward Flora McClelland and Flora Craig and Flora Anthony and now, as of this morning, Flora Buddie again.

"Well," Pam told Toughy, her mind reeling a little, "Auntie got around, when you come to remember it. And now back here, with somebody trying to kill her."

The old house was too dignified for such absurdities as Aunt Flora and attempted murder. Even now, when it had been hemmed in and, seemingly, pushed back, it was too dignified. It went up five stories and had a bow window on the second floor—the second floor if you counted the anomalous layer which was half under the earth and half above it as the first. Once it had been one of a row of dignified houses, all very like it in essentials, all representing good addresses for the right people. It had stood after most of the others had come down. Because Aunt Flora had been stubborn, it now stood in retreat, with a mountain of an apartment house on each shoulder.

It would once have been easy for Aunt Flora to sell it. The company collecting land parcels for the building on the Fifth Avenue corner had been willing to buy first, and after that the company building the apartment next door to the east had made an offer. But Aunt Flora had refused both, and the companies had shrugged corporate shoulders and gone on about their building. They had used all the ground the law allowed, coming flush to the building lines along the sidewalk, so that the Buddie house, which had once withdrawn genteelly from passers-by and only licked at them with the tongue of its brown front steps, now looked merely sunken in.

"And," Jerry had once told Pam as they stood in front looking at it, preparing to confront Aunt Flora and pay their somewhat awed respects, "and now it's merely something called 'permanent light and air.' Which means that nobody will ever make another offer."

The permanent light and air did not, however, belong to the house itself. In the house itself you looked on the outer world as through a key-hole.

Pam's room was in front, two flights up from the entrance foyer. It was wider and deeper and higher than was altogether convenient in a bedroom. Its windows were so tall and wide that it was impossible to open them for merely a little air, so that one had to choose between the resident air and a chilling hurricane. It was at a fine level to collect street noises and street dust and it had only one smallish closet, opening in the wall opposite the windows and next the door leading to the bath-room, which had a ventilator down which a peculiar, oily dust descended, when the wind was wrong, and from which the dust fell into the bathtub. But the room had dignity.

"Of course," Pam said, in a rather lonely voice, since Toughy had now joined his sister in smelling the room, "you can't have every-thing."

At the moment, she thought again, it would be nice to have Jerry. She had read his most recent letter hurriedly when she left the apart-ment to spend a dutiful few days with Aunt Flora—and to avoid look-ing at Jerry's empty bed at nights—and now she took it out of her purse to read again. Jerry said it was cold in Texas. He said it in an aggrieved tone since, being a New Yorker, he had supposed that Texas was warm, even in January. He was about a third of the way through the book, and was afraid that it was *very* like "Gone With the Wind." He missed her.

Pam curled up at one end of the big bed when she reached this part and read it carefully. He missed her very much. He was explicit to a degree and in terms which made Pam feel deliciously unlike an accepted and familiar wife.

"Wow!" Pam said, softly, and read part of the letter again. It would be *very* nice to have Jerry home. It would also be nice to find a secure place in which to sequester the letter. Pam looked around, shook her head and put the letter back in her purse. She looked at the little ball watch dangling from a chain around her neck. She dismissed Jerry from her thoughts, went to the bathroom, wiped part of the oily dust from the tub and turned on the hot water. It ran slowly, but it ran hot. The cats followed her into the bathroom and Ruffy put forepaws on the edge of the tub and peered at the water. She was about to get in to investigate when Pam caught her.

The tub was full, finally, and the cats shut out. Pam ignored their protests at this arrangement and relaxed. She wiggled her toes and regarded them. She really should, she decided, have polish put on again. But then, in the winter, what was really the point? Jerry hadn't mentioned her toes.

"Now," Pam told herself, "to get to Aunt Flora and arsenic." To start somewhere, you could start with the people in the house. So——. She went over what Aunt Flora had told her while they finished their second cocktail in front of the fire. Take the servants. Sand, the butler; the new maid, Alice Something; the cook, not new, Something Jensen— Clara, that was it. Mrs. Clara Jensen. There must be a lot of work for Alice Something in a house as big as this if Sand only butlered and Mrs. Jensen only cooked. And then there was Harry.

Where you put Harry, Pam found it hard to say. He was not a servant, certainly, although often he puttered around the house, putting in fuses, pasting down loose flaps of wall-paper, putting knobs back on drawers. It had never been easy to place Harry—Harry Jenkins, that was it. He lived on the top floor, and he was almost as old as Aunt Flora and much thinner and it had always been a question in Pam's mind whether he went with the house or with Aunt Flora. Probably, she decided, squeezing water out of a sponge and letting it flow in again, he went with Aunt Flora. Probably he was something out of Aunt

Flora's past. If things were really to be investigated, that would have to be found out.

Now you came to family. And things became complicated because Aunt Flora's family was apt to prove intricate.

"I'm the simplest," Pam thought. "Just a niece, child of a sister. After that——." Pam sighed and washed her face, absently.

It was a little simpler if you started with the Buddies, since Aunt Flora had now formally declared herself again a Buddie and since, after all, the Buddies represented the senior branch. Flora Pickering had started with the Buddies when she was a rounded, pretty girl and was visiting relatives in the Indian Territory long before it became Oklahoma. Then she had met Major Alden Buddie, of the New York Buddies, on post in country still not tame, and married him quickly and lived with him very happily until he died when they were both still young. And he had left her what must then have seemed all the money in the world and was still, Pam suspected, a good deal of it.

Of the Buddies, extant and in the house, there was first a second Alden, now also a major, and his daughters, Clem who was eighteen and Judy who was two years older. Clem and Judy, Pam gathered, were staying with their grandmother during an undetermined interim, its length eventually to be decided by the final army assignment of their father, who was now majoring at a nearby army post. In New Jersey, that was it. It was a bad time to predict the future of an army major and his daughters. The major himself stayed at Aunt Flora's when he was in the city, which apparently was often.

That evening, at any rate, there would be a fourth Buddie—Christopher. He was another grandchild, the son of Dr. Wesley Buddie, who was the second son of the first Major Buddie and Aunt Flora. All that Pam could remember about him was that he was going to be a playwright.

"If it kills him," Pam added to herself, swabbing.

That did for the Buddies immediately under foot.

"I can widen it later if I have to," Pam thought, and sighed.

After Major Buddie, Aunt Flora had married Robert McClelland, who later became a chief of police, and was now happily divorced. By

him, Aunt Flora had one son named Something or Other McClelland
and Something or Other had had, in turn, a son named Bruce, whom
Pam knew rather well and liked, and who was reporting on a morning
newspaper.

"And who isn't around," she said to herself, thankfully. "Not
tonight, anyway. But I don't know about arsenic day."

After Mr. McClelland there came, surprisingly, a baseball player,
named Craig and from him another son to Aunt Flora. She ran to sons,
Pam decided. This son was Benjamin Craig, who lived staidly at home
with his mother and who staidly managed a branch bank. He was
vague in Pam's mind, but he would be there at dinner time. There
would be a good many to dinner. Reluctantly, Pam emerged from
warm water and towelled. Remembering Jerry's letter briefly, she
regarded herself in the long mirror set into the door. She surprised herself by blushing slightly and went into the bedroom, which was chilly
enough to make her dress quickly.

In a long, dark-blue dinner dress, Pam sat in front of the dressing
table mirror and regarded herself. She nodded to herself, in reasonable
contentment and again wished Jerry were there.

"Particularly," she thought, "if there are going to be murders. But I
don't suppose there are, really. It wouldn't be like Aunt Flora to be poisoned."

She slipped through the door carefully, but Toughy was too quick
for her. He bounced past her into the hall, galloped to the head of the
stairflight, and stared down. Then he bristled, and the hall—the hall
and the whole stair well and probably the whole house—was filled
with indignant barking. Toughy snarled and bristled and a young voice
said, indignantly, "Oh!"

A brown cocker was pulling up the stairs, restrained by a green
leather leash. At the other end of the leash was a slender girl. She was
hatless and her black hair swept down to her shoulders. She pushed it
back, looked up indignantly through dark blue eyes and said, in an
indignant voice, "A Cat!" The brown cocker, his suspicions thus coun-
tenanced, bounced at the end of the green leash and barked with every
bounce.

Pam moved quickly. She swept Toughy into her arms and was rewarded by scratches which Toughy had been intending for the cocker. Toughy wriggled and stared back, still hissing. But Pam opened her bedroom door enough to push him through, closed it quickly enough to thwart the emerging Ruffy, and turned to face the cocker and the girl. The cocker was allowed to bounce on to the landing, and the girl followed him. She said, "Pam! Hullo darling. Is it yours?"

"Yes, Judy," Pam said. "Sorry if we frightened Nemo."

Judy Buddie shrugged it off.

"Although," she said, "we'll have to keep them apart. It's nice to see you, Pam. Did you just come?"

Pam told her when she had come. Judy was interested, but abstracted. She had, she explained, to rush.

"Grandma wants everybody to dress," she said. "I expect it's for you, Pam—although Grandma always likes it. She says she likes people to look pretty. Can you picture Uncle Ben looking pretty? But the cocktails will be better. They always are when we dress. Did you ever notice?"

"Cocktails always are," Pam told her. "It's because we're always more dignified and—formal. Or so Jerry always says."

"Where is Jerry?" Judy wanted to know. "Grandma didn't say anything about him."

Pam told her. Judy hesitated a moment, said "Oh" in a certain tone, seemed uncertain whether to go on or stay, and then went on rather abruptly. Judy was very young, really, Pam realized. It was hard at twenty to know when and how to end a conversation. Judy, followed reluctantly by Nemo, who wanted to investigate the door which sheltered the cat, went on up the stairs. Then she paused, leaned rather perilously over the balustrade—with casual disregard of a possible drop of better than fifty feet down the stair well—and called back, "Cocktails in the library. Be seeing you." Then, evidently conscious of social duty smoothly performed, she went on up the stairs, slim legs flickering behind the iron balusters.

Not Judy, Pam decided; it couldn't be Judy. The administration of arsenic to a wealthy grandmother, and particularly to one so unexpectedly perspicacious as Aunt Flora often proved herself, would be an undertaking requiring poise. Aside from everything else, attempted murder would embarrass Judy. She wouldn't, Pam decided, know which way to turn.

"And poisoners have to," Pam decided, going down a flight to the library. The door leading from the hall to the library, which stretched across the front of the house and was under Pam's bedroom, was open and when she entered Pam thought for a moment she was the first. But Benjamin Craig arose with dignity from a low chair by the fire and advanced toward her, a plump hand extended and a plump face smiling carefully.

"Cousin Pamela!" Benjamin Craig reported, with an air of pleased surprise, although it was improbable that he was really surprised. "How delightful!"

"Hullo, Ben," Pam said. Of course, she thought, he really is my cousin, but why make an issue of it. She looked at him. "You're looking well," she told him. Benjamin always liked, she knew, to be told how he looked. Now he nodded.

"Fine," he said. "Never better. And where's that young man of yours?"

Jerry would appreciate that, Pam thought, allowing her hand to be enfolded by Benjamin Craig's plump, warm hand. Because after all Ben couldn't be over fifty—couldn't even be fifty—and Jerry wasn't so young as all that. However—

"Texas," Pam told Cousin Benjamin. "Reading a book."

Which is strictly true, she added to herself, waiting with anticipation for Cousin Benjamin to be confused. He merely blinked and continued to regard her as if she were a long lost depositor.

"How's the bank?" Pam enquired, one thought leading to another.

The bank was doing well enough, it appeared. But Benjamin Craig permitted an expression of concern to cross his soft features, indicating that the bank was still much on his mind, however he might unbend. He was about, Pam suspected, to go into the bank in detail, but Aunt Flora intervened. Aunt Flora came briskly through the door from the hall, looking very much like a red top except that she was not spinning. She said "Oh, here you are," to Ben and, "Have a nice rest, dearie?" to Pamela. Neither remark seemed to need, or to expect, an answer.

"My feet," said Aunt Flora with feeling. "And why don't you ring for Sand, Ben? It's time for a drink." She thought this over sternly as she deposited herself in the most comfortable chair. "Past time," she added, nodding vigorously from the waist. Her wig slipped a little, Pam thought. Ben rang. Flora looked at Ben and Pam affectionately. She looked at Ben a second time and said, with a maternal note which came a little unexpectedly, that he looked tired. Ben accepted this comment much as he had Pam's assurance that he was looking in the pink. He nodded, appreciatively.

"The bank, you know," he said. "But it's nothing. A glass of sherry, perhaps."

Sand appeared momentarily at the door, but drew back to let Major Buddie precede him. Major Buddie came in solidly, one foot firm after the other; shoulders very straight and very broad; face ruddy. Sand came behind him, by way of contrast. Major Buddie marched forward, bent crisply and kissed his mother's cheek, said "How'r'y?" to Ben and turned to Pamela. He said "Hello, young lady," to Pam and took her hand firmly.

"Hello, Alden," Pam said. "You're looking—"

Major Alden Buddie, Jr., was not impolite but he was not interested. He broke in.

"Oh, Sand," he said. "Rye and plain water, will you?" Sand bowed. Major Buddie turned back to Pam, raising his eyebrows in step. "Martini," Pam told him. She went on, a little hurriedly. "Aunt Flora and I are drinking martinis today."

"Out of a small shaker," Aunt Flora reminded her. Sand said, "Certainly, madam."

"No olives," Aunt Flora said, on second thought. "You can't tell. Recesses."

Benjamin Craig and Major Buddie looked at her with vague interest and then at each other. Ben smiled and Major Buddie accepted the smile. That was the way mother was, the half-brothers agreed. Pam shook her head very slightly at Aunt Flora. Ben ordered sherry, and the major, suddenly very businesslike, demanded that somebody tell him where the girls were.

"Gadding about," he said, with disfavor.

"Not Judy, anyway," Pam told him. "She came in a few minutes ago. With Nemo. He barked at the cats. At one cat, rather."

"Cats?" said Major Buddie. "What cats? Who's got cats?" He looked suspiciously at his mother.

"I have," Pam told him. "Very nice cats."

She said it defensively. But Major Buddie surprised her.

"Of course," he said. "All cats are nice." It sounded very obvious as he phrased it. "Where are they?"

Pam told him where they were. She said that she would take him to see them, or bring them to see him, after dinner. If he liked.

"Naturally," said the major. "Always like to see cats. Some sense to cats. The others—always yapping. Bite, too."

That must be dogs, Pam decided. Then she remembered. It was a family joke; Major Buddie, who was afraid of nothing else that anyone knew about, was afraid of dogs. Or was, at any rate, unhappy in the presence of dogs. He had a chance to prove it almost at once, because Nemo entered. The cocker observed the family group, and the major observed him, haughtily. Nemo rounded the major, flattened himself at Pam's feet and smelled her shoes. He looked up at her with doubt and went to Aunt Flora. He put his forepaws on Aunt Flora's precipitous knees and looked at her longingly. She pulled his drooping ears and he extended his right paw. She took it and his soft brown eyes filled over-whelmingly with devotion.

"Hello, everybody," Judy said from the doorway. "Oh—Dad! Sorry about Nemo. Come here, Nemo."

Nemo went. Judy snapped the green leash to his collar and pulled him into the hall. She returned, alone.

"Hooked him to the banisters," she explained. "Dad doesn't like him much, do you, Dad?"

"No," the major said. "Where's your sister?"

Judy answered almost too quickly.

"She wanted me to tell you," she said. "She ran into a girl she used to go to school with and—and—. You know how it is, Dad. She said not to wait dinner, because she might be late. It was Mary Conover, I think, and you know—."

She's talking too much, Pam thought. Too much and too—too *anxiously.* But then Sand came in with a tray and bottles and glasses and Judy stopped, as if she were glad to stop. Sand put the tray down on a side table, poured drinks and passed them. Pam watched him pour martinis from a small shaker into clean glasses; watched Aunt Flora's glass until she lifted it from the serving tray. All right so far. Pam took her own drink. Sand made good martinis, but they needed lemon peel. Judy, her father's eyes on her, took sherry with her Uncle Ben. Pam remembered she was standing and that the men were standing with her and stepped backward to a chair. For a moment they sipped.

"Hello, everybody," a new voice said. "Oh, Pam! Darling! Hello!"

You would have guessed that Clem and Judy Buddie were sisters or you would, at the least, have wondered whether they might not be sisters. But still they were very different. Clem, standing in the door, was not so tall as Judy. She was quicker, brighter, more compact—and infinitely more assured. Her eyes were blue, like Judy's, but her cascading hair, uncovered, was auburn. The brightness came from her hair. It came from her reddened lips and from a kind of excitement which entered the room with her.

"Clem!" Judy said, half starting up. "I thought—."

There was a look between the sisters. And did Clem's jaunty head shake just perceptibly? Nobody else seemed to notice, and Pam wondered. I'm seeing things, she thought. It's this arsenic business.

"Stood up, darling," Clem said gaily. "Helen didn't show. Kept me—."

"Oh," Judy said, and spoke quickly. "It *was* Helen, wasn't it? I couldn't remember—I told Dad Mary Conover."

There was no pause this time.

"No," Clem said. "You were mixed up, darling. Helen. But it was only half a date, really—just one of those I'll-come-if-I-can-but-don't-wait sort of things. And apparently she couldn't. And anyway, if I'd known that Pam—."

She crossed to perch on the arm of Pam's chair, to say, "Ah, martinis!" with evidences of delight and to call to Sand across the room. Sand brought a martini for Clem Buddie.

It was family talk then for a quarter of an hour, with Ben refilling his glass and Judy's, waving his half-brother toward the whiskey decanter, solicitously carrying the martini shaker to his mother and to Pam. Then Sand announced dinner. They went back to the dining room, which occupied the rear half of the same floor. The table was long and candles lighted it. Aunt Flora went firmly to the far end and sat in the large chair; for Pam she patted the one at her right. Pamela sat down, feeling surrounded by family. She looked around the circle—Cousin Alden Buddie at her right, Cousin Benjamin at the end, opposite his mother as became the resident son, the girls opposite.

"Looking for Chris, dearie?" Aunt Flora enquired, while Sand passed soup. "Thought he'd be here myself. Telephoned Sand he couldn't come at the last minute. Something about dinner with somebody who might put on his play. Nonsense, of course."

"Well," Pam said. "You can't tell about the theater."

It seemed a safe remark.

"And Harry eats in his room when there's a crowd," Aunt Flora added. "Doesn't like crowds, Harry doesn't. Particularly of relatives." She looked around the table. "Can't say I do myself," she added. "Except you of course, dearie."

She looked around the table. Everybody was eating soup.

"I tried to get him down tonight though, dearie," Aunt Flora went on. "And I wanted Chris, too."

She spoke loudly enough for all to hear. There was something in her voice which commanded attention.

"Wanted you to see them all, dearie," Aunt Flora continued, only ostensibly to Pam. "See them all in a bunch. Because it was one of them, Pamela."

Everybody was looking at Aunt Flora, now. Her yellow wig bobbed.

"That's right," she said. "One of you. Tried to poison me, one of you did. Arsenic, it was."

She looked around at them, her eyes bright with interest.

"Nasty stuff, arsenic," she said. "People put it in soup."

There was a clatter. Benjamin Craig dropped the filled soup spoon he had raised to his lips. It clattered against the soup plate and fell in. It splashed.

• 3 •

Tuesday
8:15 p.m. to About Midnight

Dinner had not, accountably enough, ranked as a successful occasion. Sand, to be sure, moved silently and in order between the tiny serving pantry, supplied by an electric dumb waiter from the kitchen on the ground floor, and the table. Aunt Flora had, to be sure, eaten with apparent satisfaction and Pam had found time, between observations, to nibble contentedly. But it could not be argued that anybody else had really enjoyed the meal.

There had been exclamations, and expressions of shocked and incredulous amazement, and demands for further information. These Aunt Flora had squelched. She did not, she said, see any reason for discussing unpleasant things at meal-time. Even she noticed a slight inconsistency in this attitude, but met it by explaining that she had thought they would want to know before they ate. This logic escaped Pam and seemed to escape the rest; it was evident, indeed, that few of the others had left much interest in food. But all of them, under Aunt Flora's watchful eye, took token bites. They took their bites with a kind of bravado, feeling, it was evident, like kings' tasters.

Dinner ended and Aunt Flora, acting the role of hostess with uncharacteristic zeal and what Pam suspected to be sardonic amusement, suggested coffee in the library. The suggestion was not received. Benjamin Craig discovered he had some things to go over and went off, looking a little pale, to go over them. Pam caught the movement of Clem's head which summoned Judy to join her and watched the two girls, Judy so evidently uneasy and Clem so contradictorily secure, go out together. This left Aunt Flora and Pam and Cousin Alden, who drank coffee grimly and stared at Aunt Flora.

"Now, mother," the major began sternly. But Aunt Flora shook her head and said "no" with decision.

"Not right after dinner," she said. "When you're as old as I am, son, you'll learn to think of digestion."

And then, when the major had shown signs of beginning again, Aunt Flora had got up, announced that she was going to her room to rest and gone. The major looked at Pam and, after a moment, nodded.

"Now, Pamela," the major said. "What's all this? Eh?"

Pam felt that she should come to attention, but resisted the impulse. She wondered what to tell him. The major's eyes commanded.

"Well," Pam said, "your mother thinks somebody tried to poison her. With arsenic."

"Obviously," said the major. "I heard her."

"I don't," Pam said, "know all about it, of course. Only what she told me. She wants me—."

That, Pam decided, was one of the things she might better not have said. But Major Buddie only nodded.

"Yes," he said. "I've heard about you. Intelligence work. Nonsense, of course. Eh?"

It was of course nonsense, Pam agreed. She had merely happened, because she knew a detective, to have been a little involved in the investigation of one or two small matters. Small murders, to be exact. Nothing that a soldier would really regard as killing. And in them she had been hardly more than an onlooker.

"But," she added, "you know your mother. When she gets an idea—"

"Yes," the major said with conviction. "Well—go on. What did she tell you?"

The question was sharp, demanding. But then, Pam thought, the major's questions would normally be sharp and demanding, admitting of no shilly-shallying by the answerer. And what, in fact, had Aunt Flora told her—told her that afternoon, skirting the topic and rebounding from it; now direct and concise, now tricked by her own impetuosity into rather remarkable divagations? There had been in it, somehow—and at the time almost relevantly—the life story of a horse Aunt Flora had owned as a girl, and there had been a good deal, at one time or another, about the first Major Buddie. It appeared that, had he lived, he would not have permitted anybody to poison Aunt Flora.

Pam edited her account as she gave it to the first Major Buddie's son. He probably remembered that, a little over two weeks ago, Aunt Flora had been suddenly and unaccountably taken ill an hour or so after breakfast, and that for several hours she had grown progressively more ill and that, at her instruction, Sand had finally called a doctor? The major remembered.

"Something she ate," he said. "As I told her at the time."

"Yes," Pam said. "It was something she ate. Arsenic."

The major snorted, but Pam shook her head.

"Really," she said. "She had—it—analyzed. She got the report yesterday. That was why she called me up and insisted that I come to stay for a few days, with Jerry gone and everything. But she didn't tell me then. Only this afternoon."

"Well," the major said, "show you the report, did she? From the chemist or whatever it was? Showing arsenic?"

Pam shook her head. Aunt Flora had merely stated, not proved.

The major snorted again.

"Imagined it," he said. "Nobody tried to poison her. She just ate something. Getting old, mother is, and won't learn. Bad diet."

"I don't see," Pam said, "how she could have imagined arsenic into—into what she threw up. Do you?"

The major looked triumphant.

"Didn't *show* you the report, did she? Probably made it up. Or perhaps she did get a little arsenic, by accident, and—"

"I should think," Pam said, shaking her head, "that it would be hard to get arsenic by accident. Unless you were a plant."

"What?" said the major. "Eh?"

He looked at her darkly.

"Spraying," Pam explained. "It's accident to the plants, I suppose. I—oh, it just came into my head."

The major regarded her head with suspicion, but apparently decided to waive the point for one more important.

"I'll tell you what it is," he said. "All in the family, Pamela. Mother's getting a little queer." He paused. "Queerer," he said. "God knows—"

"Yes," Pam said. "I know. But I've never thought she was, really. Not that way. Not to making up arsenic."

The major's face delivered itself of an expression of concern; his voice grew lower and more solemn.

"Afraid you're wrong, Pamela," he said. "We've been worried recently. All of us—even Ben." His tone removed Ben to the outer fringes. "Been acting very odd, mother has. And that last husband of hers!" The major's tone removed the last husband to the ultimate limbo. "That in itself," the major added, sadly.

"I only met him once," Pam said. "He seemed rather—" She stopped for a word.

"Exactly." The major took over. "Of all the nasty, slippery, unwholesome weaklings I ever saw your Stephen Anthony—sorry, my dear, I mean your aunt's Stephen Anthony—is the prize." He stared at Pam, waiting for the words to sink in. "And I've seen some," he added, counter-sinking them.

"I always wondered," Pam said, "how Aunt Flora who—who'd known so many men, and seen so many things, could bring herself—. I'll admit I always wondered that. But I think she was lonely."

"Nonsense," the major told her. "Three sons, hasn't she? Counting Ben, that is. And a lot of grandchildren. And that what's-his-name—Harry—who hangs around all the time. Don't think much of him, come to that. But at least he's somewhere near her age. This young—weasel!"

"Relatives aren't quite the same," Pam said. "Even children, I should think. I mean, I'm very fond of the cats, but they aren't the same as Jerry. Not really."

The major looked a little baffled, but put himself again on the track. Years before he had tried to make a rule not to listen to Pamela North when she interrupted and said things nobody could understand. He had, even earlier and with little more success, made a similar rule as regarded his mother. They threw men off, but, after all, they were women.

"Well," he said, "can you imagine anything queerer than marrying this Anthony worm? That's when we began to wonder—even Ben. I never denied mother was odd—not in the family, anyway. But after that! Well!"

Pam felt some sympathy.

"But after all," she pointed out, "she's got rid of him, now. And gone back to Buddie."

The major nodded.

"Odd," he said, "how she always goes back to Buddie. In between. Makes it difficult for Ben, at the bank. Checks and things." This last thought seemed to please him mildly. "A bit of a blow to him too, I'd think. Never goes back to Craig, I notice. Must make Ben think." He paused. "Even Ben," he added.

"Not," he added after a moment, "that Fred Craig wasn't quite a man. Ball player, you know. I thought he was great, as a kid. Had a real spitter. Don't see those, nowadays. Held the ball like this."

The major doubled his hand in a complicated gesture, as if he were throwing a ball. He looked very interested.

"Taught me," the major said. "Had quite a spitter myself, once. Not like Fred's, of course." He moved one finger a little to the side. "More like this, it was," he said. He stared at his hand reflectively. Then he remembered that Pam was looking at him and, when he met her eyes, smiled.

"Never made anything of it, of course," he said. "Where were we?"

"You thought your mother was getting queer and imagining things," Pam said. "Because she married Anthony. And that she wasn't poisoned at all, really. But she was, I think."

The major stared at her.

"Yes," Pam said. "I think she was. I don't think she imagined it. It didn't feel as if she imagined it. When she was talking, I mean. Were you here that day?"

The major looked at her suspiciously.

"Here?" he repeated. "Yes, as a matter of fact. I was here. Didn't think anything of it; none of us did. She was all right the next day. Or pretty near."

"And the rest?" Pam said. "The girls? Ben? Harry Upstairs?"

The major nodded after the girls and Ben. Then he repeated, "Upstairs?"

"I always think of him," Pam explained, "as Harry Upstairs. I know it really isn't that—Harry Something-else. Parsons?"

"Perkins," the major said. "Yes, he was here. And Chris and young McClelland, I think. Even Anthony came in."

"Really?" Pam said. "Anthony too?"

The major nodded.

"There's the man, if it was anybody," he said. "Kind of thing he would do, you know. Funny his showing up, too."

It was funny, Pam agreed. Because he had not, before then, been around for weeks.

"A month, anyway," the major said. "She threw him out. And that day he turned up bold as brass and wanted to see her. Did, too. Ben let him in. Ben would."

"But," Pam pointed out, "Aunt Flora must have agreed to see him."

The major nodded slowly. She had agreed to see him, although she had already complained of feeling unwell. He had been in her room for almost an hour until her illness had really begun to worry her.

"Talking," the major said. "God knows what about. She's not leaving him anything."

It was a surprising remark. Pam remembered not to look surprised.

"Not a cent," the major said. "Saw the will myself. Everything to the family. A quarter each to Ben and Wesley and me and young McClelland gets his father's share. And charities, of course—things like that. And bequests. Nice penny for you, Pamela."

"That will be nice," Pamela said, sincerely but without thinking. "I mean—well, it will be nice. After all, I'm much younger."

"Obviously," Major Buddie said. "Not blaming you, my dear. Don't think you'd feed her arsenic to get it, though. Doubt if anybody would." He paused. "Even Ben," he added, thoughtfully but with less conviction. "Don't think anybody tried to kill her," he said, finally. "Lot of nonsense. Something she imagined."

"Well," Pamela said. There was no use arguing it.

"Now," said the major, having attended to the matter of the arsenic. "That's settled. How about the cats? Siamese, you say?"

"Partly," Pam told him. "On their mother's side. I could bring them down."

The major said "nonsense."

"Can't go lugging cats around," he explained. "Makes them nervous. We'll go to them. In your room, eh?"

The cats were in Pam's room, curled up together on the bed. Pam was worried, but they accepted the major with interest and appreciation. Ruffy turned on her back to be stroked and, as the major bent to reach her, Toughy, displaying glad surprise, leaped to the major's back. He flattened himself on the major's shoulders, looping behind the soldierly neck, and began comfortably to chew an oak leaf. Cats liked the major, too, and Pam said as much.

"That's what he always does with Jerry," she said. "Nobody else, though. But he tears clothes."

The major said "nonsense" again, but on second thought lifted Toughy down. Toughy chewed the oak leaf to the last but failed to detach it. The major was younger, and almost whimsical, playing with cats. He played with them for several minutes, and said they were fine cats.

"Siamese doesn't show much," he admitted, standing up at length. "However—nice to have cats around a house." He looked at Pam and shook his head. "The girls prefer dogs," he said. "Odd, eh?"

"Well," Pam said, "it needn't be one thing or the other. Dogs are all right, too."

"Handsome of you," the major said. He moved toward the door, stopped and faced her.

"No detecting, now, young lady," he said. "All nonsense anyway. But don't *you* go poking around." His expression was stern, commanding. "That's for policemen," he said. "Authority. If there were anything to detect. But, between us, just her vaporings. Not as young as she was. We've got to face it."

"I see," Pam said, intentionally vague. "Maybe you're right." There was still no use arguing it. She and the cats followed the major to the door and she was very careful not to let the cats out when he left, and he was careful to help, slipping sideways through the door in a manner which might have left an unfortunate impression with anyone who saw him. But apparently no one did.

And then, after he had gone on up the stairs, Pam found that she had remaining, of cats, only Ruffy. Toughy had been too much for them. She went to the hall and called softly and from below there came a small, responsive cry. Pam said "Damn" in a tone of resignation and went down after him. She heard him scampering ahead and wondered what dog-lover had started the libel that cats moved softly, in sneaky quiet. Toughy and Ruffy audibly trampled, even on carpets.

Toughy galloped down the hall and, apparently, into the library. Someone—Sand, presumably—had turned out the lights there, save for one small lamp near the door, since she and Major Alden Buddie had gone upstairs. Toughy waited for her near the light and then, as she approached, decided that it would be amusing to be terrified. He dashed off, tail up and twisted, and scrambled under a sofa which jutted at right angles to the wall near the fireplace. Pam went over, got on hands and knees, and reached. She touched fur with her fingers. The fur receded. Toughy made a small, throaty sound of pleasure and interest. But now there was no reaching him from this side.

Pam, moving more quietly than a cat, went around the sofa. If she were quick enough she might get him before he retreated again toward the front. She dropped, got a hand on him and heard Judy Buddie say, from near the door.

"But, Clem, I had to make up *something*. I had no way of knowing—"

"All *right,* darling," Clementine Buddie said. She had evidently said it before; her voice held amused, affectionate impatience. "Of course you couldn't know. Although why you settled on Mary Conover, when even Dad knows she's pure—drip. Not that the poor dear will think about it, I expect."

There was a little pause. Pam started to get up before things went further. And then Judy said, in a different tone,

"Why don't you give it up, Clem? Give *him* up? Because, if you are talking about poison—."

Clem interrupted. Her voice had changed, too. It was light and amused, still, but the amusement was a thin film over something which was not amusement at all.

"Hold it, Judy," she said. "Hold everything, sister. One girl's poison, another girl's meat. And I hear enough from—from other people. If I want to see him, I want to see him."

"Wherein," Judy said, rather dryly, "you and he appear to differ. If he did stand you up, as I gather."

"All right," Clem said. Her voice wasn't amused, any longer. "Skip it, darling. Something came up. He—he called me."

"Did he?" Judy's voice was without particular expression.

"Of course," Clem said. She was angry, now. "Don't get ideas, Judy. He's—he feels the same way. And nobody had better spoil it."

"All I've done," Judy said, "is to try to help. And been made to look like a fool for my trouble."

There was a little flurry. Clem was evidently displaying affection. Her voice—she can do a lot with her voice for a girl of eighteen, Pam thought—showed affection.

"Of course, darling," Clem said in a rush. "Of course you have. Don't think it isn't wonderful of you. It's—other people." She paused. "The snake, chiefly," she said. Clem repeated it, describing the snake. She gets around, Pam thought. There was a little gasp from Judy.

"Clem!" she said. "Not—him. Not the snake."

There was a moment's pause.

"I'm afraid he does," Clem said. "The—the—"

Words failed her, this time.

"I'd like to—scotch him," she said, and now she sounded as if she were almost crying. "I'd like to—I'd hate to tell you what I'd like to do, Judy. Because you know what he's after."

"What he's always been after," Judy said. "From the first. But I don't see what he could do. Or, I mean, how—who would he go to?" Her voice suddenly grew more anxious. "Listen, Clem," she said. "He doesn't *know* anything, really? I mean—there isn't anything he *could* know?" And then there was another pause, and the answer—whatever it was—came without words.

"Oh—Clem!" Judy said. "Darling—how?"

"Could I?" Clem finished. Her voice was level, and there was a kind of hopelessness in it. "Oh, darling—such a sweet darling. You can't really imagine, can you? Not *really*. My little sister!"

But that wasn't right, of course. It was really Clem who was the "little" sister; by two years the little sister. There's only one thing makes a woman feel as Clem feels toward another woman, Pam thought. Older and—pitying. However unhappy, still pitying of those who have not their unhappiness. Poor Clem. And now there was no coming out.

"An eaves-drip!" Pam told herself, bitterly. "Why do I? I'm *really* getting to—to snoop around."

And it hasn't anything to do with the arsenic, Pam thought, as she heard the two girls—who seemingly had merely stepped inside the library for the moment of their talk, and were now going on again toward their rooms at the top of the house—as she heard them, after a moment, move out into the hall and begin to climb the stairs. Obviously, it has nothing to do with the arsenic. It meant that Clem was in trouble of some sort, and of a not obscure sort, and that Judy was her confidante. It meant that somebody called "the snake" was an ingredient in the trouble, but not the main ingredient, and that Clem would like to scotch the snake. But it was absurd to think that Aunt Flora was the snake, particularly since the snake was "he." And it was Aunt Flora, if anybody, who had been scotched. "Scotch the snake, not kill him." Which was what had happened to Aunt Flora.

Pam gathered Toughy up and he tried to crawl to her shoulders, now, and was suppressed after a short tussle.

"When I'm wearing a suit, darling," Pam said. "Not when I'm practically bare."

And then she went out into the hall and heard a door close at the top of the house, which meant that Clem and Judy were safely in their rooms. She went on. This time she got both cats in at once. She read Jerry's letter again and then, finding a correspondence block in one of her bags, she sat hunched in bed and answered it. She told him about Aunt Flora and the arsenic, and about the major's fondness for cats, and something, although not all, about Clem and Judy. And then, with the news supplied, she told him about other things. She had no idea how late it was when she had finished, because she had forgotten to wind her watch. But it felt late.

She was just falling asleep, smiling over Jerry's letter and what she had said in answering it, when she heard a door slam. It sounded a good way off, but in that case it must be a heavy door, pulled hard.

"In the middle of the night!" Pam thought, just as she was falling asleep. "People oughtn't to."

· 4 ·

WEDNESDAY
8:15 A.M. TO 9:05 P.M.

Pam awakened suddenly because light was coming at her from an unfamiliar angle. She couldn't be at home, because that was not the way light came at home, so she must be in the country. But it wasn't right for the country, either—oh, yes. Aunt Flora's. Pam came awake and looked at her watch, which couldn't be right because it said 11:45. And it couldn't, obviously, be either 11:45. Then she remembered that her watch had stopped last night when she was writing Jerry. Probably it was late and she was disrupting a household schedule.

So she said "later" when her mind suggested a bath, and dressed quickly and slipped out without letting the cats escape.

"I'll bring you breakfast," she told them. "And some nice clean newspapers. You just wait."

Aunt Flora had told her that breakfast was any time, in the breakfast room. It was behind the drawing room, on the second floor, which you could call the first if you counted the kitchen-servants quarters floor, as a basement. Feeling pleasantly alive, and inclined to think that the major was probably right about the arsenic, Pam went quickly down the two flights. She was surprised when the clock in the hall showed only a few minutes after eight. She wasn't late, then. And the breakfast room proved that she was early, because as she went in one door Alice, the maid, was just coming in from the pantry with dishes and a cloth. Pam said good morning and the maid smiled and said "Good morning, Mrs. North." The table, long enough to take the family, was set only far enough out from the wall to leave room for chairs and Pam, thinking to keep out of Alice's way, went to sit behind it.

Then she thought that possibly it would be easier for Alice, and involve them both in less conversation, if she went into the drawing room until breakfast was ready, as evidently it wasn't now. Unconsciously, she put her hands down to push back the chair so that she could stand and then, although she had begun to lift herself, she froze as she was, half crouching and it got suddenly much colder in the cheerful little room.

Because, soft and unmistakable against Pam's right hand, hair was brushing. Hair that had a slight oiliness to it and was only coarsely soft and—. Pam, pushing herself to the side, looked down. And then she shrank and said "Oh! No!" and looked up to find Alice staring at her. And then, as if in slow motion, she saw the tray of dishes begin to fall from Alice's hand and saw the maid's mouth open. While the maid's scream was still beginning, Pam realized that Alice could see under the table what she could only feel. Then, frantically, Pam had pushed the table aside so that she was freed and was staring down at the body lying limply across a chair, half hidden by the table drawn close to it.

It was the body of a man and it was horrible. What should have been the back of the head was a red, shapeless mass, with tatters of black hair. And from the head, blood had run down the hanging arms and had, while it was still liquid, flowed along red fingers to the carpet, and widened there into a pool, almost black against the red of the carpet. Pam was, for the moment, very sick, and her ears were filled with the frantic, high screaming of Alice.

It was Sand who called the police, she thought. His old voice was thin and trembling. He came back and said "the police say not to touch anything, please," and took Alice away. Ben Craig was there by then, and Major Buddie, and once the major stood with his arms extended, barring the door to somebody—probably to Clem and Judy. And then Pam brushed past him, not quite so sick now, and after a moment she found a telephone in the cloak room opening off the entrance foyer.

Perhaps she could still catch Bill, she thought, and dialed his home. When she heard the answer she spoke quietly, but tried not to hurry her words.

"Dorian," she said, "is Bill there?—it's—it's terribly important. This is Pam."

There was momentary lightness in Dorian Weigand's voice as she acknowledged this last, unneeded, item of information. But Pam could hear her calling, "Bill." Then she heard running feet and what sounded like a window being raised, and again, more distantly, "Bill!" Then Dorian was back.

"He's coming," Dorian said. "Probably thinks I'm being raped—I had to yell down to him. He'd started. What is it, Pam?"

"Oh," said Pam, her voice a wail. "It's murder, Dorian! And I thought it wasn't going to be. And I need Bill."

Then, or in a moment or two, Bill Weigand was at the telephone and saying, "Yes, Pam?"

"It's murder," she said. "George Sand called headquarters or the precinct or something. But we need you. It's horribly bloody and I found it."

"George Sand?" Weigand repeated. "What, Pam?"

"The butler," Pam North told him. "It really is, and it always—Oh, Bill! We haven't time for that now. You've got to hurry. Even if it isn't Aunt Flora."

"Right," Weigand said. "I'll hurry. Who is it?"

"I don't know," Pam said. "A man. Nobody I know—but—but maybe I do, really. Because we haven't turned it over and from the back it's—oh, Bill! And Jerry's way off in Texas."

"Right," Bill said again. "Where is it?"

Pam gave him the address of Aunt Flora's house.

"Right," Bill Weigand said. "Five minutes. Keep them away from it, if you can, Pam."

Then he was gone. Pam found a chair and sat down. Sand could keep them away from it. Or the major. Or even Cousin Ben. She had to give her insides a moment's calm.

But it was only a moment. Then the doorbell rang violently and, because she was nearest, she went to the door, and threw it open for the uniformed men who stood there.

"Bill's coming," she told them. They looked puzzled. "Bill Weigand," she said. "Lieutenant Weigand, of Homicide. I called him. I'm Mrs. Gerald North."

"The hell you are," said one of the men.

The first policeman went, as Pam directed, back to the breakfast room and then, in a moment, people began to come out into the drawing room—Clem and Judy and then Cousin Ben and after them Major Buddie, not in uniform. One of the policemen came as far as the door after them, and stood looking darkly. The four stood irresolutely for a moment and the policeman said, speaking loudly because the air was quivering now with the sound of police sirens, "You can sit down. Sit down, everybody. We'll take care of everything."

It sounded consoling, Pam thought, and sat down. More consoling than convincing, however. She sat with Ben and the major and the girls and nobody said anything. Men came through the foyer and went along to the door under the stairs which led to the pantry and hence to the breakfast room. Sand and Alice, the maid, came in through the door which led directly from the breakfast room to the drawing room. Still nobody said anything, but only sat, everybody but Major Buddie looking a little smaller than life, and listened to the sirens as more police cars piled up in the street outside. Then Aunt Flora, in a red something, appeared at the hall door and stood looking at them.

"Well?" Aunt Flora said. "Enough to wake the dead! I'm surprised at you, Alden."

The major and Ben stood up and the major spoke. He said, "Sit down, mother."

"It won't wake the dead," Pam said, unexpectedly. And then to the major, who seemed most in control of things, "Who is it?"

The major looked angry. His face was red.

"Won't let us look," he said. "Nonsense, eh? Wouldn't expect it of Sand."

There were flashing lights now from the door leading to the breakfast room. That would be the photographers. And a bell clanged outside—that would be the ambulance, coming or going. Then Pam heard a familiar voice and after a second Bill Weigand stood in the doorway. Pam got up and went across to him and said, "Hello, Bill." Then she turned and faced the others.

"This is Lieutenant Weigand, everybody," she said. "Of the Homicide Squad. An acting captain, really."

"All right, Pam," Bill Weigand said. His hand touched her arm. "Quit shaking, Pam," he said. His voice was quiet and confident, as if she would quit shaking once he told her to. She quit shaking.

"Well, young man," Aunt Flora said. "So she sent for you, did she? In spite of what I told her?"

She seemed to be talking to Weigand, but she was evidently talking to Pam. And Pam answered.

"It isn't that, Aunt Flora," Pam said. "It isn't the arsenic. This is something else—a man. In the breakfast room."

"Absurd," Aunt Flora said, with vigor. "Perfectly absurd. What's he doing in there, dearie?"

"Well," Pam said, "he's dead, darling. I'm terribly sorry."

"Should think you would be," Aunt Flora said. She seemed about to go on, but Weigand held up a hand. He spoke quietly, but Aunt Flora stopped talking.

"You're Mrs. Buddie?" Weigand asked. "Pam's aunt?" He did not wait for her to answer, but said, "Right.

"I'll want some of you to look at him in a minute," he said. "As soon as the Medical Examiner has finished. It won't be pleasant but—."

"What do you think we are, young man?" the major broke in, testily. "Bunch of old women, eh? Think we've never seen dead men before."

"Well," Weigand said, his voice still quiet. "Many people haven't, you know. I gather you have, Mr.—is it Buddie?"

"Major," the major said, more testy than ever. "Naturally it's Buddie. What would it be, eh?"

"Smith," Weigand said. "Or Jones. Well, Major, we'll let you—." He broke off as somebody spoke to him from the room behind. He said, "Right, Mullins." Then he turned back and spoke to the major. "All right, Major," he said. "Suppose you have a look, since you don't mind."

"Don't be a fool," the major said. "Of course I mind. Nasty business. Nasty head wound, from the looks of it. What do you think I am, man? Eh?"

Weigand looked at him, half smiling. The major made throat sounds, but marched toward the door. Weigand let him go through, told the others to wait a moment, and followed him. There were the voices of several men from the breakfast room. Then the major came back, looking not so ruddy. He looked at Aunt Flora in embarrassment. He cleared his throat. Then he spoke hurriedly.

"It's that husband of yours, mother," he said. "Got himself killed. Sorry to tell you. Hate to be the one—."

"Don't mumble, Alden," Aunt Flora said. She looked at Major Buddie with interest. "Didn't kill him, did you, son?" she enquired. She seemed to expect to be told.

"Oh," Clem said, very suddenly. She stood up, slender in a long, fitted blue robe. "The snake—somebody's killed the snake." She turned to her sister. "Darling," she said. "Somebody's killed the snake!"

Judy looked pale. She held out her hand toward Clem. "Don't, Clem," she said. "Don't talk like that."

"I should think not," Aunt Flora said. "So you called him 'snake' did you—you—you—flibbertigibbet. I'll have you know—" She broke off. "Anyway," she said, "it was very disrespectful, dearie. When he was your—" She paused again to consider. "Your step-grandfather," she said. "Poor Stevie." She did not, it was clear, care to pretend great grief.

"She's just interested," Pam thought. "I suppose she's just run out of other feelings."

Bill Weigand was back in the door again. He looked at her a moment.

"Pam," he said. "I'd like to talk to you a minute. To start with. Not here. Right?"

"Yes," Pam said. "Of course. Can we use the library, Aunt Flora? And—and I'm terribly sorry about poor Stephen."

"All right, dearie," Aunt Flora said, sitting down in a swirl of red. "Of course you are. Everybody's sorry. But nobody's surprised, are they?" She looked around her family. "All down on poor Stevie, weren't you? All of you. Thought he was after your share, didn't you? All of you."

"Mother," Major Buddie said, "you talk too much. Too much nonsense, eh?"

His mother stared at him. Then she stared at Ben. Ben was still standing, looking a little shocked.

"Well," she said. "Say something, Ben. Unless you shot him."

If Ben planned to speak, Lieutenant Weigand's words stopped him. Weigand still spoke quietly, but his voice had a new timbre.

"What makes you think he was shot, Mrs. Buddie?" Weigand asked. "Nobody said he was shot."

Pamela looked quickly at her aunt. Aunt Flora transferred her stare to Weigand.

"Well," she said, "wasn't he shot?"

Weigand nodded, slowly.

"Yes," he said. "He was shot. Through the throat. The bullet came out his head. Did you know that too, Mrs. Buddie?"

"Don't be a fool," Aunt Flora said. "How would I know about it? But I expect men to be shot. It's natural." She paused. "And women poisoned," she said.

Weigand looked at her. His face showed nothing in particular, but Pam thought he was puzzled. She stood up and said, "Come on, Bill," and started for the door.

"The library, Aunt Flora," she said. Aunt Flora said, "Naturally." She looked at Weigand.

"Watch yourself, dearie," she advised. "Don't forget about Jerry."

Weigand said nothing as he followed Pam up the stairs. But in the library he sat down on a chair by a table and looked at Pam and then, after a moment, said: "Whew!" Pam nodded slowly, half smiling, and said, "Isn't she?" She lighted a cigarette and, after a moment during which he stared at nothing, Weigand lighted a cigarette.

"Well?" he said.

Pam started at the beginning.

Aunt Flora was her mother's sister. Stephen Anthony had been her fourth husband. "And Clem called him 'the snake,'" she added.

"I noticed," Weigand said. "And your aunt isn't much upset, is she?"

"I don't know," Pam said. "It's hard to tell. She—she's peculiar, don't you think?"

"Yes," Weigand said. "Very. Why did she think he'd been shot, do you suppose?"

Pam thought a moment, and then thought of something.

"She grew up in the Southwest," she said. "Where there was lots of shooting. She may—well, may think of murder and being shot as synonymous. D'you think?"

Weigand nodded. He said it might be that way.

"And women being poisoned," Pam went on, "because she thinks somebody has been trying to poison her." She paused. "And I think they have," she said. "But Cousin Alden doesn't."

"The major?" Weigand said.

Pam nodded. Weigand said he would try to get them straight. Starting with Aunt Flora. And her fourth husband who must, certainly, have been much younger. Pam nodded. Forty years, anyway, she thought. Younger than either Alden or Ben.

"Start with the major," Weigand said.

Alden Buddie, Pam told him. Major, A.U.S. On duty at an army training center in New Jersey. And Aunt Flora's oldest son. Son of a previous Major Alden Buddie, whom Aunt Flora had married first.

"And Ben Buddie?" Weigand enquired. "Another son?"

"Ben *Craig*," Pam told him. "A son by Aunt Flora's third husband. A baseball player."

"Ben?" Weigand asked, in surprise.

"Ben's father," Pam told him. "Don't be silly, Bill."

"Pam!" Weigand said. "And the girls?"

"The major's children," Pam explained. "Their mother's dead. And there's Dr. Wesley Buddie, who is the major's full younger brother and—."

She broke off, because Weigand was staring out through the door into the hall. He met the enquiry in her gaze.

"Somebody going downstairs," he said. "A young man. Newcomer, apparently. They'll hold onto him, however."

It might, Pam told him, be Christopher Buddie, Dr. Wesley Buddie's son. He had been expected the evening before and might have come late and stayed over. Or it might, of course, be Bruce McClelland. Weigand looked a little tired.

"Who," he asked, "would Bruce McClelland be? More family?"

Pam nodded. Another grandson, she explained. Son of Robert McClelland, deceased, who was, in turn, son of Aunt Flora and her second husband, who was also Robert McClelland. Weigand ran the fingers of his right hand through his hair.

"Jerry," Pam said. "Just like him. But this isn't my fault, is it? It's Aunt Flora's, if anybody's."

"Right," Weigand said. "Quite an aunt. No wonder—" He broke off. "Tell me about the poisoning," he directed. Pam told him. It was about two weeks ago. Aunt Flora had become violently ill a short time after breakfast and had been violently ill the rest of the day and that night. Then, slowly, she had recovered. A doctor had been called and at first diagnosed acute indigestion. But he had apparently not been easy in his mind, because he had retained specimens. And the specimens, on Aunt Flora's statement, had revealed arsenic. Weigand said it sounded fairly conclusive, and Pam nodded.

"I think so," she said. "But Cousin Alden thinks she's just sort of—sort of flighty. He thinks she imagined it, because of Stephen."

"Listen, Pam!" Weigand said. "Be helpful."

"Flighty," Pam explained, "because she married Stephen who was—oh, a worm or something. Or a snake. The arsenic, he thinks, is just another proof. But I don't know."

"No," Weigand said. "We'll have to find out, of course. Now about this murder. The butler—is he really named George Sand?" Pam nodded. "The butler seems to think you found the body. Right?"

Pam corroborated the butler's impression. She told about finding it. Her face looked strained as she remembered. Bill Weigand made con-

soling sounds. Then Pam shook it off and said, suddenly, "The cats!"
Weigand was puzzled.

"They haven't had breakfast," she said. "*Or* clean newspapers. I
forgot."

Weigand looked amused.

"So you brought Toughy and Ruffy," he said. "That must help."

Pam was a little indignant. She said it did, because they led her into
things. Already they had led her—She broke off.

"Go on, Pam," Weigand said. "You ought to know that by now."

Pam went on. She told him, quoting as exactly as she could, of the
conversation she had overheard between Clem and Judy when she was
fishing for Toughy under the sofa. Weigand seemed interested. Then
Pam remembered something else.

"Just as I was going to sleep," she said, "I heard a door slam. Could
that—could that have been the shot, do you suppose?"

Weigand was interested again. He said it might have been, if she
were far enough away. She told him where her room was, and he
thought that might be far enough. On the other hand, it might have
been a door slamming. In any event, it was worth knowing about,
because it might fix a time. What was the time? Pam looked at him,
guiltily.

"Didn't you look?" he asked. She nodded.

"Only," she said, "it had stopped. I forgot to wind it, or something."
She studied Weigand's expression.

"I'm sorry," she said. "But it was after 11:45, anyway." She told
him how she knew.

But Weigand continued to look very disappointed in her. I'm not,
Pam thought, starting this one very well.

• 5 •

WEDNESDAY
9:05 A.M. TO 9:40 A.M.

Weigand sat for a moment looking at Pamela North and then he shrugged. He said, abstractedly, that it might have been a help.

"However," he added, "what are M.E.'s for?"

"Don't you know at all?" Pam asked. "When, I mean?"

Obviously, Weigand told her, they could guess. Rigor was fairly well advanced; you could guess, then, that death had come somewhere between six and eight hours before the body was examined. It was examined at 8:35, which would make it between midnight and 2:30 or thereabouts. But rigor was a variable, depending on too many things. For one thing, it might be hastened if violent muscular activity had immediately preceded death.

"And?" Pam said. "I mean, did it?"

Weigand was still abstracted, but he smiled faintly. He said he wasn't there. However—

The course of the bullet had been rather odd. It had entered the throat below the jaw and ranged upward through the head, blasting its way out through the rear of the skull. That could happen, obviously, in several ways. For one thing, Stephen Anthony might have been lying flat on his back.

43

Pam shook her head, doubtfully. Bill Weigand admitted that the posture would, under the circumstances, have been an odd one. Other theories were more persuasive.

The killer could, for example, have been kneeling in front of Anthony, who in turn was standing. That was a possibility, although it presupposed another odd situation. Or the killer might have been sitting in a chair, with Anthony standing above him. Or perhaps leaning down toward him. That was, off-hand and until they knew more, the most likely supposition. And in that event—

"Suppose," Weigand said, "that Anthony was worked up about something and that the murderer wasn't, or wasn't showing it. Anthony was walking up and down, perhaps. Excitedly. Then he leaned over toward the murderer, perhaps put his hands on the arms of the chair and stared down at him."

"Or glared down," Pam said. Weigand said, "Precisely."

"That would have been right for the angle," he went on. "If we suppose Anthony threatening his murderer, or shouting at him. And the murderer, perhaps with the weapon concealed—in his pocket, perhaps, or in a bag—had fired up at him. The impact would have knocked Anthony over backward, probably, at that range."

Pam nodded. She thought.

"The gun wasn't there, I gather," she said. "Or you'd have mentioned it."

"No," Weigand said. "It wasn't there." He broke off and after a moment began again.

"Were they down on him?" he said. "The family—Benjamin Craig and Major Buddie and the rest. All of them, as your aunt said. Or was she—well, merely talking?"

"They didn't like him," Pam said, after thinking a moment. "Nobody really knew much about him, except that he was always hanging around places. Night clubs and places. And, of course, he was so much younger. And then there was Aunt Flora's money. Although I don't know if he gets any. Would have got any. Because I don't know how Aunt Flora felt about him, really."

"Did you ever meet him?" Weigand said.

Pam nodded. Once or twice, she thought.

"And—?" Bill Weigand prompted.

"*I* didn't like him," Pam said. "Oily, I thought. But, then, I like Aunt Flora." She looked at Bill. "I really do," she said.

"Right," Weigand said. "I've an open mind. Has your aunt a great deal of money?"

Pam said she had always supposed so. Aunt Flora had always looked like a lot of money. "And then there's this house," she pointed out. But whether these things meant merely plenty of money—"like thousands a year," Pam explained—or lots of money, like millions, Pam didn't know.

"Only," she said, "she's leaving me some. Won't that be nice?"

Weigand said it would be very nice. He relapsed into thought, and emerged from it to go to the hall and stand for a moment at the head of the stair-flight leading down. Then he called, "Mullins!", his voice cutting through the amorphous sounds below. Pam heard Mullins's heavier, blunter voice answer.

"O.K., Loot," Mullins said. And then he came largely up the stairs and, after a moment, stood beside Bill and looked down at her.

"Hullo, Mrs. North," he said. "You got a nice one this time."

"Hello, Aloysius," Pam said, sweetly. "Didn't I, though?"

"Listen, Mrs. North," Mullins said earnestly, looking suddenly rather warm. "Not so much Aloysius, huh? I didn't mean—" He looked around, a little anxiously and as if for support. "Jerry ain't here?" he said.

"Right," Pam said. "Jerry ain't here, Mr. Mullins. And don't talk as if I—as if I went out after them." But she smiled and Mullins looked relieved.

"O.K.," he said. "It was just a figure of speech."

Both Weigand and Pam looked at him with some surprise. He looked pleased. "A figure of speech," he repeated, cheerfully. "You want some of 'em, Loot?"

"Right," Weigand said. "Get your little book. And get Mrs. Buddie." He stopped, puzzled.

"Mrs. Buddie?" he repeated. "Why isn't she Mrs. Anthony?"

"She changed," Pam said. "Yesterday morning she decided to be Mrs. Buddie again. She always did."

"Listen!" Mullins said. "Sounds like she knew, don't it? I mean—she was sort of getting ready to be a widow." He looked at the others. "Sort of," he said. "In advance, like."

Weigand looked interested but Pam shook her head. She said she didn't think that meant anything.

"Because," she said, "she was always going back to Buddie. After she was Mrs. Craig, and Mrs. McClelland and now after she was Mrs. Anthony. Because she'd sent him away, you know. Stephen Anthony, I mean." Then she, in turn, broke off and her expression became thoughtful. "The funniest thing about it," she said, "is that he wasn't supposed to be here at all. Let alone dead."

Weigand nodded and Mullins looked a little puzzled.

"Right," Weigand said. "I was thinking of that." There was a momentary pause, apparently while he thought of that. Then he said, "Right. Mullins. Get Mrs. Buddie, will you?"

Unexpectedly, Aunt Flora had changed from red to black. But black did not, somehow, look like mourning on Aunt Flora. The yellow wig, the resolute complexion, defied grief. Aunt Flora continued to look like Aunt Flora. She occupied a chair and looked back at Sergeant Mullins, who looked at her with evident awe.

"Well," she said, "have you found out who killed him?" She looked at Pam, who was rising as if to leave. "Did you tell them about the poison, dearie?" she enquired. "About poisoning your old aunt?"

"Really, Aunt Flora!" Pam said. "You make it sound so—yes, I told them you thought somebody had tried to poison you."

"Thought?" Aunt Flora repeated. "Thought? Nonsense! I didn't think. Somebody gave me arsenic." She turned to Lieutenant Weigand. "What do you think of that, young man?" she demanded. "Going to let them get away with it? Or what?"

"No," Weigand said. His voice was quiet and he smiled, slightly. "We'll try not to, Mrs. Buddie." He saw Pam moving, not hurriedly, toward the door and said, "Stay around, Pam." Pam looked pleased.

"Suppose," Weigand went on, "we go into that first. Right? Tell me about the poisoning, Mrs. Buddie."

Aunt Flora told him, repeating what proved to be an accurate report by Pamela North. She had had breakfast and become afterward very ill. She had been very ill for hours.

"Sick at my stomach," Aunt Flora said, explicitly. "Sick as a horse."

The doctor had given her medicines and thought at first that it was no more than an acute digestive upset. "Old fool," Aunt Flora observed, cheerfully. And she had got better, but no thanks to him. She had insisted on the analysis because she had never had an illness like it before.

"And I've had plenty, dearie," she said, with new interest. "Always something. Mostly stomach. You never know when you're young what the stomach can do." She looked at Weigand, demanding attention. "Never!" she repeated. "If I didn't take care of myself every minute, I wouldn't answer."

"But," Weigand said, "this was different. And you were suspicious. Why?"

Aunt Flora was not clear about that. It developed that this illness was more violent than any in the past. "Not that there's anything *mild* about my stomach," she added, quickly. Then she looked at Mullins. "Scared me, this did," she reported. "It would have scared you, dearie."

Mullins looked uneasy and nodded.

"Right," Weigand said. "It's pretty late now, of course. You should have come to us as soon as you got the report, Mrs. Buddie. Attempted murder is—well, better than murder." He smiled. "For everybody," he added. "However, that's spilled milk."

"Arsenic," Pam improved. "Spilled arsenic. Under the dam."

"The bridge," Weigand told her. "Please, Pam."

"Of course," Pam said. "*Over* the dam. I get them confused."

"Be still, dearie," Aunt Flora said, equably. "You talk like your mother."

Weigand came in hurriedly.

"For example," he said, "you probably don't remember what you had for breakfast that day. What day was it, by the way? Exactly?"

"Two weeks ago Monday," Aunt Flora said. "And I had the usual."

"Which was?" Weigand prompted.

"Well," Aunt Flora said, "first the citrate salts, of course. Then prunes. I have to eat prunes every day. And take the salts."

"Right," Weigand said, again hurriedly. "And afterward?"

Afterward, Aunt Flora said, had come the usual breakfast food—hot because it was winter. And some pancakes with a little bacon. And an egg—"no, I always allow myself two eggs on Monday."

"Why?" said Pam, involuntarily.

"Because it's Monday," Aunt Flora told her. "Starts the week, dearie. You need it for Mondays."

There was a slight pause, during which everybody looked a little puzzled. Weigand aroused himself.

"Right," he said. "And toast, I suppose?" Pam listened for irony, but heard none. Neither did Aunt Flora, who nodded.

"Obviously," she said. "And coffee, of course. Oh—and a little honey to go with the toast, of course."

"Of course," Bill Weigand said. "It—it gives the poisoner—well, opportunity. Plenty to choose from."

"Listen, young man," Aunt Flora said, her yellow wig bobbing a little. "Call that breakfast?"

"Yes," said Bill Weigand.

Aunt Flora looked at him.

"Nourishment," she said. "That's what you need, young man. Pickers!"

It took time to get things out of Aunt Flora, but, with breakfast out of the way, Bill Weigand persevered. Ben Craig had been in to see her that morning, before breakfast. The girls had looked in while she was eating, sitting on the bed and nibbling toast. The major had come in, too, before she had finished and taken the girls away when he left. Harry was down to tell her they needed new fuses and to get the money to buy them. Harry? Harry Perkins, obviously. And who, while they were on the subject, was Harry Perkins.

"Harry?" Aunt Flora repeated, as if the question were absurd. "Harry's just—an old man. Don't try to make a mystery about Harry."

Weigand was patient. They were not trying to make mysteries. On the contrary. Who was Harry?

"An old friend of my husband," Aunt Flora said. It did not clarify.

"Which, Aunt Flora?" Pam said. "Which husband."

"My husband, dearie," Aunt Flora said. "I only had one *husband.* What you'd call a husband. The major, dearie."

She consented, although obviously thinking it of small import, to explain. Many years before—half a century before—Harry Perkins and Alden Buddie had been young men together and devoted friends. Harry Perkins then had been in business, successfully. But something happened—something vague and misty with years and not, it was clear, any too well understood by Aunt Flora even at that distant time. And Harry, suddenly pathetic and beaten, had gone desperately west and found Major Buddie there—a very young major, since things were moving rapidly in the army in the west in those days, and a confident one; a man of assured future, who saw no reason not to take his battered friend in charge, and as a responsibility. And Buddie had money even then, although not as much as inheritances made it before he died a few years later. And Harry—well, Harry was, in some obscure manner, part of Aunt Flora's inheritance from her young husband. Perhaps he was somehow a remembrance.

"A keepsake," Pam said, suddenly. Aunt Flora looked surprised and then nodded her head and torso, so that the yellow wig slipped a little.

"That's it, dearie," she said. "A keepsake. I've—well, kept him ever since. I suppose it's strange, but I never thought about it. It just seemed natural to keep him."

So that was Harry, explained. Adequately? Bill Weigand wondered and shrugged without moving his shoulders. They would wait and see. They would see, among other things, Harry himself; in the course of routine procedure they would see everyone. And as to last night?

Aunt Flora was not helpful. She had not expected Stephen Anthony to come to the house. She had not seen him when he did come, or heard anything of the shot which ended his life. She had gone to her room early.

"Everybody was upset," she reported, mildly. "Gabbling around. So I went to bed."

She had read a while, and then gone to sleep. She hadn't bothered to notice the time. She had noticed nothing until the sirens awakened her. Then she had come down.

"Come to think of it," she remarked, "I still haven't had breakfast. You have breakfast, dearie?"

"No," Pam said. "No, I guess I didn't. I don't know—."

"Nonsense," Aunt Flora said. "Keep up your strength, dearie. Feed all of you, if you like."

Weigand shook his head, first for himself and then for Mullins, who had begun to look receptive. But then he nodded at Pam.

"Good idea," he said. "Coffee, anyway."

Pam said, "Well—" and then, when Weigand nodded again, more emphatically, followed Aunt Flora out. The two detectives looked after them.

"Quite a dame," Mullins said. He paused. "Quite a dame," he repeated. He looked at Weigand. "Wears a wig, don't she?" he added.

"Right, Sherlock," Weigand said. "Let's talk to the major."

"Yeah," Mullins said. "Put him through it."

He got the major. The major came in at the march and offered a stiff hand to Weigand. Weigand shook it and said, "Sit down, won't you?" The major looked rebellious for a moment, but sat down.

"Damn foolishness," he said. It was not entirely clear what was foolishness. But apparently the murder and everything that went with it. "I can't hang around here all day," he added. "Not like you civilians." He looked at Weigand. "No offense, Lieutenant," he said. "Can't help it, probably."

Weigand took him over the course. About the attempt to poison his mother—no definite opinion, expressed at considerable length in crisp, emphatic sentences. Inclined to think, the major was, that it was a lot of nonsense. Doubted if anybody *had* tried to poison the old lady. A bit flighty, mother was. However—not for him to say. She'd been sick all right, and the doctor had taken specimens. He knew nothing of the report. Nasty shock, having her come out with it like that at dinner, eh? First he'd heard of it. He didn't know who had been in his mother's room before or during her breakfast, except that the girls had. Yes, he had dropped in. Seemed to remember that Ben had been there or just left. Anthony had come after the breakfast things had been removed, he thought.

"And Harry, of course," he said. "Always around. Ever since I can remember, always around."

He was not, boiled down, particularly helpful. He had talked for a while with Pam North after the others had gone to bed. He had stopped by to see the cats.

"Like cats, Lieutenant?" he wanted to know.

"Yes," the lieutenant said. "Some cats."

The major approved; was glad to hear it. Very well, he had stopped to see the cats. Very nice cats, eh? He had gone on up to bed and thereafter heard nothing until morning. He had awakened a few minutes before "that girl screeched." He had come down to investigate. He had tried to keep the women out of the breakfast room. Then the police had come.

He knew no specific reason why anybody should have wanted to kill Stephen Anthony.

"Or," he said, "wanted him to go on living, come to that. Nasty specimen, that Anthony. But he wasn't worrying anybody, particularly—not even mother. I'd have thought he was out of the picture."

Weigand nodded.

"Although," he said, "nobody's really out of the picture, with a lot of money around. There is a lot of money, I gather."

"Plenty," the major agreed. He looked at Weigand shrewdly. "But," he said, "we all get along. I get along, Wes gets along. Even Ben, although it's a surprise, eh? Nobody needs money, that I know of. Suppose Anthony did get some, and I wouldn't put it past mother. There'd still be plenty. Must be some other reason, eh?"

"I don't know—yet," Weigand told him. "We have to think of everything. Suppose, for example, he were to get it all under your mother's will. Is that possible?"

It wasn't. The major was emphatic.

"Mother isn't a fool," he said. "Flighty, yes. Coddles herself, marries men like Anthony. Fills herself full of damned fool patent medicines. But she isn't a fool. You'll never get anywhere on that line, Lieutenant. Shrewd, mother is."

"Right," Weigand said. "As a matter of fact, that's what I would have thought. Do you know, then, what provision she has made about the money?"

The major did; there was no secret about it. There were, naturally, specific bequests. The balance was divided into four parts, one to each child—the major himself, his brother Wesley, his half-brother Ben, and the part which would have gone to Robert McClelland and would now go to his son, Bruce. If one heir died before Aunt Flora, without issue, his share was divided among the survivors.

Weigand nodded. Wills like that had been known to make trouble. But there was no point in telling the major that, and starting an argument. He let the major go and summoned Benjamin Craig. Benjamin came in softly, soft hands swinging limply and soft face expressing gravity and concern. It was, he told the lieutenant, a dreadful business. The lieutenant agreed. He sat as requested, and made intricate diagrams with the fingers of his two hands. He made tents and church steeples with his fingers and more intricate patterns. It was evidently a mannerism, unconscious; one could see him doing it at the bank, as he listened to people with financial difficulties. It was, Weigand found, distracting. Mullins stared at the fingers, fascinated.

Ben had, he said, gone to bed early the night before; he had not expected to see, and had not seen, Stephen Anthony. He had heard nothing. It was impossible to imagine a more innocent night than Benjamin Craig, all eagerness to be of help, described. Weigand switched him back to the day of the poisoning, which Ben remembered in detail. He had gone to see his mother, as he customarily did, before going to his office. She was awake and awaiting breakfast; she was just finishing a frothing glass of the citrate salts with which she always started the day. After she had drunk the salts, he stayed with her for a time, drinking a cup of coffee from her pot. He had not suffered any ill effects. He confirmed what the major had said about the disposition of the Buddie fortune; he, like the major, was unable to think of any motive for either the attempt on his mother or the murder of Anthony.

But, unlike the major, he expressed complete belief in the authenticity of the poisoning attempt.

"Alden is very—abrupt," he said. "Inclined to be cavalier with—less assured and commonsense people. Everything is 'nonsense!' to the major, I'm afraid. Perfect digestion, perfect everything, including perfect adjustment. My brother is very certain about everything, as you've probably decided. And very impatient of people's small failings and—weaknesses. He is always badgering mother about her medicines, for example, because he himself has never needed medicines. He ridicules me for the same reason."

Ben smiled pleasantly. It was apparent that he bore no malice, and had only the small contempt of the sensitive for the flagrantly healthy.

"I have to doctor a good deal myself," he added, amplifying. "A sinus condition. But Alden doesn't believe in that, either, his sinuses being in excellent shape. I'm afraid he thinks me an old woman. He is very fortunate."

"Right," Weigand said. "I've no doubt he can be difficult." He let his sympathy find acceptance. "By the way," he said, "you probably don't remember. But these salts your mother took—a powder of some sort, to be dissolved in water, I suppose?" Ben nodded. "Was the bottle, or whatever the receptacle was, full?" Weigand wanted to know. "Or didn't you see it?"

Ben's expression indicated that he was sending his memory back. It returned, evidently laden.

"Why yes," he said. "It looked like a new bottle. It was standing on the bed table. It seemed nearly full."

He looked expectant, but after a moment the lieutenant thanked him and said that there were, for the moment, no more questions. Benjamin Craig went away, gently. Mullins looked enquiringly at the lieutenant.

"Why," he wanted to know, "spend all this time on the poison? The dame's all right. It's the guy who ain't—the guy downstairs, unless they've hauled him away. I don't get it, Loot."

Weigand said he wasn't sure he got it himself. But the supposition was that poisoning and murder tied together. Somehow, somewhere.

Because you could never start with a belief in coincidence; coincidence ran counter to all detection.

"I'm afraid, Sergeant," he said, "that we'll have to try to find out all about everything." He watched the expression on Mullins's face. "Yes," he said. "It's a nuisance. Murder is, Mullins. Get me one of the girls, next."

"Either one?" Mullins said.

"Either one," Weigand repeated. "No—make it the younger one, Judy."

"She ain't the younger one, Loot," Mullins told him. "She's two years older. You wouldn't think it, would you?"

Weigand agreed that you wouldn't. But he'd still start with Judy.

• 6 •

WEDNESDAY
9:40 A.M. TO 10:55 A.M.

Pam drank fruit juice and coffee and nibbled at toast and then, for several minutes, watched in admiration while Aunt Flora crunched contentedly through a much larger breakfast. Pam had tried to talk to Aunt Flora but Aunt Flora had been firm.

"Too unpleasant for meals, dearie," Aunt Flora said, shifting an egg from platter to plate and regarding it with affection, her wig a little over one eye. "Taxes the digestion, you know. When you're my age, you'll not take any chances on your digestion." Aunt Flora lifted the cover of a dish she had overlooked, beamed on the contents and said: "Sausage, eh? Something like." She took sausages to bear company to the egg.

In its fashion, it was admirable. It was monumental. And Aunt Flora, although she ate a great deal, ate very nicely. But it occurred to Pam that only Aunt Flora was really getting anywhere. Pam stood up, pushing back her chair from the table which Alice had set up under one of the windows in Aunt Flora's room. Aunt Flora's room—which was really an enormous bedroom and dressing room and bath—was on the same floor as Pam's room. The window looked down on the little yard at the rear of the house and on the tops of barren trees.

"Oh!" Pam said, with the air of one who has just thought of something. "The cats! I've forgotten to feed the cats!"

Aunt Flora, easily perturbed by the thought of hunger, however remote, was solicitous. She shook her head over Pam's thoughtlessness, the wig shifting a degree or two. She offered cream from the table and, after a moment of painful thought, one of the remaining eggs. She suggested that they be stirred together, and offered a dish for the stirring. She offered to spare a sausage or two and was a little surprised when Pam doubted that sausages were good for cats.

"Nonsense," she said. "Never hurt me, did they?"

"Cats are different," Pam told her. "Especially very young cats. But the egg and the cream will do, and later I'll get them some raw meat. But I better take this to them now, because the poor dears must be starving."

Pam carried the dish away and along the hall to her own door. As she opened the door, she could hear the cats talking, but not indignantly. She had closed the door behind her before she discovered the cats were not alone. Bruce McClelland was bending over them as they did cat gymnastics on the bed. He straightened and turned to Pam, smiling. It was a long smile, made by a long mouth in a thin face. Bruce was tall and rather gangling and his hair grew down to a bristling point on his forehead.

"Homely as anything," Pam thought, regarding him. "And very nice." She said, "Hello, Bruce."

"I'm hiding, Pam," he told her. "Hiding from the police."

He seemed, Pam thought, to be only half joking.

"That's nice," she said. "I always do. The motorist's reflex, probably. Only not really, and I wouldn't."

The last was for Bruce, whose smile had faded.

"Actually," he said, "I've been waiting for you, Pam. I want advice. From the family dick."

"Shamus," she told him. "Don't talk newspaper slang, Bruce. What advice?"

But Bruce McClelland seemed hesitant about beginning. He asked about Jerry, and was told about Jerry. He shuddered carefully when he heard of Jerry's employment and predicted that no good would come of it.

"My God," he said, "It might really *be* another 'Gone With the Wind.' Just as we'd begun to forget."

"What advice?" Pam insisted. "Or won't you talk?"

Bruce turned to face her and folded himself onto the edge of the bed. Toughy, presented with the irresistible, climbed to his shoulders and peered around. Bruce raised a hand and tickled Toughy absently behind the ear.

"I was here last night, Pam," he said. "Nobody knows but Judy. I'll have to talk to Weigand eventually but I want—well, to check things first. There might be some things—" He let it trail off.

"No," Pam said. "Tell it all, Bruce. Or I will. So if you don't want it told, don't tell me. Because even if I wanted to, I wouldn't keep anything from the lieutenant."

Bruce heard her out.

"Anyway," he said, "listen. You can at least tell me whether it fits in. Then we'll both go to Weigand, if you like."

He paused. "Understand," he added, "I think he's O.K. But this is family."

Pam waited and Bruce talked. He said he had planned to drop in during the evening, but a late assignment had held him up.

So he had come when he could, which was a little after midnight. He had let himself in with the key he always carried; Aunt Flora was generous with keys. He had found nobody around and had gone upstairs to the top floor. He had—

"Well," he said, "you can guess where I went. I wanted to see Clem. Is that enough?"

"Whatever you want," Pam told him. "You wanted to see Clem. Only if you think it's a secret—"

Bruce smiled at her, crookedly.

"All right," he said. "I'm that way about Clem." His smile faded. "In spite of—everything," he said. "Is that enough?"

"For me," Pam said. "I hope for Bill. But she's up to something, Bruce. I don't know what but—some man, isn't it?"

"She's a fool kid," Bruce said, darkly. "If you call him a man, yes. Ross Brack."

"Not—" Pam said. "The—"

Bruce was grim.

"Precisely," he said. "The—. Almost anything will fill it in. Crook of all trades. Policy racket. Drugs, the Feds think. Maybe—well, women. And nothing, at the moment, they can hang on him. Nice, huh?"

It wasn't nice. It was—

"The fool kid," Pam said, as if nobody else had said it. "How on earth?"

Bruce said it didn't matter. They had met somewhere, with some-body. Presumably Ross Brack had thought she looked like money, per-haps he merely liked her looks. And she had been—well, call it excited.

"I hope that's all," Bruce said, simply. "I'm in love with her, you know. And they're sending me off."

That was news.

"Yes," he said. "War correspondence. And God knows where. The Pacific, perhaps. Or London to start with. At any rate, a long way off. And I've got to go to Washington tomorrow for papers. Perhaps I'll get back; perhaps I won't. I mean before I start to look at wars. And so I had to see Clem. Just to see her and—well, to talk about Brack." His voice was younger than usual; it was tight. "My God, Pam," he said. "I can't just leave her to him—not without trying!"

"No," Pam said. "Did you see her?"

Bruce McClelland shook his head. All the lightness had gone out of his manner, now. His attentive fingers left the cat's head and Toughy, deserted, dropped back to the bed.

She hadn't been in her room. She and Judy occupied connecting rooms which split the front part of the fifth floor, both opening from the hall under the skylight. He had known the girls would be in those rooms, but not which room was Clem's. He had knocked, at first gently and then more loudly, at one of the doors. And after a moment, the other door opened and he faced Judy. Judy had been crying.

"She's a fine girl," Bruce interpolated. "I don't know why—" He broke off.

Judy had shaken her head and, before he asked, had said, "She isn't here, Bruce. And I'm afraid——."

They were both, without further words, afraid of the same thing. Brack. Bruce had taken the girl by the shoulders. He had taken her, he thought, rather roughly by the shoulders. He was keyed up. And he had had a couple of drinks. He thought, now, that he had frightened Judy.

"Because," he said, "she seemed to know where Clem had gone. With Brack, or to meet Brack. But she was afraid to tell me, probably because she thought I might follow and make trouble. For all I know, she was right."

She had tried to persuade Bruce to leave, but he had refused to leave. She had insisted that Clem was all right, wherever she was. Finally she had said that she would go herself and try to find Clem, and that Bruce should wait. This he refused to do.

"I couldn't let her go, all over town, maybe, by herself in the middle of the night," he said. "I said she could come with me, if she would tell me where to go. But she was afraid, still, I'd make trouble. Then I suggested her father."

Judy had said at first, "No, not Dad. Clem would never forgive us." But then, when Bruce insisted, she had agreed.

"She may have intended merely to quiet me," Bruce admitted. "I suspected that at the time. So I told her we would both go get the major, and that if he would go with her, I'd wait."

Judy had, after a little while, agreed to this, astonishing Bruce.

"I didn't think she would," he admitted. "Because it was, after all, going behind Clem's back. But she seemed—well, to take it more seriously than she ever had before. To feel that we had to do something. And that made me more anxious than ever. And more worried. I thought—well, that she had found out something I didn't know about. Something that frightened her."

Pam nodded, involuntarily, thinking of the talk she had overheard the night before between the sisters. Judy had found out that it wasn't merely a flirtation between Clem and—now it was evident—Ross Brack. And so she was frightened.

Bruce caught the movement of Pam's head and broke off.

"There is something!" he said. "You nodded. You know what it is!"

"No," Pam said. "I just nodded because I was listening. That was all. And for you to go on."

Bruce looked at her and she looked back. He seemed only half satisfied, but he went on.

He, with Judy, had gone down to the floor below to waken Major Buddie. They had knocked on the door and, when the major did not answer and they heard nothing—"normally," Bruce interjected, "he snores. Or so Judy says"—they opened the door and called. Then there was still no answer and they went in.

"And then," Bruce said, "there was no major. He'd dressed, and gone out. But apparently not in uniform. His uniform was hanging on a chair."

It was a dead end, for the moment. Bruce and Judy had gone back up the stairs, and he had told her good night at the door of her room. He had pretended to be licked, he said, and had let her think he was going home. And she had tried to reassure him—tried at the same time to reassure herself, he thought. And then he had started downstairs and come opposite the door of the back room occupied by Harry Perkins. The door was open and the light in the room was on.

Bruce was not clear what impulse had led him to look into the room, but he had looked into the room.

"Maybe," he said, "I thought Clem had come back while we were downstairs and was waiting in Perkins's room until I left. I don't know what I thought I'd find."

What he had found was, for the second time, an empty room. Harry Perkins was also elsewhere, with a bright, empty room behind him. It had meant nothing then; now it was—well, something to remember.

Bruce had gone on downstairs, and then it was, he thought, about 12:30. He was passing the drawing room door on the lower floor when he thought he saw a light in the room—a very faint light. He had looked in, but found the light was in the breakfast room. But even there it was faint and now, thinking back, Bruce believed it had come into the breakfast room from the adjoining pantry, through a partly opened door. He had not thought much about it then, and was not sure now there was much to think.

"The liquor's in there, you know," he said. "I supposed, if I supposed anything, that it was Harry having a nightcap. He has them, you know. And now—well, I still think it was probably Harry having a nightcap."

Then Bruce had gone out. And thereafter, for several hours, he had gone to bars and cafes where he had thought he might find Clem and Brack, and had found nothing except, he admitted with a wry smile, an eventual hangover. Today he had come back, still wanting to see Clem, and had run into the murder. And then, taking a chance he knew which was Pam North's room, and wanting to see her before the police, he had slipped in and played with the cats while he waited. And now?

"Now," Pam told him firmly, "you talk to Bill Weigand. And tell him all of it."

"Brack?" Bruce said. He was serious. "If it's important," he said, "we'll have to tell him; if things lead to it, he'll find out anyway. But it may be entirely irrelevant, and then there's no point in his knowing. Suppose I leave out Brack—I just wanted to see Clem because I am going away, and Judy and I thought she might be with her father downstairs—and now we suppose she and her father had gone out somewhere. How's that?"

"Passable," Pam said. "Bill won't believe it, but it makes a story. Actually, you know, he'll want to know where all these people were—the major, and Harry and even Clem. Because that must be pretty close to the time."

That was evident, Bruce McClelland told her. He told her that he'd met a couple of policemen himself, in the course of getting around.

"Sic 'em, Toughy," Pam said, agreeably. Toughy looked at her with interest. "Making fun of your mother, the man is," Pam told Toughy. "Come on." This last was evidently to Bruce. He came on. The cats found the dish Pam had set on the floor when she entered, and began to push each other away from it. They were so preoccupied that they let Bruce and Pam go out the door unchallenged. Bruce and Pam went down a flight to the library and looked in. Weigand was talking to somebody half hidden in the big chair by the fire, and Mullins was sit-

ting at a small table, on a small chair, making notes. Weigand heard
them and looked up. He smiled amiably.

His voice was almost hearty and he said, uncharacteristically, "Well,
well!"

"Come in," he said. "We've been waiting for you, Mr. McClelland.
And Mrs. North."

"Hello, Lieutenant," Bruce McClelland said. He saw who was in the
chair. "Hello, Judy," he said. His voice was expressionless.

"Damn," said Pam. "I guess we're a little late, Bruce."

"Right," Weigand said. "Always glad to see you, however. And
now, Mr. McClelland, Miss Buddie tells me you and she had a little
talk last night. I gather from what she says that you were a little worried about Miss Clementine Buddie. Because of Ross Brack." He
paused. "Which," he added, "is understandable. I would be myself. Or
would have been if I'd known."

"He was coming to tell you, Bill," Pam said. "Be yourself."

"Right," Weigand said. "I'll be myself. Let's hear it."

Bruce McClelland told him about things. Since he seemed to know
already. But he had not, it developed, known either that Harry
Perkins's room was empty or that there was a light in the pantry off the
breakfast room. He said that the points were interesting, and advised
Mullins to make notes of them. Mullins said "O.K., Loot." Then Bill
Weigand let Judy and Bruce McClelland go but, with an eyebrow, intimated that Pam should remain. She remained.

"And so," Weigand said, after a moment, "the lies begin. Like old
times."

"If you mean Bruce," Pam said, "I don't think so."

Weigand shrugged.

"Bruce," he said, "or the others. Or Bruce *and* the others. The major
was safely tucked in all night, says the major. He was up and out, says
young McClelland. But they don't all lie well. Your cousin Judy didn't
lie at all well and had to admit it. She is your cousin, as I figure it?"

"Removed," Pam told him. "Or something. I always get confused.
About her sister, you mean?"

At least about her sister, Weigand agreed. At first, Clem Buddie had been in her room all night and nobody had interrupted either of them. And there had been no conversation for Pam to overhear in the drawing room. Then there had been a conversation in the drawing room—finally there had been the story of Ross Brack, and of Bruce McClelland's visit and, reluctantly under shrewd questioning, an account of the whole night which matched McClelland's.

"Perfectly," Weigand admitted. "So it's true or carefully cooked. You can take your choice."

"True," Pam said. "Do I get a prize?"

Bill Weigand didn't know. Perhaps she did. He would tell her later if she did.

"I've sent for Brack," he said. He paused. "You may as well know," he said. "Brack and Anthony were—well, partners in a fashion. At least, we think so. They were together a good deal, and Brack is careful about his company. Keeps it in the firm."

"What is the firm?" Pam wanted to know. "What business?"

Weigand shrugged again.

"Anything that's dirty," he said. "Wine, women and song—dope, women and dives. Also policy. Probably a little fencing, not with foils. All the rackets that come handy—intimidation, union racketeering, what they call 'protective associations.' He gets around."

"My!" said Pam. "Why not arrest him for something?"

They did, Weigand told her. Every few months. And he got away. Legally or quasi-legally. Meanwhile they collected evidence, a bit here and a bit there. A time would come, he assured her. But it hadn't yet.

"And Clem's mixed up with him?" Pam said. It wasn't funny.

Weigand nodded.

"Apparently," he said. "We're checking. They're seen together." He paused. "Don't think of him as a thug, Pam," he warned her. "He's very smooth—very smooth and very vicious. Young McClelland's right to worry about her. It would make, at the least, what we used to call a scandal."

"Would?" Pam repeated. "*Isn't* it a scandal?"

Weigand said that it was a funny thing, but it wasn't. It was one of those things which, really, only a few people knew. "Everybody" would know about it, and it would be a scandal, only if somebody forced the issue; brought it from the backs to the fronts of "everybody's" minds. Or if there were some drastic turn which compelled general acceptance of the implications of the facts. If, for example, Bruce McClelland did get excited and try to take it out on Brack—and probably get half killed for his pains. Something that would bring it into the newspapers. Then it would make trouble for everybody.

"For the major, particularly," Weigand pointed out. "A major's daughter, and Caesar's wife. Or for the major's brother, Dr. Buddie, even. For your aunt, although probably she would take even that in her stride. Say there were letters, and say it could be, somehow, thrown into court. That would do it. Letters from your cousin to Brack, for example. That some of the newspapers, if the letters became privileged through court action, would print." He paused. "If they could," he added. "Or as much as they could. Depending on the letters."

Pam said, "Oh!"

"McClelland knows something," Weigand told her. "It isn't that Clem has had a drink or two with Brack somewhere. Did you think it was?"

Pam shook her head slowly.

"I suppose not," she said. "Oh—the poor little fool!"

"Right," Weigand said. "Now—suppose Anthony had some way, or thought he had, of forcing the issue. Breaking the story, as McClelland would say. And suppose—well, suppose he saw an opportunity for a little blackmail. And suppose he discovered, as a good many black-mailers have, that it isn't a healthy occupation. For example—I shouldn't care to blackmail the major, should you?"

Pam said, "Oh!" again. Then she said, "Oh, Bill!"

"Right," Bill Weigand said. "I'm sorry, Pam. But the major was up and about. Clem herself was up and about, and Judy and young McClelland, who seems to be in love with Clem. And Harry Perkins, your aunt's keepsake. Who might be devoted to the family, or at least to her, and might let his devotion carry him a good distance. A good many people were up and about, Pam. Perhaps more than we know about. And some of them are lying. Right?"

Pam sighed. She said, unhappily, "Right, Bill."

So, Bill Weigand told her, they were going to talk to Harry Perkins. And he had sent out for Brack.

"Who'll come," Weigand assured her. "He's very affable—when we haven't got anything on him and he knows it."

"And," Pam said, "Cousin Alden again. Now that you know."

"Right," Weigand said. "And—all right, Stein. Bring him in."

But Detective Stein, who had appeared at the door and waited to be seen, came in alone. He shook his head.

"Can't find him," he said. "Not in his room. He's not in the house, as far as we can find out. Looks like he took a powder."

Weigand looked tired. But his voice did not change.

"Find him," he said. "He shouldn't have got away, you know. That's what you're for, Stein—you and the rest."

Stein said he was sorry.

"But we don't know he's been around this morning," he pointed out. "Nobody's seen him since early last night. We can't keep him in if he isn't in to start with, Lieutenant."

"All right," Weigand said. "Just round him up, Stein. We'll go into all this later, if we need to. Now I want him here."

Stein went back through the door.

"That was supposed to be Harry Perkins," Weigand explained. "Seems Mr. Perkins isn't in. And—"

But now Stein was back. He was not alone this time.

"Here's Brack, Lieutenant," Stein said. He said it with distaste. "Go on, Brack," he added.

Weigand stayed in his chair. It wasn't necessarily true that the standing man had the advantage; often the reverse was true. Brack came in and stood and looked down at Weigand and then, curiously, at Pam. He didn't look at Mullins, who looked hard at him.

Pam had expected a dark, evil weasel of a man. Brack wasn't. He was tall and square and looked like anybody until you saw his eyes. His eyes looked as if they had been shaped and polished and set in his head. Also he was a little better dressed than seemed either necessary or desirable. He looked down at Weigand out of the hard eyes.

"How are you, Lieutenant?" he said. "Want me for something?"

"Hello, Brack," Weigand said. "Why did you think I had you brought in?"

"Was I brought in?" Brack said. His voice had no inflection. It revealed nothing. "I thought I was invited. And accepted the invitation."

"Did you, Brack?" Weigand said. It was not a question. "Do you want to be thanked?" That was not a question, either.

The hard Brack eyes shifted a little and swept over Pam. They almost held an expression of curiosity, but it was restrained.

"Well?" Brack said.

"Right," Weigand said. "Where were you last night, Brack? When your friend Anthony was knocked off?"

Brack did not seem surprised, but he said he was. He said he didn't know Anthony had been knocked off. And he didn't know when.

"Where were you, Brack?" Weigand repeated.

"With a lady," Brack said. There was a movement of his lips which created part of a smile—the harder part. "What does it prove, Weigand?"

"With Miss Buddie?" Weigand asked.

"It could be," Brack said. "Or it couldn't. I'd have to know the score."

"Murder," Weigand said. "That's the score, Brack. Where were you?"

"Out and around," Brack said. "With this person and that. With this lady and that. I'll let you know if it gets important."

"Well," Weigand said. He spoke almost pleasantly. "I guess we'll have to take you down again, Brack. The boys will like that."

Brack did not seem impressed. He said he doubted if the boys would have much chance to like it.

"However," he said, "I didn't cool the rat."

Weigand said he was glad to hear it. The rat was Anthony? Brack nodded.

"A small timer," he said. "A small time rat. I wouldn't bother."

"No?" Weigand said. "Were you out with Miss Buddie, Brack?"

"I—" Brack began. But then there was a sound of sudden movement in the hall, and a heavy voice said something angrily. And then Major Buddie was in the room, moving very fast for a short, stocky man, and throwing off the hands of a detective with a violence unexpected in a man in his fifties. And Major Buddie knew where he was going.

He told Brack what Brack was as he went toward Brack, and the last few feet he covered in a jump. His fist found Brack's face before Mullins, coming up violently from behind the small table and sending it cracking to the floor, could reach him. There was a lot of weight in the little man, and a lot of violence. Brack was half a foot taller, and a good many pounds heavier and a good many years younger. But he staggered.

He staggered and then he was cold and deadly as he came back. His hand reached the major once and the major went back off his feet and brought up against a chair. Then the major came back and his hand was reaching for a pocket and he was telling Brack what he was in a voice Pam had never heard before from anybody. And then, caught in midair, Major Buddie stopped. Weigand had him from behind; his longer arms pinned the major's to his sides.

And at the same time, Mullins had Brack. But Mullins had him with a small, heavy blackjack and was lowering him into a chair. Brack wasn't out, but he looked dazed for a moment. The hard eyes filmed. Then they cleared and he stared at Mullins. Then he said a few words to Mullins, and the voice was still without inflection.

"Yeah?" Mullins said. "Try it, mug. Any time."

Major Buddie quit struggling. He made no objection when Weigand took from his pocket the automatic he had been reaching for. Weigand let him go.

"All right," the major said to Weigand. He stared across at Brack.

"I'd like to kill you, Brack," he said. "You lousy, small-time crook!"

Brack answered unexpectedly.

"You've got it wrong, Major," he said. "I didn't see her. I was stalling the copper here. Thought maybe it would be useful if I had seen her." He stared at the major. "What the hell," he said. "She's jail bait anyway, the little bitch. I'll stay bought, Major." The last was still without inflection. But there seemed to be irony in it.

The major looked puzzled, and the anger faded a little from his choleric face.

"She went to meet you," he said. "I saw her."

"Could be," Brack said. "But I wasn't there. What the hell? You paid off. You didn't see us together, did you?"

The major shook his head.

"No," he admitted. "I—"

"Right," Weigand said. "Take him out, Mullins. And have the boys hold on to him." He looked across at Brack. "Assault, Brack," he said. "We saw you jump the major."

Brack said one word. It made Pam jump.

"Without provocation," she said. "We all saw it."

Brack stood up.

"It won't stick," he said. "You know that, copper."

Weigand said he didn't know. Maybe it would stick.

"If we need it," he said, easily. "We'll just keep it in mind for a while. And keep you around. Maybe we'll want to ask you some more questions, after we talk to the major here."

He nodded to Mullins. Mullins took Brack out. He did not touch him. He merely stayed very close to him, with one hand in a pocket. Brack went without looking back.

· 7 ·

WEDNESDAY
10:55 A.M. TO 12:45 P.M.

Weigand told the major to sit down. Weigand sat too. He still held the major's automatic, and now he turned it in his hands, abstractedly.

"Well, Major?" he said, after a moment.

The major looked at him. The major was not so confident as usual; he looked, on the whole, embarrassed.

"Made a damn fool of myself, eh?" he said, after a moment. "Spilled the beans."

"Yes," Weigand said. "Although it's understandable, I suppose—under the circumstances. How long have you known about Brack and your daughter, Major?"

The major moved his thick body in what might have been a shrug. He stared commandingly at the lieutenant, who did not wilt.

"This is all damned nonsense," the major said. He said it a little hopefully. The expression on Lieutenant Weigand's face apparently did not sustain the hope. "Nothing to do with all this," the major said, decisively. Weigand nodded.

"That's quite possible," he said. "It is also something about which the police will have to make up their own minds. If it doesn't mean anything, in the end, we'll forget it. But it's something that's come up. So—"

The last syllable was final, demanding.

"All right," said Major Buddie. "Months—three or four months. But the girl don't know it."

So, Weigand said, he had gathered. So—?

"Tried to stop it," Major Buddie said. "Naturally. Can't have Clem going around with a fellow like Brack, can I?"

"Right," Weigand said. "I wouldn't. In your place."

But he hadn't, the major explained, gone directly to Clem herself. He didn't know whether Weigand would understand. "Know these young people, do you?" he demanded. "Who does?" Weigand answered him. The major approved. The point was, he said, that anything he said to Clem would make her more difficult than ever. Stupid old parent interfering. "That sort of thing." So he went, instead, to Brack.

"After I'd tried other things," he admitted. "Tried to interest her in some young officers at the post. Fine young fellows, as the young ones go. In uniform, too."

That should, the major's tone implied, have decided it. But Clem was incomprehensibly immune to fine young fellows, even in uniform. The major had tried sending her away—South. She had come back. And when these things failed, he had gone to Brack.

"Nasty customer," he said. "Didn't want to listen; couldn't talk to him, y'know. So it came to money."

Brack had listened when it came to money. The major had—and in his own mind Weigand echoed it—a shrewd suspicion that the affair was of no real importance to Brack. Brack could, the major intimated, take Clem Buddie or leave her alone. In spite of everything, this thought clearly infuriated the major.

"Damned guttersnipe," the major commented. Weigand nodded. Brack was all of that.

So, with Brack only casually concerned, the money tipped the scale. Brack promised to avoid the girl.

"Just a flirtation, anyway," the major interjected, and his voice seemed to seek reassurance. "Nothing in it—really. Eh?"

"Possibly," Weigand said. The major looked at him.

"You don't think so, eh?" the major demanded.

"If you will have it," Weigand said, "no. But I don't know. I'm only telling you what I think. It wouldn't—well, necessarily make any difference to Brack's attitude. He wouldn't feel—obligated. Not particularly."

"He's a swine," the major said. "A——swine." Then the major noticed that Pam was still there. He got very red.

"Sorry, Pam," he said. "Not responsible, eh?"

"But he is," Pam reassured him. "He's worse than anything you can say about him. It's—it's what he *is* I mind."

Weigand broke in. He said there was no use, now, trying to make up their minds precisely what sort of object Brack was. There were other matters. For example—

"How much money?" Weigand said.

The major hesitated.

"A lot," he said. "For me."

"How much?" Weigand was insistent.

"All right," the major said. "Five thousand. We had—we had a damn auction. Better have shot him and had done with it. Might have known he wouldn't stay bought. Nothing to do with men like that but shoot them. Eh?"

Weigand said he could see the temptation. But he could not, obviously, approve the major's suggested cure. And, in any case, what reason had the major to believe that Brack had not stayed bought?

"How long ago did you give him the money?" Weigand added.

"Three days or so," the major said. "Wait a minute. Last Saturday night."

"And he's been seeing your daughter since?"

"Well," the major said, "where else did she go?"

That, Weigand said, brought them to the next point. Suppose, in view of new events, the major revised his story about the night before. The major looked a little surprised.

"You weren't in your room around midnight, or a little after," Weigand told him. "We know that. Neither was your daughter Clementine. Presumably that's what you meant when you wondered where else she would go than to Brack. Now—let's start with that."

The major tried the quelling stare on Weigand again. Weigand smiled faintly and shook his head.

"Let's have the story, Major," he said.

The major gave the story. It began, so far as he was concerned, with his going up stairs to his room after visiting Pamela and the cats. He had not, as he had insisted earlier, gone at once to bed. "Wasn't sleepy," he said. "Damn coffee at dinner." He had read for a time, but he had been worrying about Clem. He had been suspicious when she had been delayed the night before by a reported meeting with some girl. Judy's effort to explain had not, it appeared, fooled her father. His voice softened when he spoke of Judy. "Good girl, she is," he reported. "Tries to help everybody."

It was a little after 11 o'clock when he heard someone going downstairs past his door. It could only be one of the girls, or Perkins. It hadn't sounded like Perkins. On an impulse, prompted evidently by his uneasiness about his younger daughter, he had gone to a window of his bedroom—a window facing the street. Because the house was set back from the sidewalk, he could easily see anyone who left the house as the person leaving reached the walk. And he had seen Clem.

She came down the steps leading from the house, hesitated a moment on the sidewalk, and turned west toward Fifth Avenue. The major, watching, decided instantly that she was going to see Brack— that the five thousand had been thrown away, serving no purpose. It was clear, even through his clipped description, that many emotions had taken hold on the major—fear for his daughter's safety and her future, rage at Brack for leading her on, the normal fury of a self-confident man who finds himself cheated. He had decided to go after Clem and find her with Brack and—

"You had this with you?" Weigand inquired, shifting the automatic in his hands. The major looked at him.

"What do you think?" he asked.

"Right," Weigand said. "I thought you had. And I gather you didn't find them?"

The major hadn't. He had been in uniform and realized he must change. Changing took time, finding his coat and hat in the hall closet downstairs took other moments. Getting to the corner of Fifth Avenue, he had found no sign of Clem.

But he knew the place Brack frequented—an odd, dark place, half old-fashioned saloon, half night-club, altogether sinister, beyond Eighth Avenue in one of the Forties. On the chance, he had gone there and, after a drink at the bar, he had asked for Brack, not seeing him. There was a stairway in the rear of the barroom, leading up to what were evidently other rooms of the "club," and he had started for them. But "a couple of thugs" had barred his way, unobtrusively but finally. The major, saving his temper for Brack, had pretended to be looking for the men's room. After that he had waited around for perhaps a quarter of an hour and left.

He had not returned to his mother's house immediately, however. It occurred to him that Brack and Clem might have gone somewhere else and he had tried a few of the better known and more likely spots. He had had a drink at the bar in each and then, cooler, had realized the futility of his search. Clem and Ross Brack might be anywhere in the city, up town or down, east-side, west-side. The major, finishing a final night-cap at a final bar, gave it up. He went back to the house and let himself in.

"And," Weigand said, "went on to bed?"

"Naturally," the major said. "Two o'clock by then. Late for me, eh?"

"Not," Weigand insisted, "stopping anywhere?"

"Obviously," the major said, sounding a little puzzled. "Oh, I see what you mean. Bathroom, of course."

"Nowhere else?"

The major started to shake his head and stopped. Then, slowly, he said, "My God!"

"I went into the breakfast room," he said. "Through it, anyway—to the pantry. Sand leaves cheese out for us. And things."

"Yes," Weigand said. "And you saw the body?"

"So help me," the major said. "There wasn't any body. There wasn't anything. I just went through the room, which was dark, went into the pantry, lighted a light, got a sandwich, turned out the light and went back through the breakfast room and—went up stairs." He stared at Weigand.

"You believe that?" he challenged. "Better. I didn't kill Anthony. Why should I?"

"I don't know," Weigand said. "There might be several reasons, Major. Perhaps he was going to get too much money under your mother's will. Because, Major, somebody tried to poison your mother. And, perhaps, after that attempt failed, remembered—or found out—that Stephen Anthony would get a large part of the estate if she died. And then decided to kill Anthony first, before having another trial at Mrs. Buddie. Does that sound reasonable, Major?"

"Not to me," the major said. "Damn nonsense. Sounds like the theory of a fool."

Weigand was unperturbed. He said there could be other theories. Then he spoke quickly.

"By the way, Major," he said. "Wasn't it Anthony who first told you about your daughter and Brack?"

The major stared at him.

"What if it was?" he said. "You don't kill a man for doing you a service."

"Right," Weigand said. "You don't kill a man for doing you a service. If it is a service. And if he doesn't want to be paid too much for it." Weigand leaned forward suddenly, intentionally dramatic. "What was Anthony blackmailing you about, Major?" he demanded.

The major's face was not normally expressive. It was hard, now, to tell what he thought. But to Pam, watching, it seemed that the eyelids blinked over the blue eyes, as if protecting them from a threatening hand. But when the major spoke, his voice was quiet—almost too quiet.

"Blackmailing me, Lieutenant?" he repeated. "Damn nonsense. He wasn't blackmailing me." There was the faintest possible emphasis on the last word, as if the major's mind had tricked his voice. Apparently he heard it. "Or anybody," he added, quickly. "So far as I know."

Weigand looked at him for long seconds. Then he leaned back in the chair.

"All right, Major Buddie," he said. "That will be all, now. Thank you."

The major stood up. He looked down at Weigand.

"How about my gun?" he said. "Do I get it back? It's an issue gun."

Weigand looked up at him and slowly shook his head.

"Not right now, major," he said. "Eventually—I hope. But right now the boys in ballistics will want to look it over." He paused. "You see, major," he said. "Right now it's the only gun we've come across. And Anthony was shot." He looked at the gun. "With a .45, probably," he added. "Like this. We'll know more when we find the bullet."

The major stared at him.

"That's not the gun, Lieutenant," he said. He said it in a tone of finality. But Weigand's face revealed nothing.

"I hope not, Major," he said. "For your sake, I hope not."

Weigand and Pam and Mullins watched the major turn on his heel and march to the door. There was a faint smile on Weigand's face.

"I *do* hope not," he said. "I like your cocky little cousin, Pam. I'd rather pick on someone else."

He continued to gaze after the major. Then he brought his attention back.

"And so I must," he added. "Get Miss Clem Buddie, Mullins, will you?"

Mullins said, "O.K., Loot," and rumbled off. Weigand laid the automatic on a table nearby. He looked at Pam and half-smiled and shook his head. She misinterpreted the gesture and started to get up.

"No, Pam," he said. "Stick around. You may be useful."

Pam stuck around.

Clem came and she was lovely and all bravado. She had seen Brack in the house, or had been told about him, and she was armed against questioning. Her first remark was to prove her confidence and indifference.

"Lieutenant," she said, standing in the door. She was wearing slacks, now, and a pale green sweater and she looked as if she were masquerading in the clothes of a little girl. "Lieutenant, I think it's absurd with all you policemen around. But somebody's gone off with Nemo's leash. His new leash."

Weigand looked at her, as if she had made a reasonable and expected remark.

"Come in, Miss Buddie," he said. "Sit down. Perhaps we can find it for you. I gather Nemo is a dog?"

"Definitely," Clem Buddie assured him. "A cocker. And the leash is green and made of braided leather. Judy just got it for him the other day, and it's gone."

"Well," Weigand said, "we'll let you know if we come across it. We probably will. Meanwhile, there are one or two other things." He paused and looked at her, saw her get ready. She was not as poised as she thought she was, he decided. "About Ross Brack, of course," he said.

She was ready for that.

"Ross Brack has nothing to do with any of this," she said. "Or with you. He doesn't like policemen."

"No," Weigand said, "I don't suppose he does. But that isn't the point, Miss Buddie." He broke off, began again. "I won't pry into anything, Miss Buddie," he told her. "Not unless it becomes necessary. All I want now is to know where you and Brack were last night. And don't tell me you were here in the house, because we know you weren't."

"I went out," Clem said. "By myself. Not with Ross."

"You left the house some time after eleven," Weigand clarified. "You went by yourself. You were not with Brack. Where were you, Miss Buddie? Who were you with?"

"Whom," Pam thought to herself. But it was no time to bring it up.

"I wasn't with anybody," Clem Buddie said. "I—I just went for a walk. I couldn't sleep."

Weigand looked amused. She didn't like him to look amused, and showed it.

"Try again, Miss Buddie," he suggested. "Make it better, this time."

"I may have dropped in some place," she said. "To get warm. I wasn't out long."

"A drug store?" Weigand suggested. "A lunch counter? Or a bar, perhaps?"

"What difference does it make?" she demanded. "What business is it of yours?"

There was a man dead, Weigand explained, as if to a child. She didn't like that, either. He had been killed somewhere around one o'clock, earlier or later. He was investigating the murder. He had to find out where everyone was.

"You're old enough to appreciate that, Miss Buddie," he said. "You're not a little girl. And I doubt if you're a fool—enough of a fool not to understand that you have to account for your time. Or enough of a fool to go walking around New York in the middle of the night without reason. Where did you go? And why?"

She didn't say anything.

"You went out to meet Brack," he insisted. "Did you meet him?"

Still there was no answer.

"Or did he stand you up?" Weigand went on, pressing. "As he did earlier in the evening."

The girl stared up at him. She was flushed.

"Leave me alone, can't you?" she demanded. "Leave me alone!"

"When you tell me," Weigand said. "You went to meet Brack. He didn't show up. Where?"

He waited, giving her time, leaving it up to her and leaving her conscious of the weight of time and of his certainty.

"All right," she said. "All right. Damn you! The Grand Central."

"Why?" he said. "Why the Grand Central?"

"Oh," she said. "Because there are always people there—and a girl can be alone there without attracting attention. We—we often meet there. And maybe go into the oyster bar and then go some place else." She defended herself, unexpectedly. "Lots of people do," she said.

Weigand nodded. It seemed reasonable.

"And he didn't come," he said, stating a fact. "How long did you wait, Miss Buddie?"

"About half an hour or—longer." Her voice was low, but she wasn't fighting him now. "Then I knew he wasn't coming. The way he hadn't come for cocktails, after he promised."

She sounded miserable.

"Somebody's done something," she said. "Somebody's made him change."

Now she sounded, as well as looked, like a little girl. Pam wanted to go to her, and her wish was reflected in the small beginning of a movement from her chair. But Bill Weigand caught her eye and shook his head, just perceptibly. She looked hard at him, trying to tell him something.

"Don't tell her about the money," Pam tried to tell Bill Weigand with her eyes. "Don't tell her he was *paid* not to meet her."

There was something in his eyes which made her sure Bill had caught her message. Or had not, even without it, planned to tell Clem Buddie that Brack was for sale; that, to him, she was for sale.

"So," Weigand said. "You went to meet Brack. You didn't meet him. You waited half an hour or so. Then you came home?"

"I had an oyster stew," Clem said, her voice very small. "I was hungry."

It was disarming, Pam thought—utterly disarming. And it made her feel better about her young cousin. Something which wanted to be a smile twitched at Bill Weigand's lips and was sent packing. His voice was quiet and level, and revealed nothing.

"Then you came home," he said. "After the stew. When did you get here?"

She didn't know, exactly.

"I wasn't thinking about time," she said. "It was late. It was—wait a minute. It was about one when I left the station. I remember a clock. I took a cab home. It took about—oh, ten minutes. Perhaps fifteen, from the time I saw the clock. It must have been about a quarter after one when I got here."

Weigand was interested. Pam could tell it from his voice, and from his eyes.

"And you saw nothing?" he said. "Heard nothing. In the breakfast room, I mean?"

The girl shook her head.

"I didn't notice," she said. "There wasn't, anyway, anything big enough to notice. I didn't see anybody, or hear anything. I suppose you mean a shot?"

"A shot," Weigand agreed. "Or anything else."

She shook her head. Then she seemed to remember something.

"There was a funny smell," she said. "Like—like Fourth of July, in a way. That—" She broke off then, and her eyes grew wide. She was very much like a little girl, now.

"Yes," Weigand said. "A powder smell, but this time not from fireworks. You got here—well, within a few minutes. Anthony had just finished dying."

"But I didn't see anyone," the girl insisted. "Or hear anyone."

"Then," Weigand said, "you were lucky."

She waited, saying nothing. After a moment he told her that was all, for now.

"But," he said, "I may have to have the whole story—later. Be thinking that over, Miss Buddie."

She still said nothing. She was still lovely when she went out, but she was no longer defiant.

"The poor child," Pam said, watching her and looking after her still when she had gone out of sight down the hall. "The poor child—what a mess!"

"You believe her, don't you?" Weigand said. His voice held no comment.

"Of course," Pam said. "Anybody could tell. It was just as she says. Don't you?"

"It would be nice to know, Pam," Bill told her. "You think it's obvious?"

"Of course," Pam said. She was very decisive. "Nobody could make up the oyster stew."

Weigand smiled. Oddly enough, he told her, that was the point he had hit on. Nobody could make up the oyster stew—or, rather, nobody *would* make up the oyster stew. Pam said she was pleased with him.

"Now what?" she said.

Now, Weigand told her, some odds and ends. An automatic to be sent to ballistics; reports to listen to. "And," he said, gloomily,

"Deputy Chief Inspector Artemus O'Malley. Dear old Arty. He likes to be in on things. And George Sand to talk to." He hesitated over the name.

"At first," Pam said, "I always used to think of George Eliot. And once I called him Silas Marner. Although they were really quite different, except for the names."

Weigand was already thinking of other things.

"It sounds dull," Pam said. "Particularly Arty. I think I'll go see the cats. The poor morsels aren't seeing *anything*."

Bill did not object. Pam went up to her room and talked to the cats. But the cats were engrossed with each other, and merely used her to run across. They were so active that it tired her to watch them, and then she thought of telephoning Jerry. It was thoughtful of Aunt Flora, Pam thought, to have an extension in the guest room.

There was somebody—some policeman, probably—talking on the phone when she first tried. She hung up, waited a moment and tried again. This time the line was clear. She dialed the operator.

"I want Houston, Texas," Pam told the operator. "Mr. Gerald North. At the hotel."

Pam waited. There were small buzzes and distant voices, one of which said "St. Louis." Then there was a snapping noise, which apparently was Houston. Then Pam's own operator said, "What hotel for Mr. Gerald North?"

"Oh," Pam said, "the—the—" And then she couldn't remember it. Because surely she had known it. "The best one, I guess," she said. There was a little, baffled pause. Then the operator spoke, apparently to Houston. "She says the best one," the operator said. "She doesn't know the name."

There was another long pause, and then a distant operator.

"Mr. North was registered at the Gladstone," she said. "He has checked out."

"But he can't have," Mrs. North said. "He's reading a book."

"Our report is that Mr. Gerald North has checked out," the operator said, formally. "Excuse it, please."

"All right," Pam said. "Only" she added as she cradled the telephone, "I don't understand it. It isn't like Jerry." Then, as if it were answering her, the telephone bell rang and, knowing that it was for her, she took the instrument out of its cradle.

"Is Mrs. Gerald—" a voice began, but Pam interrupted.

"Jerry!" she said. "I knew you hadn't. Was it?"

"No," Jerry said, in a voice that was small and distant. "It wasn't a 'Gone With the Wind,' baby. But what hadn't I?"

"Checked out," Pam said. "They just said you had."

Even over the telephone, and from a long way off, Jerry North's voice had a familiar sound in it.

"Who said I had checked out?" he said. "Of what, Pam?" Pam could almost see him. He was running a hand through his hair. "That's why it's getting thinner," she said. "Because you rub it so much."

"On the contrary," Jerry said, "massage is supposed to be very good for it. Who said I'd checked out of what, Pam?"

"The hotel in Houston," she said. "But there you are."

"Houston?" Jerry repeated. "I'm in Kansas City."

"But look," Pam said. "I called Houston. How did you get to Kansas City?"

"I flew," Jerry told her. "I just got in. I'm at the airport now."

"You know," Pam said, "I think the telephone company is wonderful, don't you?"

"What?" Jerry said.

"The telephone company," Pam repeated. "To follow you all the way to Kansas City. By air."

"Darling!" Jerry said. "The telephone company isn't following me." He paused. "Listen," he began, slowly and carefully. "I called you up to tell you I was on my way home. It was so early when I left Houston that I didn't want to waken you. Now I'm in Kansas City. At the airport. Talking to you. How's everything?"

"Listen," Pam said. "*I'm* calling you. Everything's fine. Except for the murder and Aunt Flora's arsenic."

"One of us is crazy," Jerry said. Then, apparently, he heard her. His voice got much louder and nearer. "*Murder!*" he repeated. "Aunt Flora *murdered* somebody? With arsenic?" Then he spoke very hurriedly.

"Go straight home, Pam," he said. "Don't get in it. It's bad enough when I'm home."

"Bill Weigand's here," Pam told him. "And both cats. I can't go home. You come here, Jerry. And help. It wasn't with arsenic, but with a gun. And Aunt Flora *took* it, not *gave* it."

"Listen, Pam," Jerry said. He was being patient, now. "You said arsenic. And nobody can *take* a gun—I mean, not that way. Not fatally."

"I don't," Pam said, "see how you get things so mixed up. Somebody tried to poison Aunt Flora with arsenic. And then somebody shot Stephen Anthony. Her last husband. And now she's Mrs. Buddie again."

"Listen, Pam," Jerry said. "A plane just came in. Right by the booth. I didn't hear anything you said. Who did she poison?"

"Whom," Pam said, using the one she had been saving. "She was poisoned, darling. Maybe you'd better come right home, because you sound sort of—jumpy. And don't worry. Mullins is here, too."

"That's—that's fine," Jerry said. "I think I'd better. I'll be there some time tonight. Only it's just started to snow here."

"*Jerry!*" Pam said. "Weather information. It's—wait a minute." She put down the phone and went to look out the window. "It's starting to snow here, too," she said. "Maybe you'd better come by train."

"No," Jerry said. "Not unless I'm grounded. I think I'd better be there. Listen, Pam—be careful what you eat. Hear?"

"Of course," Pam said. "I haven't had any bread for days. Goodbye, darling."

There was a slight intermediate sound from the other end of the wire. Then, "Goodbye, Pam."

It is wonderful Jerry's coming home, Pam thought. He really understands things better than anyone. She sat, patting the telephone, for a moment and then made up her mind. It was a fine time for a bath.

Pam had finished her bath and was doing her hair, wearing a long robe, when somebody knocked at the door. She said, "Yes?" And Mullins opened it. Mullins looked embarrassed and said, "Oh. Sorry, Mrs. North."

"Why?" she said. "I'm covered. Come in, Mr. Mullins."

"That's all right," Mullins said. "I won't come in. The Loot says do you want to go to lunch with him. And me?"

Pam said she thought it would be lovely, and in ten minutes. Mullins went away from the door, still looking a little embarrassed. He's sweet, Pam thought, and finished her hair. Men were funny about things; it was her not having her hair done, and being in the act of doing it, which had embarrassed Mullins. It was very funny about men.

· 8 ·

They had lunch at a Longchamps not far away, Bill Weigand and Pam sitting on a bench along the wall and Mullins facing them. Pam said that, as long as they were detectives, they could tell her how the telephone company followed Jerry from Houston to Kansas City and got him in a telephone booth at the airport. Mullins looked at her and said, "Huh?" Bill Weigand got the rest of the story.

"Oh," he said, "obviously coincidence. He just happened to call you at about the same time. It was odd, of course."

"Do you suppose," Mrs. North said, "telepathy? Sometimes I think so. Because often Jerry says something I'm thinking, just when I've begun to think of it and when it's a long way off. I mean, when nothing leads to it."

Bill said he didn't know, but that there were usually easier explanations. Sometimes trains of thought, starting from a given station—a spoken remark, say—followed parallel tracks and reached the next station—perhaps another spoken remark—simultaneously.

"Do you," Pam enquired, "call that easier?"

Or, Weigand said, there was always coincidence. Simon pure. Pam nodded.

"The other night," she said, "we were playing bridge and the first four cards I picked up in a hand were aces. All there together, in a row." She smiled, reminiscently. "Very nice, too," she added. "I bid slam, of course."

"Right away?" Mullins asked, doubtfully. He had played bridge once with Pam North and it had ranked as an experience.

"Obviously," Pam said. "There's no use fooling around when the gods give four aces in a row. And if Jerry'd had anything, we'd have made it. Anything but tens. That would be coincidence."

Bill said he supposed she meant the aces. It would, he said.

"But," Pam pointed out, "you don't believe in coincidences in murders. You've said so."

"It isn't," Weigand told her, "that I don't believe in coincidences. I do—every case is full of them. Coincidences in time, for example. You find some person, not really involved in the case but exposed by the investigation, doing some strange, unrelated thing. It is coincidence that he happened to be doing it, perhaps, just when somebody else was doing some related thing, like killing. And then you may get coincidental results. Sometimes rather tragic results. But you can never investigate on the assumption that these things are merely coincidental. You always have to assume relationships until you have proof to the contrary."

"Like," Pam said, finishing her cocktail and embarking happily on lobster thermidor, "Aunt Flora's arsenic and poor Stephen being murdered. You're going on the assumption they are related, aren't you?"

He was, Bill Weigand told her. Obviously.

"How?" Pam enquired.

He shook his head. There she had him. He looked tired, suddenly. He said he wished he knew.

"It's a screwy one, Loot," Mullins told him. "A sure enough screwy one." He thought. "Ever since we met the Norths," he said, thoughtfully, "they've been getting worse." Mullins stared at his chops. The other two watched him, smiling faintly, as his face reflected nostalgia for the good, pre-Northian days of murder that was simple and direct.

"When you could round them up and give them a going over," Pam said. Mullins looked startled. "Trains of thought," she said. "Making simultaneous stops."

"Local stops," Bill added. "A very short trip, that."

"Listen, Loot," Mullins began. Then he saw their faces and grinned. "O.K., Loot," he said. "Where were we?"

"Arsenic," Weigand told him. "And shooting. A couple of weeks apart and different people. But the same setting, same cast. What do you think?"

"I'd think the same play," Mullins said. "Right?"

"Right," Weigand said. "So would I."

"Well?" Pam said, and waited.

Well, Bill Weigand told her, they'd picked up a few things while she was away. One of them was not, however, Harry Perkins. He was still missing.

"But," Pam said, "it couldn't have been Harry. He's a little, thin man, about my aunt's age. He wouldn't kill people."

Neither the administration of poison nor the use of a gun required physical strength, Weigand pointed out. Or, for that matter, youth. It was quite possible that Harry Perkins had tried to kill Aunt Flora, for some reason they didn't know, and had succeeded in killing Stephen Anthony, for the same reason or for another reason they didn't know. It was also possible that somebody had killed Harry Perkins, and hidden his body. Again for reasons they didn't know.

"And," Mullins said, "maybe he knows something and is hiding out."

"Right," Weigand said. "Maybe he knows something and is hiding out. If he's alive, he's certainly hiding out. But we'll find him, given time."

"If you're given time," Pam commented.

There was always that, Weigand agreed. On the other hand, it might be of no importance. Another coincidence, like four aces in a row.

"But you don't think so," Pam said.

Weigand agreed he didn't. And that, he said, was all about Harry. They had sent out an alarm for him. Weigand had also talked to Inspector O'Malley, who had wanted news for the press.

Then Weigand had talked to the servants—to the cook, the maid and Sand, the butler. From the first two he had got nothing of importance; from Sand a curious thing. A puzzling thing.

It had come out more or less by accident, and because Weigand was covering all possible ground. Sand had been asleep in his room on the ground floor, had been awakened by something and not known what, and had gone back to sleep, not bothering to look at his watch. He had not seen the body until after Pam and the maid had discovered it, although he had gone through the breakfast room to the drawing room a few minutes earlier. Since the body was partially concealed behind the table, this was not remarkable.

Weigand had taken him back to the morning of the poisoning, and at first got nothing. The maid had taken Mrs. Buddie's breakfast up and insisted that there had been no opportunity for anyone to put arsenic in any of the food.

"Which," Weigand interjected, "is valueless." It could have been put in in half a dozen ways, without the knowledge or help of any of the servants. In the coffee pot, for example, before it was filled from the percolator. In the sugar, during the night. Stein was going over such possibilities, checking and re-checking, possibly—even probably—wasting his time. But it had to be done. You had to look into everything.

So Sand, being little concerned with breakfast service, had at first appeared to have nothing to contribute. And then, half by chance, something came out. Sand said it had been puzzling him.

Mrs. Buddie—who was then still calling herself Mrs. Anthony—had discovered late the previous evening that she was out of the medicine she took every morning on waking up. Wilson's Original Citrate Salts. She had told Sand to go out to a drug store and get her a bottle and Sand had gone. But it was a medicine not widely stocked, and the usual druggist had been out of it. Sand had gone to several other stores without success and then, thinking Mrs. Buddie would be growing impatient, had telephoned the house and reported his lack of success, offering to continue the search. But that, he said, Mrs. Buddie would not allow. He had, she told him, traipsed around enough, and should come home and go to bed. She could miss one morning.

But—she hadn't missed the morning. Because the next morning she had, on her own statement, taken her usual dose of the medicine. So—

"Wait a minute," Pam said, "are we sure it was the same medicine? Because she takes such an awful lot of stuff, because she eats a lot and never exercises." Pam pushed back the empty lobster shell, regarded it and rescued a morsel she had overlooked. "Perhaps it was something else."

That was possible, Weigand agreed. But if it was something else, it must be something very similar to Wilson's Original Citrate Salts. Because she had described what she took as "the citrate salts" and, although she might not have seen the bottle, she would certainly have noticed anything which tasted decidedly different.

"And the fizz," Mullins said, suddenly. "Whatever she took would have had to fizz."

"Do they?" Weigand asked, interested. "How do you know, Mullins?"

"Took some once," Mullins said. "Met a guy who said they were fine for—well, for the next day, you know. So I tried them."

"And were they fine for the next day?" Pam wanted to know. Mullins shook his head, sadly.

"I couldn't see no difference," he said. "I felt lousy, just the same. But they fizz all right."

Then it was practically certain that what Aunt Flora took as medicine that morning was either the customary salts or something almost identical. Which brought up another odd point.

"Because," Weigand said, "the next day—the day after she was so sick, and while she still thought it was merely a digestive upset—she had Sand go out again for Wilson's Citrate Salts. This time he got them and, on her instructions, opened the package and put the bottle in the usual place in the medicine cabinet in her bathroom. And the place was empty, waiting for the bottle which was always kept just there, between the mineral oil and the pepsin tablets, on the shelf under the bicarbonate and the milk of magnesia. So Sand says, in detail. It was a blue glass bottle, he said, the small size. Probably a four-ounce bottle. She always got the small size because she thought it spoiled if it was kept."

"But then," Pam said, "what did she take?"

"Right," Weigand said. "What did she take? And what happened to the bottle she took it out of—the special bottle, out of which she seems to have taken only one dose?"

Pam looked at him a moment and then said, "Oh!"

"So that was where she got it," Pam said. "The arsenic was in the medicine. And that's why nobody got sick when they nibbled off her tray. She was the only one who took the medicine."

"Right," Weigand said. "She was the only one who took the medicine. And the only one who got poisoned. And the bottle which contained the medicine appeared mysteriously and disappeared mysteriously. So when we find out who brought it, and who gave it to her—if she didn't give it to herself, maybe we'll know something."

"Probably," Pam said, "she had somebody mix it for her. She would—the maid or one of the family. A lot of them were in that morning, she says. Only the person who mixed the medicine—I mean the person who served it to her, in water—needn't have known it was poisoned. Need she?"

"She?" Weigand repeated.

"Well," Pam said, "I should think she'd have asked the maid. Or one of the girls. Why don't you ask her?"

"I did," Weigand said. "Obviously, Pam. She doesn't remember. It might have been one of the girls, or the maid, or Ben. Or even Harry Perkins. When you pin her down, she isn't sure of the order in which different people came to her room. She's inclined to think now that Perkins came in first, even before the maid. She says he always gets up early."

"Well," Pam said, "that's something to work on, isn't it? What else?"

"Well," Weigand said, "I asked everybody, of course—everybody who was in the room that morning, except Perkins, whom we can't find. And nobody gave her the medicine. But she's sure she didn't get up and prepare it herself—says she never gets up until she's had some coffee, and never has coffee until she's had citrate salts."

"But then—then it has to be Harry," Pam said. "Unless—"

"Right," Weigand said. "Unless one of the others is lying. Which is certainly a possibility."

They thought it over, drinking coffee. Pam started the conversation again.

"Hunch?" she said. "Have you got one?"

Weigand shook his head. He had no hunch, only a few inadequate facts and guesses. Aunt Flora was poisoned by arsenic—"there's no doubt about that," he interjected. "I've seen the report"—and the arsenic presumably was administered in medicine. Two weeks later, Stephen Anthony was shot, possibly as he stood in front of a seated murderer, the bullet entering his throat and blowing out the back of his head. The bullet had been found in the wall, high up, badly battered. It might or might not still be useful to the men in ballistics. There was an abundance of suspects.

Anyone in the house, and anyone with a key to the house—and almost everybody in the family apparently had keys—might have shot Anthony. Almost anybody might have substituted the poisoned bottle of medicine for the harmless bottle.

"Not," Pam objected, "unless they had sneaked in that night. Because there wasn't any bottle the day before."

"Right," Weigand said. "But anybody who was in the room would have brought the bottle with him, anybody with a key could have got in during the night and left the bottle. Your aunt says she hardly ever gets a wink of sleep, but that doesn't have to be true. She—"

"She always says that," Pam said. "She sleeps like—well, I don't know like what. She stayed with us in the country a few days last summer and she slept beautifully. You could hear her all over the house. I think anybody could have gone in in a full suit of armour, clanking, and never waked her."

Weigand nodded. He said he had suspected as much. "She's built like it," he said. So anybody could have committed either crime, assuming he had a key and was lying about his actions. As, under the circumstances, he would be.

"The major could have come home earlier than he says and shot

Anthony," Weigand pointed out. "Because Anthony was blackmailing him about Clem, or because he wanted to eliminate an heir to his mother's money. Or for some other reason we don't know about. Ben Craig says he was in his room and heard nothing. But perhaps he was out of his room and heard and did a lot. Perhaps he had some grudge against Anthony we don't know about. Perhaps there was the same money motive the major might have had. The other brother—the major's brother, Wesley—might have come in the night, used his key, shot Anthony and gone home. I don't know what he says about it, but I'll see him this afternoon. Young McClelland doesn't have to have gone straight out after he looked for the major and found him missing. He could have stayed long enough to kill Anthony. Clem Buddie could have come back early enough—we're trying to check times at the Grand Central, and particularly at the oyster bar, but we've got to chase the night men. And she may have been there as late as she says, and nobody may remember her. Probably nobody will, which will prove nothing.

"And," he went on, "your aunt may have poisoned herself for some purpose—according to the physician she had a very small amount of arsenic, enough to make her ill but not enough to kill her under any predictable circumstances. She may have thought it would lead suspicion away from her if she decided to kill Anthony. Maybe she did kill him. Maybe she wanted to be a widow again."

"Don't be foolish," Pam told him. "She never cared that much, one way or another. Except with the first."

Weigand didn't, he said, mean that as a real motive. But perhaps there was a real motive. Perhaps Judy Buddie had a motive, too. Perhaps it was a motive of her own; perhaps she was acting to protect her younger sister.

"Toward whom," he added, "she is obviously very protective, although she tries to hide it from Clem."

"Yes," Pam said. "I think so."

And there was always Harry Perkins.

"Why?" Pam said.

"Well," Weigand said, "maybe he wanted to get Anthony out of the way so he could marry your aunt himself. Maybe he's been wanting to marry her for years." He said it smiling, but slowly sobered.

"And that," he said, with more interest in his voice, "isn't necessarily as absurd as I thought it was when I said it. Maybe Harry's been in love with your aunt for years—from the time she was first married to his friend Buddie. Maybe he thought after Buddie's death that he would get her, and was disappointed and hung around. And maybe his hopes went up after the divorce of her second husband, and went down again when she married Craig. And still he stuck around, hoping—hoping and getting older and more bitter. Perhaps he thought that when they were both old she would change and he finally would win—get for a few dusty years the woman he had wanted all his life. And then Anthony came along—came along young and confident and hateful. And perhaps that was the last straw, so he decided to kill them both. But perhaps he couldn't force himself really to kill the woman he'd loved all his life, and subconsciously miscalculated her dose, giving her only enough to make her ill. But he had no such compunctions about Anthony."

Weigand broke off.

"It makes quite a story," he said. "Don't you think so, Pam? Worked out, I mean—with the psychological detail put in? Something Dreiser might have done, in his day."

Pam nodded.

"Perhaps," she said, "almost too much like something by Dreiser. Or don't you think so?"

"Well," Weigand said, "'An American Tragedy' was real, you know. It happened. This might have happened. It will be something to talk to Perkins about—when we catch him."

"As a matter of fact," Pam said, after a moment. "It is the best motive you've got yet, really. Only I don't think Harry did it, somehow. He's always been so—meek."

"Right," Weigand said. "Which is precisely the way he would seem if the story were true, isn't it? Part of the character."

Pam had to agree with that. They had finished coffee and cigarettes. Weigand looked at his watch.

"So there we are," he said. "Nowhere much as yet. One poisoned, one dead, one missing; suspects to the right of us, suspects to the left of us. Everybody with opportunity; almost everybody with motive. A pistol missing; a bottle missing; a hunch missing. So Mullins and I go whistling back to work. Coming back, Pam?"

Pam thought swiftly. She didn't much want to go back. It was really snowing now and it was a beautiful snow. Pam said she thought she would do a little shopping, now she was out. And watch the snow for a while. If anybody asked, she'd be back about cocktail time. If, with things as they were, anybody was going to serve cocktails. And if Jerry called again, would Weigand have somebody take a message?

"Except," she said, "that he's probably in a plane and he can't call from that, very well. If they're flying in this . . . "

The weather, Weigand reassured her, might be local—a purely coastal storm. It was hard to tell, now that there were no weather reports. It made them both think, suddenly, about the war.

"Jerry's still trying to get in," Pam said, as they stood for a moment at the door of the restaurant, and waited for Mullins to retrieve his hat and coat. "He doesn't get anywhere, though. Apparently he can't see well enough for *anything*. Anything more about you, Bill?"

Bill Weigand shook his head. Apparently, he said, he would continue to devote his time to murder at retail. He looked down at her.

"Of course," he said, "other things come up now and then. We—cooperate, as they call it. It's something."

Probably, Pam assured him, it was a great deal. And it was what he was trained for. He flagged a cab for her, and she went off in it through the snow. Mullins and Weigand scuffed back, kicking the white powder on the sidewalks, to the dark Buddie house, slunk back between the apartment buildings.

It was a little after four when Pam North's taxi turned off Fifth Avenue, skidding a little, and sloshed down the block to the dark Buddie house. It was snowing hard, now, but it was warmer. In the streets, warmed by subterranean passages and pounded by tires, the snow was a dirty slush and already a grayish-brown. But on the sidewalks it was whiter and more like snow. The air was thick with it; it swirled down

over the roofs of buildings and spiraled through the channels the
streets made. Gusts caught it and threw it back; here and there it
almost reached the ground and was tossed back into the air and fell
again. There was a strong wind which seemed to be coming from all
directions, so that you could never satisfactorily brace yourself
against it. Snow found temporary lodgment on roofs and piled up
there, and then was torn from its refuge by the wind and sent stream-
ing out in banners. Janitors shoveled it from sidewalks into the streets,
and some of them yelled back and forth at one another, enjoying the
phenomenon like children. Others, red-faced and with mufflers
wrapped under their chins, worked doggedly, in a kind of anger. Cars
starting up skidded in the slushy snow and went off like crabs,
straightening out only to skid disconsolately once more when they had
to stop again. In Fifth Avenue cars which had skidded together and
locked bumpers were stalled helplessly, and little knots of drivers and
bystanders stood around and for each one man stood on the bumpers
and bobbed up and down. But except for the angry shovelers and
some of the traffic patrolmen, the snow seemed to make people jovial
and when they bumped together, caught in wind eddies and half blinded, they laughed and bumped away again, their faces red and pleased.
It was quite a snow.

But Pam was not enjoying it. She had shopped a little and then
stopped at a news-reel theater, because obscurely she did not want to
go back to Aunt Flora's. But one of the pictures showed what remained
of an airplane which had crashed into a mountain in a snowstorm and
suddenly Pam thought of Jerry and was frightened.

"Only," she kept telling herself, as she waved frantically at taxicabs
before one stopped, "only they won't let them fly in this. They never
let them fly in this."

Fear rode home with her, and as they skidded off Fifth Avenue into
the right street, it grew larger, because in a moment she would know
whether there was any word and the seconds which kept her from
knowing were unendurable. She stared ahead at the house, willing it
nearer, and that was how she saw the man going in.

He was vague and shadowy in the snow, even from a little distance, and oddly helpless. He was rather tall, and very thin, and the wind whipped his overcoat about him. He moved slowly, carefully, pulling himself up along the rail as he climbed the steps to the front door. Once he faltered, but then he went on into the house while the sloshing taxicab was still some doors away, and suddenly Pam knew who he was. Harry Perkins had come back, groping his way through the snow. She was excited for a moment, thinking how soon, now, they might know whatever it was he could tell them. And then she saw Jerry in an airplane groping through the smother toward the side of a mountain—a very high, vicious mountain—and forgot Harry Perkins.

By the time the cab had stopped and been paid off, and Pam had been blown across the sidewalk and half up the steps, and then had pulled herself up the other half against a wind which had now turned on her, and gone into the foyer, there was no sign of Harry Perkins. But on the table where mail collected in a silver tray by the vase of daffodils, there was the yellow of a telegram.

Pam was so sure that it told about Jerry that she hardly looked at the name looking out through the transparent panel on the front of the envelope. She thought, afterward, that she would have opened it, probably, no matter whom it was intended for. It was merely good luck that it was really for her—and beautiful, almost unbelievable, luck that it was from Jerry. She stared at the beautiful words:

> "Grounded at Pittsburgh coming on by train stop
>   don't eat arsenic love.
>   Jerry"

Pam realized how frightened she had really been and put a hand on the little table to steady herself. Trains were all right; she believed in trains. Nothing happened to them, she told herself, except that they were usually late. Now Jerry would be all right. And now she could find Harry Perkins, who had already almost certainly been found by Weigand, and perhaps by the time Jerry got there everything would be settled. Then they could take the cats and go home and watch the cats play while Jerry told her about the book and she told him about how worried she had been. Pam dropped her hat and coat on a chair in the foyer and went into the drawing room.

It was remarkably full of people, including Mullins and Weigand. Mullins and Weigand were standing up, looking like men about to go away, and Weigand was finishing a sentence.

"—ask you more later, when I know more questions," Weigand was saying, in a tone which had disarmed a good many people, sometimes to their drastic disadvantage. He turned and came toward Pam and saw her and smiled.

"Jerry's all right," she said. "He's grounded. Have you—?"

Weigand shook his head. Just odds and ends, he told her. "And," he added, "an experiment or two. I'll tell you later. Routine, for the most part. And we're leaving, now, for a while."

"But—" Pam said. "What did Perkins say?"

"Perkins?" Weigand repeated. "We haven't found Perkins. What made you think—."

"But, he just came in!" Pam told the detectives. "A moment before I did. I saw him climb the steps."

That got them moving, because nobody had seen Perkins. Weigand whirled on the people who seemed to fill the drawing room and demanded information sharply. Perkins had just come in. Had any of them seen him?

The major stood up, bristling a little, and said "no!" Ben Craig, sunk in a chair, shook his head. Aunt Flora shook her torso. Nobody, it turned out, had seen Perkins. Quickly, Weigand and Mullins, aided by Detective Stein and one of the precinct men, searched the house. There was no sign of Perkins. He was not in his room, or in the library above or in any of the bedrooms. Sand, answering for the servants, denied that he had come down to the kitchen or the quarters on the ground floor. Sand insisted, further, that without being seen he could not have gone along the corridor of the ground floor and to the door leading to the sub-cellar, used for storage and the heating plant. Perkins had appeared and disappeared, and Weigand looked a little doubtfully at Pam.

"Of course I'm sure," she said. "He's so sort of wispy. You couldn't make a mistake."

Weigand seemed worried, then, and said he didn't like it. He said it so that all could hear.

"He worries me," Weigand said. "Now you see him and now you don't. And obviously he's hiding."

"Knows something, Loot," Mullins came in. "Scared, that's him. Maybe he saw the guy plugged."

"Or plugged him," Weigand suggested. "Or knows something about the poisoning. At any rate, I want him. Tomorrow, if he doesn't show we'll get enough of the boys here to take the house apart. Meanwhile, I'll leave a man here—keep an eye on things."

"O.K., Loot," Mullins said. He followed Weigand, who went without saying anything further. Pam looked after them for a moment, and then went on into the drawing room and found a chair. This time it was the whole family and no fooling, she thought, looking around.

Major Buddie was still standing and now that she was officially in the room, other men stood. Dr. Wesley Buddie, taller and heavier than his brother, impressive and professional but with a friendly smile, stood up and said, "Hello, Pamela." Bruce McClelland, who had been sitting on a small sofa with Judy—"Yes," Pam repeated to herself, "Judy!"— stood and grinned at her and said nothing. Christopher Buddie stood, looking as unlike his father as possible, and said, with a kind of mockery, "Good afternoon, Mrs. North." It was hard to tell what Christopher Buddie was mocking. Ben Craig half stood, sluggishly, and sat again, but made up for it by a special smile of greeting. Pam said, "Oh, please sit down everybody," and sat down herself, near Aunt Flora.

"Now," said Aunt Flora, smiling rather horribly, "we're going to have a family council, dearie. Everybody—including the murderer."

She beamed around the family circle.

"*And* the poisoner," Aunt Flora added, jovially.

"Must you *always* be a character, darling?" Christopher Buddie enquired, still mocking. He was dark and thin, with narrow lips. Narrow lips, Pam suddenly realized, looking around, were an un-Buddielike characteristic. The other Buddies, including Aunt Flora herself, had full lips. Which meant, probably, that full lips came from Aunt Flora, since she had them and—yes—Cousin Ben had them, too. There was less color in his, so that you noticed it belatedly. But Christopher's lips were thin and flexible. His nose was thin and looked as if it might be flexible too, although at the moment it was not flexing.

"Who's a character?" Aunt Flora demanded. "Character yourself, Chris." She stared at him. "What *are* you making fun of, dearie?" she demanded. Chris was not as assured as he thought himself, Pam decided. He looked taken aback. But so often did much older people when Aunt Flora spoke to them.

"He's a playwright, mother," Dr. Wesley Buddie said, easily. "An observer of life—an amused observer. Incipiently, a Noel Coward. We're just for practice."

But he smiled at his son affectionately, and Chris Buddie smiled back. His face was no longer so sharp when he smiled.

"Well," said Aunt Flora, "tell him not to practice on me, Wesley. I won't have it."

But she didn't mind having it, Pam thought. It amused her, and in some fashion gratified her. It singled her out, and of that Aunt Flora always approved.

When nobody said anything, Aunt Flora looked at the small watch on her plump wrist.

"My God," she said. "Cocktail time! Why didn't somebody say something?"

Christopher Buddie rang the bell which summoned Sand and turned back to Clem Buddie. They had their chairs drawn so that they formed an intimate V. And Bruce McClelland was absorbed, evidently, in Judy. Bruce and Judy were talking, indeed, as if they had only just met, and as if they had to talk fast to make up for time lost. But Bruce was supposed to be devoted to Clem, not to Judy. Pam wondered if what had happened the night before had changed things; if, meeting late at night in the lonely house, finding themselves united by the little emergency of the disappearances of Clem and the major, Bruce and Judy had found more than they had expected. It was conceivable, even, that Bruce had discovered that, for him, it was really Judy all the time.

Things like that could happen. Certainly they were acting as if something very like that had happened.

It was hard to tell about people, Pam thought as she watched drinks being passed and sipped her own, as she listened, with half a mind, to the conversation which with the drinks was resumed around her. It was hard to tell who was in love with whom, and that was one of the easiest things. (It was easier in the later stages than it was before "anything" had happened. Pam smiled inwardly at the "anything." People had such odd, fragile defenses against words they were afraid of.)

And if it was hard to tell about a thing which went so much by pattern, how much more difficult to tell—well, for example, whether one person out of several was a murderer. That was the crux of it. Here, supposing that neither Harry Perkins nor the servants nor some outsider called "X" had killed Stephen Anthony, was a murderer. He or she was drinking with the rest, talking with the rest casually, remembering little family jokes with the rest and saying with them, "Remember when we all—" and laughing when they laughed. And perhaps the murderer, sitting there with the others, almost forgot at times he was a murderer, because even a murderer cannot always remember, as the grief-stricken cannot always remember grief.

But it must come back again and again, that sense of being a murderer. Sometimes it must come in the middle of speech, confusing a thought already formulated—it must go round and round in the head, the knowledge of murder and of pursuit. The thought that shrewd men and clumsy men, intelligent men and dogged men, men in blue uniforms and men in slouch hats, were everywhere after you must make a coldness in your mind. Here a man was talking to somebody, and perhaps a word would give you away. Here a man was peering through a comparison microscope at tiny scratches on a piece of metal, and perhaps some scratch would give you away. Here a man was sifting through papers, steadily, unwearingly, looking for some written word that would give you away. And when he was tired, another man would look. And somewhere men in white uniforms were probing with knives into the body of the man you had killed, looking for something which would give you away.

All over the city, you would think, men would be searching for
you—in words and in metal, in scraps of paper, in the things you did
yesterday and the things your victims had planned to do tomorrow—
and there would be no stopping them. Because, whatever they tolerat-
ed, the police did not tolerate murder, or ever give up looking for a
murderer. And the men you saw—men like Lieutenant William
Weigand of the Homicide Squad, and Sergeant Mullins and Detective
Stein, and uniformed and ununiformed men from the precinct—they
were only the men nearest, most visible. Behind them there were many
times as many anonymous men, all with their hands against you. And
behind them there was something greatly vaster and more anonymous—something so anonymous that you could not give it a name, or
could give it many names. The People of the State of New York
against you; the Public against you; Society against you; Law against
you; Civilization against you. You could call it anything, and it was
always against you. But, looking around at the others, Pam realized
that you—the strange, not quite imaginable Murderer—You—could
remain resilient. You could chat and remember and laugh, and outsiders could not see the fear that must be in your eyes.

You did it because you could stop thinking about it, not for long but
long enough for surcease. You could get your second wind, in a way,
and then start over. And the people looking at you, if you could
remember that, would be people with dull eyes, who could not really
see.

If I could really see, Pam thought, I could see which one was the
murderer, and it wouldn't matter about times and motives. She was
looking, she found, at Aunt Flora—Aunt Flora with the applied complexion and the uneasy wig, with the bright amused eyes and the full
lips and the remarkable necklessness; Aunt Flora who had married four
times and had once, remarkably, managed to get a husband who was
chief of police locked up in one of his own station houses for drunken-
ness; Aunt Flora who could be so boisterous one moment and so
shrewdly sympathetic the next and who immediately thought of shooting when she thought of the sudden deaths of men. Aunt Flora could
shoot a pistol, if you came to that; Aunt Flora was apt to be impatient

of people who got in her way; Aunt Flora was, Pam suspected, essentially amoral. Could Aunt Flora kill a man? Probably. Had she? Pam
peered and peered with her mind, and could not tell.

And there was, after Aunt Flora, Cousin Alden Buddie, the choleric,
stubby little major. Naturally he could kill. It was his profession, and
there was grim evidence enough in the world that the line between public and private murder was a wavering one. But if he killed, would he
not kill openly, defiantly, as a man who had a right to kill? "Eh?"
Would he not kill contemptuously, and carry until the last a bristling
scorn for those who criticized him, even if their final criticism was the
drastic one of electrocution? Or was he more subtle than he seemed?
For men of the army were no longer trained to advance in long lines,
their chests manfully inviting bullets, bands playing to advertise their
presence and flags fluttering to focus fire. Now they manoeuvered, and
perhaps the major, if he decided to murder, would manoeuvre, too. And
what would make him murder? Pam looked at him. Almost anything he
didn't like, she decided, suddenly—given the right time and the right
place, the right intensity of disapproval, and the major might murder
anybody. But had he, in this case? It was hopeless. Pam went on.

She looked at Clem Buddie, slender and animated and, just now,
very poised. There was less to know about the young—it was hard to
tell how deep veneer went, and how hot the fires were underneath. The
very young counted so much on veneer because they were so uncertain—some of the very young did. And some of them were perhaps
hard almost all the way through and some of them only very thinly surfaced with hardness. It was difficult to tell which Clem was, but Pam
thought only surfaced. But the very young are, to outsiders and often to
themselves, capable of almost anything. And perhaps in this case anything included murder. But you couldn't tell.

Nor could Pam tell, knowing him only slightly, much of anything
about Christopher Buddie, except that he was intelligent, and not so
sure of himself as he thought and probably violent only mentally. Judy
was not, Pam thought, violent at all, for herself. But for Clem, her
younger sister, Judy might be violently protective—emotion might
catch her and do what it wanted with her and perhaps even carry her

on to murder. She's the best of all of us, Pam thought, and the least-considering. But wasn't murder, when you came down to it, an action possible only to those who were, essentially, unconsidering; to those who saw only what was nearest and could not really see that other things came after, or if they saw could not emotionally realize?

If that were true, it would bar Ben Craig as a murderer. Because Cousin Ben was a man who considered, carefully. He looked before he leaped, and then he did not leap but moved forward cautiously. He was listening, now, with a smile to something the major was saying across the room, and seemed completely relaxed and comfortable. He looked as if he would prefer to husband all his resources, even to the extent of saying as little as possible. And yet he managed to remain entirely affable. Which was shrewd of him. He was, probably, a man shrewd even to the point of meanness, and she had already thought that murder was not the act of a shrewd man but of an unconsidering one—of a violent and emotional one. It was, Pam considered, difficult to imagine Ben Craig doing anything which required as much initiative as murder, and as much hotness of blood.

And if hotness of blood and violence were required, there was Bruce McClelland. He and Judy were a match in that—they were generous, emotional people. Bruce was shrewd enough in his way, probably. Pam knew him well enough to think that, and Jerry said he wrote well, which was a kind of shrewdness. And his newspapers thought well of him and gave him important jobs to do, and papers did not so put their faith in people who could not tell which side of the bread had butter on it. But there was no question of his initiative and little, Pam thought, that he could be violent if a cause arose. Probably he might kill, under the right circumstances. Had not there been such circumstances?

"I can't tell anything," Pam said, to herself.

"Can't you, dearie?" Aunt Flora said, comfortably. "I must say you don't say much this afternoon, dearie. But I didn't know that it was because you had secrets."

Pam was momentarily confused. Then she smiled, with only a little embarrassment, at Aunt Flora.

"Darling!" she said. "I must have been talking out loud again. I *did* think I'd given it up after—after that awful time. Because once, you know, I almost talked myself to death."

Aunt Flora was very interested. She insisted that Pam tell her all about it, then and there. Pam did.[1]

1. The story of Pam's almost fatal conversation with herself has been told in *Death on the Aisle*.

· 9 ·

6:15 P.M. TO THURSDAY, 12:15 A.M.

The mood of the whole family had somehow changed during dinner, Pam thought as she undressed a little after 11 o'clock that night. When they were scattered through the drawing room, they had seemed to talk normally; it seemed that they had all, including whichever of them was hiding murder, forgotten Stephen Anthony's violent death in the adjoining room. The doors to the room were closed and Sand had not used it as a passage from the pantry, as he sometimes did, but had come and gone through the foyer. But it was always near and, under everything else, it had always been in Pam's mind. But there was nothing to indicate, before they sat down to dinner a little after 7:30, that it had been in the minds of the others.

It was hard to understand how then, almost as they sat down in the dining room, the atmosphere had changed. Perhaps it was the comparative darkness of the room, with only the table lighted by candle flames which twisted now and then with the movement of the air. Perhaps they felt the shadows behind them. Perhaps only one felt it first, and felt suddenly a fear which was conveyed, no one could tell how, to the rest. Perhaps it was merely that, when the pattern of casualness they had established in the drawing room was necessarily broken by the physical movements necessary to get them upstairs and regrouped around the long table, it was broken irretrievably and each mind fled back to fear.

Whatever the cause, the pattern of casualness—of sufficiently secure men and women talking idly in an atmosphere also secure—was not re-established after they moved to the dining room. At first they merely sat, each as if waiting for the conversation to resume. And then, while they were still waiting, it became hopeless. It seemed to Pam that she could almost hear the silence change from something merely accidental to something permanent and nerve stretching; could feel, almost physically, and in the air, the passing of the time when it was still possible for some one of them to speak casually into the time when anything said by anyone would of necessity be portentous.

It was Aunt Flora, characteristically, who broke the silence, which had endured through Sand's distribution of the soup and continued momentarily thereafter, with all of them looking at the plates as if they could not imagine what the plates held or how they came to be there.

"It was one of us, you know," Aunt Flora said. Her tone held nothing except flat statement, but Pam, looking at her, thought that her face had somehow shrunk under its unvarying surface. Aunt Flora looked slowly down one side of the long table and up the other—looked at her sons and her grandsons, looked at Clem and Judy and included Pam herself in the stare which did not change. "One of us is a murderer."

There was still no emphasis.

"Now, mother," Ben Craig said, and seemed to decide that any possible addition would be inadequate. "Now mother."

His mother waited rather obviously for him to say something more. He said nothing more.

"Can't deny it, can we?" she said. "You can't deny it, can you, dearie?" The last was specifically to Ben. "Somebody here killed him. And fed me arsenic."

"Don't be ghoulish, grandmother," Chris Buddie said. Pam could feel him trying to regain the crisp mockery that was his manner. Aunt Flora looked at him.

"Ghoulish?" she repeated. "Don't be a fool, dearie." She dropped him and looked around the table again.

"Well," she said, "why doesn't one of you speak up? Eh? Tell the truth and shame the devil. Alden?"

The major had, apparently without knowing it, started to eat his soup. His spoon clattered as he put it down. He met his mother's eyes and for a moment their gazes held.

"Drop it, mother," he said. "You'll not get anywhere. Drop it, I say!"

After he had spoken, he continued to stare at her. It was as if commands were clashing between them, and then Pam realized that the major—miraculously she thought—was winning. It gave you a new idea of the major. It was Aunt Flora who broke the passage between them, suddenly looking down and taking up her spoon uncertainly. It was as if, suddenly, she had become afraid—afraid to look any longer at Major Alden Buddie, afraid to look at any of those around her. And Pam, watching the others, saw that each of them seemed similarly affected. It was as if each were embarrassed among the others, and afraid to catch the eyes of the others because of what might be in them, whether of guilt or accusation or, possibly, fear. It was as if each feared the dreadful embarrassment of finding disclosure in the eyes of one of the others. And after that no one spoke—literally, so far as Pam could remember, slipping on a robe and going to a window to watch the snow—literally, after that, no one spoke. Or spoke only, as it became necessary, to Sand, or the maid, Alice, waiting on them silently. Even Sand, Pam thought, had been a little odd, but perhaps he had merely felt the strain so palpable around the table.

And after the meal had been finished, the family had melted away. Dr. Buddie and Chris had, Pam thought, left the house, going to their own apartments—the doctor's a few blocks up Park Avenue, Chris's in a shambling old building in one of the Forties. The others apparently had gone to their rooms and closed their doors after them, as Pam herself had done, and perhaps found in being alone some of the lifting of weight Pam herself had found.

Pam had found also the two cats, indignant at being so long deserted by the human society they prized. They had been all over her; Toughy had climbed to her shoulders, as he so often did to Jerry's. He crouched there now, looking out with her at the snow; now and then making the small sound of a cat asking attention. Pam reached up and stroked his head idly, and felt Ruffy tugging at the cord of her robe. It was snowing as hard as ever; snow was pouring down through the cones of light made by the street lamp opposite; snow was scratching faintly at the window. A car went along the street with snow thick in the beams of its headlights. It seemed to be groping.

Pam turned away and walked across to dump Toughy on the bed. He clung and was dislodged; he voiced mild protest and was diverted by the alarming vision of his own tail. He jumped at it and revolved madly, his tail swelling. Toughy was pretending to be greatly alarmed by this unknown which pursued him as he pursued it. Ruffy jumped up on the bed and regarded Toughy with evident disdain. She began to wash herself.

And then there was a tiny knocking at the door of the room—a secret knocking. Pam heard it and stiffened and she could feel her heart beat suddenly faster. She waited and did not move, and heard the knocking again. It was a little louder this time and gave the impression of urgency. Pam told herself, fearfully, that there was nothing to be afraid of and went closer to the door. But she did not move to open it.

"Who is it?" she said. "What do you want?"

The voice was low and secret, too—low and hurried and frightened.

"Harry," the voice said. "Harry Perkins. I've got to tell you—"

Pam did not wait for him to finish. She recognized the voice and quickly drew the door toward her. But she let it stop against the toe of one foot after it was open only a little, and looked out. She could not have told why it seemed safer, but it did seem safer.

The light was dim in the hall. On each floor a small bulb burned throughout the night, and now only the small bulbs were lighted. But there was enough light for Pam to see that it was Harry Perkins. He stood very close to the door, as if he had been flattening himself against it.

The light fell on him from above and behind, so that it fell on his thin, disordered gray hair and his narrow, old shoulders. Somehow the light made him even thinner and more frail than Pam remembered him—more frail and more helpless. His voice was thin, too, and he was trying to keep it low. But it had a penetrating sound, as if excitement lifted it in spite of Harry Perkins's efforts.

"I've got to tell you something," Harry said. "I know—"

Then he broke off and looked back over his shoulder, and the light caught his thin, gray face. It was the face of a man utterly exhausted and desperately frightened.

"Did you hear anything?" he demanded, after a moment of listening. "I thought I heard something."

"No," Pam said. "Come in, Harry."

Harry shook his head.

"Not here," he said. "I think I heard something. They'll come after me. I—"

While he talked he had thrust out his hand. There was a small package in it and his eyes told her to take the package. He moved it toward her urgently, and after a second she took it. The eyes thanked her. Then Harry stood for a moment listening.

"Maybe I was wrong," he said. Now he was whispering. "Maybe there's nobody. But I can't take a chance. I've got to tell somebody."

Pam was whispering too, she found.

"What, Harry?" she whispered. "What do you know?"

But Harry was listening again. His whole body concentrated on listening. The hand which had held the package motioned her to silence. She listened, too, and heard only Harry's hurried breathing.

"There's nobody," she told him, her voice low. "Nobody. You'll be safer here, anyway. For what you want to tell me."

Harry turned back to her, but there was still fear in his face. He leaned close.

"Upstairs," he said. "They won't get me there. In my room?"

The last was a question. Will you come to my room, where we will be safe?

"But—" Pam began. But there was no use pointing out the obvious. Harry was not listening to her—he was merely listening. He has lived in the room a long time, Pam thought. It's the place he's safe in.

"All right," she said. "You go on. I'll come." It was drafty in the hall. "I'll put some clothes on and come," she said. "You go on and wait for me."

There's really no danger, Pam told herself. But if there is any, it is in the hall. In his room we can lock the door. I'll have to go to his room.

Because there was no doubt in her mind that Harry had something to tell her—something to tell someone. Bill had promised to leave a man in the house. But if he had left someone, the man he had left would be hard to find in the dark house, and while she searched Harry might slip away again. Because there could be no doubt that, whether he had reason or not, Harry Perkins was terrified.

The old man nodded to show he had heard her, and then in a moment he had slipped away. She could hear him going along the hall toward the foot of the next flight of stairs; she could imagine how he was going, creeping, close to the wall, looking around him wildly in the half light.

She closed the door and was conscious only as she started to take off the robe that she was holding something in her left hand. She put it down and zipped off the robe. She fumbled through the larger of her bags for sweater and skirt and pulled herself into them. Somewhere she had crepe-soled walking shoes, but there was no time to look for them. Slippers would do. She had caught from the old man at the door some of his desperate urgency.

The cats stared at her. When she went to the door and through it, they tried to follow her. But she pushed them back and pulled the door closed behind her. The hall was empty now, and silent; it was dim and cold. She was shivering, partly from cold.

She looked back over her shoulder, as the old man must have done, when she went toward the stairs leading up. There was nothing—nothing but shadows and emptiness. She went up the wide stairs, still looking back and along the hall above. She was halfway to the last flight leading to the top floor when she heard an odd, scuffling sound. It came from above, and was beyond description. It was a sound of something rubbing against something else; a soft sound, as of cloth rubbing. For a moment she stood still, gripping the rail that ran along the side of the stair well. It was above her head—almost directly above her head.

Something was moving above her and, as she sensed it, Pam North threw herself back against the wall. She stood there, her arms out and her hands lifted level with her shoulders, instinctively in an attitude of defense. And then she looked up. Her neck muscles seemed to resist the movement.

For a moment, in the half darkness, she saw nothing. Something was between her and the light. And then, horribly, she saw that she was looking at the bottoms of a pair of shoes! They were half a dozen feet above her head, and they were moving slowly in a kind of circle—a kind of awkward dance. A dance upon the air.

And then, sickly, Pam knew. Somebody had said that about a man hanged! *She was looking up at a man hanging!*

She made herself go on—go on along the hall, and part way up the last flight. Then she was almost level with the hanging man. The head was twisted to one side, and the body was turning slowly in a circle. She knew when she saw the back of the head, but she could not move, or cry out. She was held there, helplessly—staring helplessly—until the body turned so that it faced her. The face was distorted; it was hard to recognize the frightened, gray face of Harry Perkins.

The body hung quietly and from the twist of the head Pam thought the neck was broken. The rope, or whatever it was, was taut from the neck upward, and Pam followed it with her eyes. It was knotted to one of the balusters at the head of the stairs. The body hung down into the stair well.

The rope was dark and irregular. Then Pam, after a moment, knew what it was. It was dark because it was green and the light was dim; it was irregular because it was braided. Nemo's lost leash had been found.

And then the light on the landing above her, and the lights on the landings below, went out together. And Pam, for the second time, threw herself back against the wall, with hands raised, and waited. And now she heard movement above her.

She wanted to run, but she was afraid to run. The darkness was too complete; the stairs pitched too sharply downward. But whoever was above her would have to be cautious too, at least until his—or her?—eyes were adjusted to the dim light which came through the skylight above. Pam began to slip down the stairs, her back to the wall and her hands against it, steadying her.

As she moved, waiting for her own eyes to adjust to the darkness which was already not quite so complete, she tried to get her feet out of the slippers. On the carpeted stairs she could run, barefoot, and not fall. She could make herself small and run. One slipper came off. The other caught, half on and half off.

Balanced precariously, one hand groping for support on the smoothness of the wall, she reached for the slipper. She lost balance as she tugged, swayed perilously for a moment, and got the slipper off. There was reassurance as her feet felt the carpet. But now whoever was above was visible as a darker shadow—now there were two dark shadows at the same height. But only one of them was swaying in the air. That was the body of Harry Perkins—hanging in the darkness, turning slowly, making a shadow against the pale light from above. The other shadow was moving down toward her. It moved with a horrible, slow sureness.

The other shadow, as she looked up at it, seemed enormous. And by now whoever made the shadow could see her—not so distinctly as she could see, perhaps, because the light was behind whoever was creeping down the stairs toward her. But clearly enough, perhaps, to risk a shot. Pam North made herself small against the wall, and went down from step to step. The shadow followed. The shadow, too, was afraid to run down the steep stairs.

And perhaps there lay safety, if the shadow did not have a gun, or could not risk the alarm of a shot. Now—if she ran!

She was only a few steps from the bottom of the flight when she started, crouching as well as she could but not looking back. She ran down stairs and stumbled when the stairs suddenly ended before they should. She stumbled and fell to her hands and knees, and scrambled on until she could regain her feet. The shadow was running too, but there was no shot.

She could almost see where she was going, now, as she ran on along the hall to the next flight, her left hand touching the rail for guidance.

She was halfway down the flight when she heard running steps in the hall she had just left. She went headlong down, half falling, clutching at the carpet with her bare feet, clinging with the hand that slid down the rail. But the shadow was gaining.

She would not have time to open the door of her own room, she realized—the murderer who had hanged Harry at the end of the dog's green leash would catch her as she tugged at the door or, if she got the door open and got inside, would force in after her before she could grope for and use the key. So she ran on past her door, and along the third floor hall and then, blindly, along the hall of the second floor. She might have stopped there, and hidden somehow in the library, but she could not think. She could only run down flights of stairs which seemed to have no end.

But they did end in the entrance foyer, and here there was more pale light coming in through the panes in the heavy doors. She started for the doors, hesitated and turned back. Perhaps the murderer wanted her outside the house— out in the whirling snow, where he could hit her down and leave her in the snow and the cold for them to finish—to finish and conceal! She ran, gasping for breath, into the drawing room. There was a little light there, too; furniture loomed around her.

Pam was not thinking, now. She was thinking only that she had to get behind something, or under something, and that was not thought. That was instinct—the instinct in peril to be hidden by something, and protected by something; to put some barrier up. Pam ran across the room; a low table caught one of her legs and sent sharp pain through it and she fell. And then she crawled on, on hands and knees, until she was behind the larger sofa. And there she crouched, trying to quiet her gasping breath.

And then sanity came back, and she thought she had done precisely what the pursuer would have chosen to have her do. She had trapped herself, limited her freedom. When he found her there she could not run, but only look up at death and shudder away from it and try to scream. Whereas, she could have screamed as she ran—ran past occupied bedrooms in which her screams would have been heard. But she had forgotten to scream—or been afraid to scream, or had too little breath to scream. It was afterward you screamed, or when you had only a scream left, not while you were running.

Pam crouched and waited and stared at the door leading from the hall, where the shadow would appear. But the shadow did not appear; the door remained a gray blankness against the darker walls. Pam cowered, terrified, and nothing happened. She listened, and she did not hear anything but her own drawn breaths. Miraculously, she was no longer pursued.

But perhaps the pursuer was wily; perhaps he was waiting for her to move—waiting just outside the door. Pam waited—and waited. And nothing happened. She began to notice that she was cramped and cold, and nothing happened. There was not even any sound.

And then the idea came to her that she might creep, if she were careful, back across the drawing room and into the foyer, and across it to the coat closet by the stairs and to the telephone there. If she could get into the closet and close the door without being detected, she could use the telephone and get help. She could get Weigand and Mullins, and they would take care of her—they might even catch the person who had hanged Harry Perkins before he got back into his bedroom, if he had come out of a bedroom, and pretended sleep and innocence.

Pam waited a little longer—five minutes, ten minutes, there was no way of knowing. She waited, crouched behind the sofa, and listened and heard nothing. And finally, with infinite slowness and care, on hands and knees, she began to creep across the room toward the door. Halfway across she stopped, because she thought she heard someone in the hall, and waited. But it was only the wind, she decided, tugging at the house, battering against the closed doors which shut it out. She crept on.

Not until she reached the door did she stand, and then she clung to the side of the door to steady herself against the darkness. At first she thought the foyer was empty and then something moved. A man moved away from the door of the coat closet—moved silently and carefully, and stood at the foot of the stairs, apparently looking up. Pam shuddered back and she did not know that she gasped, or made any other sound.

But she must have made some sound, because the figure moved; moved slowly, it seemed stealthily, as if the man did not want his movement detected—as if he were tensing his muscles to leap toward her. And then Pam knew that she had fatally miscalculated; that the man had been waiting in the foyer, knowing that if he waited long enough she would come creeping toward him. As she had.

And now, she thought, I can't turn my back to run! Now he's got me, and if I turn—

· And then she remembered the heavy vase on the table near the door. If she leaped first, with the vase grasped by its narrow neck; if the surprise was hers, and the weapon, these might be enough. It was a chance—

Pam had the vase in her right hand and was swinging it up as she half jumped, half ran, toward the figure at the foot of the stairs. Water was draining out of it as she lifted the vase, and cascading into her face; she could feel it cold through her sweater and down her body. And she was, ridiculously, showered with yellow daffodils as she leaped toward the threatening figure, which was turning, now.

If the water and the flowers had not so ridiculously blinded her, Pam might have realized sooner. Even as it was she realized in time to let out a small, horrified, "Oh!" as the vase began its descent on the unprotected head in front of her. But she did not realize in time to deflect, or greatly retard, the blow.

The bulbous end of the vase descended with a crack upon the head of Gerald North, home at last from Texas to the arms of his loving wife. It hit and broke, and Jerry North went down under it, shards dropping from his head and water showering around him. And Pam, at almost precisely the same moment, went down beside him.

Jerry was not unconscious; he did not seem even to be much hurt. But he was remarkably surprised. He sat with his eyes wide open and stared at Pam, and he raised one hand in a familiar gesture before he spoke. The hand lingered in his wet hair as he regarded Pam, kneeling frantic-eyed beside him.

"For God's sake, Pam," Jerry said. "For God's sake."

"Darling!" Pam said. "Darling! Oh Jerry—it's you! And I *hit* you!"

"You certainly did," Jerry said. He did not sound so helplessly astonished, now. "You certainly hit me, all right. And what the hell—?"

"Jerry!" Pam said, and because it sounded so fine she said it again. "Jerry! You've come!"

"Well—" Jerry North said, doubtfully. He looked at her, and in spite of everything he looked as if he were about to smile. "I seem to have picked the hell of a time for it," he remarked. "What was the idea, Pam?"

"Oh," Pam said. "I thought you were trying to kill me. But you're not the one."

"No," Jerry said, with finality. "I'm certainly not."

"He's killed Harry Perkins, now," Pam said, and now that she knew Jerry was not much hurt, there was a new terror in her voice—a remembered terror. "Harry's hanging up there, Jerry. At the top of the stairs. By Nemo's leash."

Jerry put a wet arm around his wet, and convulsively shaking, wife. He pulled her toward him, and as he held her, stared up the stairs into the darkness. He held her more closely, reassuringly. Then, quietly, he pulled himself and her to their feet. His voice was very low, and he kept his arm tight around her.

"Hold it, baby," he said. "Hold it. Where's the phone?"

Pam pointed toward the door of the coat closet. They went toward it, and as they went both of them kept looking sidewise up the stairs.

· 10 ·

WEDNESDAY
11:30 P.M. TO THURSDAY, 1:15 A.M.

There was no light beating in Ross Brack's eyes and nobody stood over him with a length of hose. He was comfortable enough in Weigand's small, shabby office, sitting on the wrong side of Weigand's scarred desk. The light beat down on the detective and on Brack more or less impartially; it glared down, also, on Mullins, who sat like a man with nothing to do, and on the police stenographer, who kept busy. Brack did not look as tired as Weigand, and was smoking a cigarette. But it would have been easier for Weigand to leave the office than for Brack to leave.

"You worked with Anthony," Weigand said, not in the form of a question. Brack said "no."

"Or he worked with you," Weigand amended. "Say he was small-time."

"No," Brack said. "I knew the punk. He didn't work with me." He paused and regarded Weigand and smiled. "Though I wouldn't know what you mean by work," he added.

Weigand told him he could skip it.

"I've nothing on you," he said. "Not at the moment. Later, I hope. I want to know about Anthony."

"Nor any other time," Brack told him. "Anthony was a punk."

"Right," Weigand said. "What kind of a punk, Brack?"

"Just a punk," Brack said. "He wasn't working for me. On his own. Punk stuff."

"Such as?" Weigand said. Brack stared at him. "He's dead," Weigand pointed out. "It won't be a squeal."

Brack continued to stare. Finally he said, "The hell with it.

"Shake-down," Brack said. "Small time stuff. Dames. Old dames, mostly. Before he ran into the Buddie dame."

"And after?" Weigand said. Brack shook his head. Weigand waited for him.

"Maybe," Brack said. "How the hell should I know?"

"You get around," Weigand told him. "You're not a punk."

Brack said "Thanks."

"You know something about Anthony," Weigand insisted. "The boys might find out."

"I wouldn't, copper," Brack said. "I sure as hell wouldn't." He looked at Mullins, who smiled at him with unkind affection. "Nor you, copper," Brack said to Mullins. Mullins continued to smile at him, and then looked across at the stenographer. The stenographer had quit making notes, and was smiling too. His smile resembled that of Mullins.

"Think of that," Mullins said. "Think of that now—punk."

"Skip it," Weigand said. "Both of you. This is just a little talk."

He turned to Brack, and pointed out that it was no skin off Brack. He told Brack to be himself.

"It's nothing to you," he explained. "If you talk, maybe we'll remember it. Later." He looked at Brack. "What the hell," he said. "This is a killing, Brack. None of yours. You're just a guy who knows another guy. Who was he shaking?"

Brack seemed to be thinking it over. He drew on his cigarette and exhaled a cloud of smoke between himself and Lieutenant Weigand. The smoke floated away.

"I wouldn't know," he said. "Maybe the old girl. Maybe the army guy. Maybe the kid."

"Clem?" Weigand said. "Clem Buddie?"

Brack said it could be. He paused, and seemed to make up his mind.

"Want to get that guy out of here?" he said, jerking his head toward the stenographer. Weigand didn't look at the stenographer, but he said, "All right, Flanner." The stenographer closed his notebook and got up. "How about him?" Brack said, jerking his head at Mullins.

"No," Weigand said. "He stays around. Be yourself, Brack."

Brack waived it with a shrug. He said "O.K." He remarked, echoing Weigand, that it was no skin off him.

"He had some letters," Brack said. "The punk did. From the kid to me." Brack smiled as between men. "That baby sure wrote a letter," he said.

Brack went on talking. He was very careful. But a picture appeared. Anthony had dropped around to "my place" one afternoon. "The hotel place," Brack said. "You boys know it."

Weigand nodded. They did.

"And a hell of a lot it ever got you," Brack added, with pleasure. "So the punk comes around."

Brack had been alone in the hotel rooms and let Anthony in. Anthony stuck around for an hour or so, having some drinks. Before he came there were "a couple" of letters from Clem Buddie to Brack in a table drawer. After Anthony left, there were no letters. Brack had been annoyed and had sent a couple of the boys around the next day to get the letters. But the boys had missed Anthony, somehow and, before Brack took any other steps, Major Buddie had talked to him—had talked and met Brack's price. After that the letters weren't worth bothering with.

"What the hell?" Brack said. "Let the punk make a yard or two. They were asking for it."

The letters? Brack was not reticent; Brack leered a little. It was evident that the letters, in wrong hands, would not enhance Clem Buddie's reputation.

"The kid was nuts about me," Brack said. It pleased him.

"You're a punk, Brack," Mullins told him, conversationally. He described Brack further. Brack did not seem offended; he seemed to regard it as a tribute.

Did he know what Anthony had planned to do with the letters? Brack smiled and shrugged. How would he know?

"Put the bee on her old man," he suggested. "Or on the old lady. Or on the kid. How should I know? Or on the whole family. He was quite a punk, for a small-timer."

The letters had disappeared about ten days earlier. Did Brack really know that Anthony had taken them? Brack shrugged. Anthony had had the chance; he didn't know anybody else who had had the chance. Was he out of the room while Anthony was there? Sure—they'd been drinking, he'd said. Did they think he was a blotter? Had he seen Anthony since? He had not. Was he looking for him? Hell no! As far as he was concerned, that was all washed up. When he was paid off he stayed paid off.

"Sometimes," Mullins interjected. "You're a jerk, Brack."

Brack told Mullins he talked too much. He said Mullins might talk himself into trouble, some time. Mullins said "Yeh?" with heavy skepticism.

"Skip it," Weigand told them both. "All right, Brack. Go peddle your papers." Brack stood up and looked down at Weigand. "And watch yourself," Weigand added.

Brack grinned at him, crookedly.

"I'm a business man, copper," Brack told him. "Strictly legitimate."

Mullins made a noise, but Weigand only stared up at Brack. Finally he said, "On your way, punk." His voice was full of contempt, but Brack appeared not to notice it.

Mullins and Weigand watched Brack go out and after he had gone Mullins remarked, in a conversational tone, on what Brack was. Weigand said, "Right."

"However," Weigand said, "he gave us something."

Mullins agreed that he had.

"What this guy Anthony was doing ain't healthy," Mullins said. "People don't like to shell out, sometimes. Sometimes they do something about it."

Weigand nodded. People had been known to do something about blackmailers. Men like Major Buddie, for example—it was hard to imagine the major taking blackmail lying down.

"Or the rest of them," Mullins pointed out. "The girl herself. Or the old lady. Or damn near anybody."

There was, Weigand admitted, a complication. Anthony might have tried to sell the letters to Clem's father, accompanying his offer with a threat.

"Yeh," Mullins said, a little uncertainly. "But what did he do to them if the major wasn't having any? Peddle them to the papers or something?"

Weigand thought not. For one thing, the papers wouldn't have them. "No privilege," Weigand pointed out. "And I don't know any paper that would touch them anyway. But there was always Mrs. Buddie."

Mullins thought it over and nodded, but still a little doubtfully.

"Mrs. Buddie has the money," Weigand pointed out. "She can leave it where she likes, to those she's fond of. The letters wouldn't make her any fonder of Clem. She might even turn the girl out. She might even take it out on the major."

Mullins nodded, with less doubt.

The same threat—to show the letters Clem had written to her grandmother—might work against Clem herself, Weigand pointed out. Or against her sister, Judy. Mullins looked doubtful. Weigand nodded.

"Judy'd go a long way for her little sister," he assured Mullins. "It sticks out all over her. Use your eyes, sergeant."

"O.K.," Mullins said. "O.K., Loot. Anybody else?"

Bruce McClelland, assuming the authenticity of his apparent devotion to Clem, might go an equally long distance to protect her, Weigand pointed out. Nor was it possible entirely to ignore Mrs. Buddie herself. Assume she was the tolerant one, and the major intolerant. Suppose instead of the major's keeping the letters from his mother, she were keeping them from him. And suppose she, instead of he, got tired paying. It was perhaps not so likely, but it was possible—it depended on the people.

This much was evident, if Brack had put them on the right track; if Anthony had died because of his use of the letters. Somebody got tired paying him. The major, either of the girls, Bruce, Mrs. Buddie. You could take your choice.

"And the letters?" Mullins asked. "Where—?"

The telephone interrupted him. Weigand scooped it up and listened and said, *"What?!"* He listened again, and Mullins, watching him, could tell from his face that something had happened. After a moment, Weigand said, hurriedly, "Right. We'll be along," and put the telephone back in its cradle, hard. He sat for an instant, and spoke vividly into the air. Then he spoke at Mullins.

"Somebody got Perkins," he said. "The little guy who was hiding out. And Jerry's back. Pam seems to have hit him on the head with a vase."

"Jeez," Mullins said. "It gets screwier and screwier. I thought Jerry was in K.C."

They were at the door, Weigand leading the way. It seemed, he said over his shoulder, that Jerry North had come home.

They were running down the stairs toward the car; they were in the car and roaring up town, Weigand driving and the red lights blinking. The siren was silent, except in extreme emergencies; sirens were not popular in New York that winter.

"It must have been quite a jolt to him," Mullins said. "Being conked. Why?"

Weigand, intent on the snowy pavement, shook his head. Jerry hadn't said, he told Mullins.

"He did seem sort of surprised," Weigand admitted, as he swerved around a bus. "And he says somebody has hanged Perkins."

"Hanged him?" Mullins repeated. It evidently puzzled him. "Why hang him?" he said. Weigand said he didn't know; that they would have to find out.

They swung, skidding on the hardened snow, off Fifth Avenue and slid to a stop in front of the Buddie house. At the door, Mullins started to ring, but Weigand stopped him.

"Door's unlocked," Weigand said, turning the knob. It was unlocked. "Unlocked when Jerry got here, he said," Weigand amplified. "And that's a funny thing."

The Norths were waiting in the foyer, without a light. They looked a little damp and subdued, and Jerry now and then rubbed his head spec-

ulatively, feeling the bump. It was Weigand who flashed on the first
lights, and almost as he did so the commotion began in the street, as
police cars piled in and the squad assembled. Now it was all to do over
again—pictures, doctors, fingerprint men, statements—all the rest of
it. Weigand sent detectives to wake the family, and peremptory knocking sounded on bedroom doors. Shepherded by detectives, the people
in the house assembled—sleepy eyed, heavy witted, hair standing on
end. Before Weigand thought to warn, the girls were awakened and
brought down, and so were brought past the swinging body of Harry
Perkins, dangling in the stair well with the green leash around its neck.
And Clem screamed, and buried her face against Judy's shoulder. And
Judy, very white but silent, held her and, without letting the younger
girl look again, led her by the hanging man.

Flashlights flared in the topmost hall of the old house and cameras
were aimed up and down at the hanging figure. And only then, while a
precinct man held the body and drew it toward him, leaning himself
perilously out over the stair well, did Mullins saw at the leash with a
sharp knife until it parted. The precinct man carried the body back up
the stairs and laid it in the hall.

"He's light," the precinct man said. "For a stiff."

Weigand watched the body lowered to the floor.

"It looks like a broken neck," he commented, and knelt beside the
body, touching the neck with long fingers. It was a broken neck; Harry
Perkins had been hanged neatly enough to satisfy the most demanding
professional executioner. Weigand stepped back to let the fingerprint
men and photographers go on. When they finished, he knelt again by
the body and examined the knot which had held the noose in the green
leash. It was not, as he had half expected, a hangman's knot. But it was
approximately as interesting. It was a bowline—around Harry Perkins's neck it had been a running bowline—and the knot itself had
come behind his left ear. Weigand said "Well," thoughtfully, and went
to look at the part of the leash still fast to the baluster.

That had no knot at all. The murderer had taken advantage of the
tongue and hook fastener with which the leash was normally affixed to
Nemo's collar. He had merely run the leash around the baluster and

hooked it upon itself. This was not so expert; the hook might have broken. Weigand took it off and looked at it. The risk had been slight; the
leash had been made for a heavier dog than little Nemo. But a bowline
at this end too would have been safer, if you wanted to keep Perkins
hanging.

Safer and, Weigand added to himself, slower. Even if you could loop
a bowline expertly—and it would take someone better than a fumbler
to put the knot in the rather stiff leather thong—it would take a few seconds. And use of the snap saved the seconds which must have been of
value. But if seconds were of value, why hang Perkins at all? Why not
merely hit him over the head, if you had a weapon? Or strangle him if,
for reasons not entirely clear, you preferred to use the leash?

Weigand left the squad to it and went back down to get Pam's story.
On his way up, he had left the Norths at the door of Pam's room. Now
they were behind the door, and opened it when he knocked. And Pam
threw out her hands in a gesture toward the room and said: "Look!"
Weigand looked.

"At first," Pam said, "I thought it was the cats, because they can tear
up almost anything. But they couldn't open my suitcases, so I knew it
wasn't the cats. So this must have been where he was all the time. And
I thought he was after *me*."

Pam seemed a little affronted, as she looked about the disordered
room—the room in which, since the cats could not open suitcases,
somebody had been conducting a search for something; a search so
hurried that it must have been almost frenzied.

"All the time I was down there hiding," Pam said, somewhat bitterly, "he was up here tearing things apart. Or she. Why?"

"Because," Weigand said, reasonably, "you had something he wanted—or he thought you had. Did you?"

Pam looked puzzled and shook her head.

"I can't think of anything," she said. "I haven't found anything. Or
lost anything."

Then somebody thought she had, Weigand told her. He looked
across at Jerry, who was sitting sadly in a chair with one hand to his
head.

"Aches," he announced, briefly, when Weigand looked at him. He looked aggrieved. "I wish, Bill," he said, "that you wouldn't leave Pam in a house full of murderers." He felt his head. "And vases," he added, darkly.

Weigand admitted it was a mistake. It wouldn't happen again. Meanwhile—what had happened?

Pam told him about Perkins—about his appearance at her door, his evident terror, her agreement to go up to his room to hear what it was he had to say.

"Something about the murder, of course," Pam said.

Weigand wanted to know if he had said so. In so many words.

Pam, remembering back, didn't think he had. But he had said something—surely it was something he had said?—which she could not now remember.

"If he did," she told Weigand, "what happened afterward chased it out of my head. Finding him and being chased and hitting Jerry and all."

"I wish people wouldn't talk about heads," Jerry said from his chair. Nobody paid any attention to him. Encouraged by Weigand, Pam told her story in all the detail she could remember. It was clear now, she thought, that whoever had been chasing her—and was presumably Perkins's murderer—had quit chasing her when she fled down past the door of her bedroom. Instead, the murderer had abandoned her, no doubt being sure that he had not been recognized, and instead ransacked the room.

"And you didn't recognize whoever it was," Weigand said. It was not a question, but Pam shook her head. "He turned off the lights," she pointed out. "There is a switch on each landing which controls all the lights or, if you prefer, only part of them. So that people can go up in the light and turn off from the top of the stairs. Only the lights usually burn all night."

Weigand nodded. He rubbed fingers down Toughy's spine, as the cat sat on his lap. The fingers were abstracted, but Toughy purred in ecstasy. Weigand turned to Jerry North.

"I got in by train," Jerry told him. "I checked everything but a small bag and came up here. Everybody had gone to bed, apparently. So I started to ring."

But he hadn't rung, because there was snow on the bottoms of his shoes, and in the tile-floored vestibule he had slipped as he reached out toward the bell. Clutching wildly, he had grabbed the nearest knob of the double doors and saved himself. And, more surprisingly, felt the knob turn in his hand. The knob turned and the door opened and Jerry, surprised but grateful, went into the warmer foyer.

"I supposed Pam had pushed the little thing-a-ma-jig," Jerry explained. "So that I could come in without waking people. But she says she didn't."

Pam shook her head.

"The button, he means," she explained. "The thing that makes it not lock. You know?"

"Yes," Weigand told her. "But you hadn't?"

Pam hadn't. Weigand was interested. Because evidently somebody had, which opened up new avenues. There had been an arrangement which would let somebody, but presumably not intentionally Gerald North, come into the house that night without ringing the bell or using a key. Evidently because the person expected didn't have a key and did not want, or was not wanted, to ring. Which let in outsiders. Weigand made a note of it and heard the rest of Jerry's story, which was brief.

Jerry had been surprised to find the hall lights out, but there had been enough light from the door to show him the coat closet, and he had hung his wet overcoat and hat in it. Then, with the small bag on the floor at his feet, he had suddenly become doubtful as to which was Pam's room. Normally, he had decided, it would be the front guest room on the third floor, and he had been speculating about it, making up his mind to chance knocking on the door of that room, when he had heard a noise behind him.

"Pam was flying at me," he said. "Like a mad cat. And before I could say anything I was all covered with flowers and water and pieces of vase. And had this." He fingered the bump on his head. "A hell of a greeting," he added, but he smiled at Pam.

"I don't think you ought to call me a cat," Pam said. "And I've said I was sorry. But you wouldn't want me just to let him kill me, and not *do* anything, would you? I mean, if you had been the murderer, instead of you."

"All right," Jerry said. "You did fine. If it had been the murderer, you'd have had him. You certainly had me."

Somebody knocked at the door. It was Detective Stein, with word of the arrival of the assistant medical examiner. It wasn't Dr. Francis, this time, Weigand found, but a crisp young man the lieutenant knew only slightly. The physician's interest was distant and professional. The conditions were what one would expect if a man were hanged—with a drop.

"About what you'd get in a legal hanging," the doctor agreed. "Cervical spine fractured or dislocated. Spinal cord crushed." He was kneeling beside the body.

"Feel the jaw," Weigand suggested. The medical examiner felt the jaw. He nodded.

"Hit first," he said. "Probably knocked unconscious. There's not much swelling—wasn't time, evidently. But you can just feel it. Is that what you expected?"

"It would have been easier that way," Weigand said. "And quicker. And also silent. The murderer was in a hurry."

"Was he?" The assistant medical examiner did not seem much interested. He got up and dusted the knees of his trousers. He said Weigand could send the body down whenever he wanted. They'd take it apart for him. Weigand nodded, abstractedly, and watched the doctor go down the stairs without seeing him.

The murderer must have been in a hurry—either in a hurry or extremely lucky. It looked as if he were in a hurry. If he were in a hurry, it would be because he knew Pam North was coming up to hear what the old man had to tell her. And that meant that he had heard the conversation between Pam and Perkins outside the bedroom door. It would mean that he had followed Perkins to the top of the house, passing Pam's door while she was dressing; come up behind Perkins, struck him brutally on the jaw—he'd have had to whirl him around to do that, and Weigand thought of the final terror of the old man, only a few feet from what he thought safety, when a hand had suddenly wrenched at his shoulder, turning him to face death—struck him on the jaw, knocking him out, and then hanged him.

But why, if you were in a hurry, bother with hanging? You had the leash, presumably picked up and secreted with its purpose in mind, and almost certainly the plan had been to strangle. Why had the plan been abandoned? Presumably because hanging served the turn better. Then Weigand realized why.

Assuming you knew you would not fumble with knots, it was literally quicker—quicker if you wanted to be sure. Strangulation, with its slower death by suffocation, took time if you wanted to be sure you had finished the job. And you had to wait until the job was finished, which was risky, but no riskier than leaving the job half done. But if you resorted to hanging, your part was finished quickly. Perkins might still have died of strangulation, if the drop had not broken his neck. But you did not have to wait for him to die. You could leave that to the leash, and the old man's slight weight, which would nevertheless be enough. Hanging, Perkins did half your job for you.

It had seemed bizarre at first glance. But it was not intended to be bizarre. It was merely intended to be effective. As it had been.

With the hanging attended to, the murderer was cut off from going down the stairs by the fact that Pam was presumably coming up them. So he had stepped out of sight, perhaps in Perkins's own room, and waited. Perhaps Pam would be frightened when she saw the body and run without waiting to investigate further. In that event, the murderer could count on the confusion to shield him, and, if he were a member of the family, appear later with the others, as sleepy and disheveled and horrified as any of them. Presumably, however, if Pam had gone on it would have been necessary to do something about her. It was lucky she hadn't gone on.

When she retreated without screaming, the murderer had followed her down, but probably not really in pursuit. Probably he had merely wanted to get away from the top floor, which indicated he was not sleeping on that floor. (And hence "he" was not either Judy or

Clem?) When Pam had gone on past her room, the murderer had proved himself an opportunist and had searched the room. For what? Something Pam had and had forgotten she had, presumably; something she had got since she came to the Buddie house, probably. But what?

• 11 •

THURSDAY
1:15 A.M. TO 2:35 A.M.

Pamela North had told Jerry what had been happening in the old house, but she had told it in fragments, breaking off now and then to look around the disordered room.

"And the major paid this Brack creature five thousand—" Pam said. "Jerry! I don't understand it. What *could* he have been looking for?"

"Well," Jerry said, "something small. Something small enough to be in the bottom of a bag, under other things."

He was looking at one bag. The contents had been strewn around it; the searcher had gone at the bag with both hands, like a dog digging. And then he had moved on to the other bag. He had searched the clothing which Pam had unpacked, and tossed it aside; he had stripped the covers from the bed and thrown them over the foot, so that they dragged disconsolately on the floor. He had broken the string which held a hat box closed, and grabbed at the hat, crushing it. He had, it was evident, been in a hurry.

"I can't think," Pam said. "There must have been something. Because it couldn't have been the cats."

The cats sat on the disordered bed and looked at the Norths. Toughy started to scratch an ear, became bored on the instant, and sat ridiculously with his leg cocked up. Ruffy looked at him and decided that something was biting her tail. She bit her tail angrily, seeking the marauder. Then, with no interval, she pretended that there was something of fascinating importance between the spring and the side board of the bed. She lay flat and reached a long forearm down, hooking at it.

"I wish her tail were bigger," Pam said, thoughtfully. "Toughy's got a much better tail." Toughy, hearing his name, pranced to the end of the bed. He walked on tip-toe and his hind legs advanced more rapidly than those in front, so that his body curved. It was a kind of dance. His tail stuck straight up and twisted at the end and grew rapidly in circumference. Toughy was scaring himself, making up terrors for amusement.

"You're crazy," Pam told him. "There's nothing there."

Toughy advanced, gingerly, and batted at something. Then he sat down, his tail subsided and he fell to washing his chest. One would have thought, watching him, that he had had, for hours, only chest washing on his mind.

"You know," Jerry said, interestedly, "I sometimes think he's a little crazy, don't you?"

Pam said, somewhat indignantly, that she thought he was very sweet.

"He does distract easily," she admitted. "But they all do."

Ruffy was not proving that. Ruffy was still angling for the prize between the mattress and the side board of the bed. She would almost have it, apparently, and then it would get away. It was a long way down, evidently; perhaps it was lying on the end of a slat which helped support the springs. She wriggled closer and dug deeper. Then she flicked.

She had it now. It was on the bed. Ruffy went around it in a circle, reached out one slender paw and tossed it again. Then she jumped over it; then she pawed it under herself and sat on it and laid her ears back. Then she leaped away and pretended to look at Toughy and not to remember that she had trapped her prey. Toughy abandoned chest washing and advanced. Ruffy laid back her ears, leaped and tossed her own—her own, so personally captured, so infinitely desirable—prey to one side. Toughy sat down.

Ruffy advanced again and flicked the prey delicately. Then she crouched over it and got it between her teeth and, with her mouth full, growled warningly at Toughy. Toughy stood up, regarded her intently and sat down again. He seemed to have nothing in mind; he looked at Pam with an air of boredom, indicating that he was not being taken in. Probably, his look said, she hasn't anything; certainly she had nothing an intelligent cat would want.

Ruffy dropped her prey, drew back and, unexpectedly, tossed it toward Toughy with a flick of her forepaw.

"Did you ever notice that they're usually left handed?" Jerry inquired, interestedly. "They usually strike with the left paw, by preference. What do you suppose she's got?"

"Whatever it is, she hasn't got it now," Pam told him. "Toughy's got it."

Toughy was heavier in play than his sister. His paws were heavy at the ends of sturdy legs. Where Ruffy had whisked the prey, Toughy cuffed it. He knocked it to the floor and fell headlong after it. He landed in a heap, and rolled.

"Anybody else would look awkward," Pam remarked. "And he does, beside Ruffy. But I wish I could do it."

"Fall out of bed and roll?" Jerry enquired. "I don't see where it would get you."

"Anything," Pam said. "Not necessarily out of bed. But do everything—oh, all of a piece. We gangle. Who was it said we should have started out as cats? Instead of monkeys, I mean."

Jerry said he didn't know. Clarence Day had speculated about it, he thought. It would have had advantages.

"For instance," he said, "paws couldn't get hold of vases." He sobered. "Or tie knots in ropes," he added. "It would have had its points."

"Yes," Pam said. She watched Toughy, who had rolled back toward the prey and was lying on his back and reaching for it. Ruffy had come to the edge of the bed and had her head stuck over and was staring down at him in evident amazement. She couldn't, it was clear, imagine what he was up to. "We made a mistake back there, somewhere. Jerry! What *have* they got?"

"Anything," Jerry said. "Probably a piece of mattress. Or a piece of the bed. I wouldn't put anything past them."

Toughy reached the prey and knocked it across the floor. It hit a leg of the bed and clinked.

"Probably your fountain pen," Jerry said. But Pam was staring.

"Oh!" Pam said. "That's what it was!"

She dropped to her hands and knees and brushed Toughy from his plaything. It was a small plaything, twisted in newspaper and hard and round.

"Jerry!" Pam said. "It's what Perkins gave me! I'd forgotten. And it's a"—she felt it—"a bottle!"

She was up with it, now, and had begun to strip off the haphazard wrapping, already loosened by the play of the cats. Then Jerry was beside her, holding out his hand.

"Don't touch it!" Jerry said, quickly. "Or only the paper."

He took it from her, holding it gingerly. Carefully he pulled the paper down from the small bottle, exposing the neck with the cork half pushed in. He stripped the wrapping further until, still not touching the bottle, he could read part of the label. There was, just where the bottle started to swell from the neck, a blue crescent pasted on the bottle and on the crescent, in white, the words: "Professional Sample." Below that was another label. This one was white, with black letters, and the first word was "Folwell's." Jerry peeled the wrapping down until he could read the next line: "Fruit Salts." The bottle was of green glass and Jerry tilted it. There was some sort of powder inside, filling about half the bottle.

"Arsenic!" Pam said, excitedly. "It's half full of arsenic! That's where Aunt Flora got it!"

Jerry nodded. He admitted that it seemed probable; there was a bottle missing—a bottle which had appeared mysteriously and disappeared overnight. It was a fair guess that, arsenic or not, this was the bottle. And it was a fair guess that there was arsenic in it. Jerry held the bottle gingerly and said to Pam, "Come on."

They found Bill Weigand in the library, with Mullins and Aunt Flora. Aunt Flora wore a remarkable garment of purple with decorations and her wig was pushed back perilously from her forehead. The makeup was undisturbed, confirming Pam's suspicion that she kept it on day and night. But the blue eyes did not snap. They were clouded. For the first time she could remember, Pam was seeing Aunt Flora in tears.

"Of course I was fond of him, dearie," Aunt Flora was saying. Her voice was little changed by emotion, and she still spoke with authority. "I was used to him. We remembered—the same things." Aunt Flora had hesitated for a moment and gone on. Then she saw Pam and Jerry.

"Gerald!" she said. "What happened to you, dearie?"

"What?" Jerry said. "Why, Aunt Flora?"

"Bump." Aunt Flora said. "Bump, dearie. I didn't even know you were here."

"Oh, that," Jerry said. "Pam hit me. It doesn't matter. I've got to talk to Bill for a minute, Aunt Flora."

"Why don't you?" Aunt Flora said. She turned to Bill Weigand. "You through with me, dearie?" she enquired. "If you are, I'm going back to bed." She looked around at the others. "Tired," she said, firmly. "Old women get tired, eh? Nobody remembers I'm an old woman." That, it was evident, pleased her. "Don't coddle myself, that's why," she said. "But all this—" she broke off. "Poor old codger," she said. She was not talking to them now. "Such a long time ago," she said. "Such a long time."

"Right," Weigand said. "I'm sorry, Mrs. Buddie." He stood up, and Mullins stood up. At a nod from Weigand, Mullins moved beside Aunt Flora, his hand hovering near her elbow. She looked at him and smiled faintly. It was an odd smile—an odd, touching smile.

"That's right, dearie," she said. "I'm an old woman."

Mullins's hand came under her elbow, supporting her. Weigand and the Norths watched them to the door.

"The poor old thing," Pam said, softly. "The poor—They were

young together, Bill. She and Harry. And remembered the same things."

"Yes," Weigand said. "However—" He seemed a little on the defensive, and turned back from the door, his manner dismissing the moment. "What have you found, Jerry?"

"The cats," Pam answered for Jerry. "They found it—what I'd forgotten. What Harry gave me, and I forgot all about it. And must have dropped when I was by the bed, changing. And it fell down the side—inside. Before he said anything, he gave it to me."

Jerry held "it" forward, touching only the paper. Weigand took it from him and stared at it and after a moment said he'd be damned.

"So this was it," he said. "And you didn't remember it, Pam!"

"Listen," Pam said. "With all that's been going on. And being chased. And Jerry. You'd have forgotten, too. And, after all, you've got it now. Is it the bottle?"

Certainly, Bill Weigand told her, it was *a* bottle. And if its contents held arsenic, *the* bottle. And Harry Perkins had risked his life to bring it to her, and it had remained for the cats to find it.

"But," he said, "we have got it now. And maybe—" He broke off and stood staring thoughtfully at the bottle. Mullins came back while he was still staring and looked at the bottle and said, "Jeez!"

"Perkins gave it to Pam," Weigand told him. "Somebody tore her room apart looking for it. And one of the cats found it."

Mullins looked at the bottle incredulously.

"You sure got to hand it to cats," Mullins said. He looked at the bottle more carefully. "Pawed it open, though," he said. "Got prints all over it." He stared at Weigand. "Jeez," he said. "Now we got cat prints."

"I opened it," Jerry said. "The cats didn't. And it won't have my prints, except on the paper."

"Probably," Weigand said, "it won't have any prints. But—have the boys gone, Mullins?"

The boys hadn't, Mullins said. Weigand was pleased.

"Have them work on it," he said. "And if they find anything, check with what we've got."

Mullins took the bottle gingerly and went away with it.

"What have you got?" Pam said. "Prints, I mean?"

Everybody, Weigand told her. At least, they hoped everybody. From toilet articles, from glasses, from here, there and everywhere. In some instances the identity of the prints was only hypothetical; in others they could count on it. But it was optimistic to count on prints being where they meant anything.

"Except," he added, "that people forget. Or get hurried. Then you find prints. And juries love them. Do you know anything about knots, Jerry?"

"Knots?" Jerry repeated. "What kind of knots? Tying knots? Or speed knots?"

"Tying knots," Weigand explained. "In this case, a hanging knot. A bowline."

"No," Jerry said. "I wasn't a boy scout. Or a sailor. Or—or what?"

Weigand shrugged.

"A rigger," he said. "A cowboy for all I know. A yachtsman. Almost anybody."

"No," Jerry said. "Who tied a bowline?"

If he knew that, Weigand told him, he'd know a lot. The person who had hanged Harry Perkins.

"You can say 'man,' I think," Pam told him. "Because he must have been thrown *over* the bannisters, and that couldn't be a woman. Or bowlines either, whatever they are. Women always tie grannies. At least Jerry says I always do."

"That I do know," Jerry put in. "A square knot from a granny. Because I have to tie up the Christmas packages. And the things Pam sends people."

Bill Weigand stopped them. As far as throwing Harry Perkins over the bannisters was concerned—and Pam probably was right in thinking that necessary—it needn't have been beyond the strength of a reasonably strong woman. Harry Perkins weighed hardly more than a hundred pounds. And he could have been propped up against the balustrade and slid over. He need not have been lifted and dropped. In either event, he would have fallen from the rail of the balustrade to the end of the leash about his neck, and that would have been drop enough.

Pam shuddered and sat down suddenly and looked rather white.

"It's—terrible," she said. "It's always seemed—oh, more horrible than anything else, hanging. The second of falling and knowing and then—"

Jerry sat on the arm of the chair and drew her to him.

"Don't think about it, Pam," he said.

"Right," Weigand said. "And in this case he was out. He didn't know what was happening."

He told them that Perkins had, apparently, first been knocked unconscious. Only then was the rope knotted about his neck and made fast to one of the balusters, and his body pushed over the rail. He admitted it still didn't bear thinking of.

"But," Pam said. She leaned her head against Jerry's shoulder for a moment and said, "All right, darling—I'm all right now" in a low voice—"but could a woman have knocked him out?"

Weigand nodded, and said it was possible. Particularly if she used something as a weapon.

"But to get back to the knot," he said. "The bowline is a common enough knot—among people who know anything about knots. But most people only know square knots, and perhaps not even those by name. Or grannies. You don't need a bowline to tie packages."

"What is it?" Pam asked. Weigand looked nonplussed.

"I don't know how to describe a knot," he said. "It goes—well, you take an end, loop your line, lay the end across the standing part, loop the standing part around the end, bring the end around behind the standing part and through the little loop and—does that make it any clearer?"

"No," said Pam, decisively. "I don't think anybody could tie a bowline, from what you say. Or even imagine a bowline."

"It doesn't matter," Jerry pointed out. "As long as you know what it is, and somebody tied it in the leash. You don't have to explain it."

"Right," Weigand said. But he still looked a little taken aback. "But it ought to be possible to explain it, you'd think. You take the end of a line and make a loop and then—"

"Please, Bill," Pam said. "Not again. After awhile we'll get you a piece of rope or something and you can show us. But don't explain it."

"Well—" Weigand began. But then Sergeant Mullins came back, and he looked excited. He said "Loot!" from the door and "We got a break!" as he advanced. He held the little green bottle loosely in a handkerchief.

Weigand stood up and took a step toward Mullins and said, "Prints?"

Mullins nodded, vigorously, holding out the bottle. They bent over it and Pam North was beside them, looking too. There were several clear impressions, outlined in black, on the bottle.

"And?" Weigand said.

"Craig's," Mullins told him. Mullins's voice was happy. "Benjamin Craig's. As neat a set as—"

But Weigand, looking down at the bottle, seemed puzzled and not to share Mullins's evident happiness.

"And nobody else's?" he said. His voice was sharp, demanding. Mullins looked less happy.

"Nope," he said. "Just Craig's." His voice was very worried. "That's all right, ain't it, Loot?" he enquired. His voice was very worried. Weigand looked at him and slowly shook his head.

"That," he said, "is not so good, Sergeant. I think somebody's kidding us."

"But why—?" Pam began. Then she stopped and nodded too. Jerry got up and came over and looked at the bottle and looked perplexed. "Of course!" Pam said. "Where are the others?"

"Right," Weigand said. "Where are the others?"

"Because," Pam explained, more to herself than to anybody, but a little to Jerry, "because there *ought* to be others. There'd almost have to be. Unless—"

"Right," Weigand said. "It ought to be a blur. Somebody packed the bottle and left prints, somebody unpacked it and put it on a shelf, somebody took it off a shelf—a dozen times it must have been handled."

"By people without fingers," Pam said. "And that's ridiculous. Or gloves?"

"Why?" Weigand said. Nobody knew.

"Obviously," Jerry offered, "somebody wiped the bottle off."

Weigand was still staring at the bottle and after a moment he said, "Right."

"And *after* it was wiped off, Ben Craig picked it up," Weigand said. "Which doesn't make sense."

"Which doesn't make *one* sense," Pam corrected. "It doesn't make the sense that it was Ben who poisoned Aunt Flora. But it makes sense, if somebody wanted it to look as if Ben poisoned Aunt Flora—somebody not very bright."

"Listen," Mullins said, in a rather desperate voice. "We got prints, ain't we? What do we want, huh?"

"Sense, Sergeant," Weigand told him. "As Pam says. Did they test the cork?"

Mullins shook his head.

"They say it ain't no use, Loot," he said. "Not that cork. They say a good cork, maybe, but where do you get good corks now days?" He looked at the lieutenant defensively. "That's what they say, Loot," he added. Weigand nodded again.

"So what we get is too good to be true," he said. "All very neat and easy and somebody is being very bright."

He looked, Pam thought, more than expectedly upset. This was not merely an annoyance; it was in some fashion a frustration.

"This messes things up, doesn't it, Bill?" she said. "I mean—you had it worked out, and this is all wrong."

It was something like that, Bill Weigand admitted. Jerry went back and sat down and felt the bump on his head. The three continued to look at the bottle as if it might explain itself at any moment. Jerry watched them.

"If it doesn't mean something," he said, presently, "why did Perkins give it to Pam? Or did he merely think he had something when he didn't have?"

Pam came over and sat on the arm of Jerry's chair and waited for Weigand to answer. Weigand walked to a table and stood with his fingers drumming on it, and then turned to them.

That, he told them, was only part of it. Where did Perkins get the bottle? When? How long had he had it? Why had he hidden out and then returned? Did he know that there were prints of Ben Craig on the bottle and if he knew it, how did he know it?

"Because," Weigand put in, "you couldn't see them unless they were brought up."

"Presumably," Jerry suggested, "he got the bottle after it was used— after the contents were used— on Aunt Flora. The same day, probably, since the bottle was missing. It was missing that day, I gather?"

"So do I," Bill Weigand told him. "I couldn't prove it in court, probably. It's—it's one of those tenuous things a lawyer can make confusing. But I gather the bottle appeared one night, was used the next morning, and disappeared some time that day. At any rate, it wasn't there when Sand brought back the usual bottle of citrate salts. So presumably Harry Perkins took it. Then he kept it two weeks, being careful not to get prints on it, and gave it to Pam last night. And then got himself killed. And then somebody tears Pam's room apart looking for the bottle." He broke off and stared at them. "It looks almost," he said, "as if somebody were determined we would find the bottle and pay attention to it. And that looks as if somebody wanted to lay the poisoning on Craig. So we get Craig, who is the only one to whom the bottle points, as the only one who wouldn't want us to find it."

He sighed and crossed back to his chair and sat down. He looked up at Mullins.

"Sit down, Sergeant," he said. "And don't look so damned hurt. It isn't your fault."

Mullins said "O.K., Loot," and sat down. He stared reproachfully at the bottle. Nobody said anything. Then Pam said, "What's in it?"

"Folwell's Fruit Salts," Mullins read. "What the hell's that? And it says: 'Professional Sample.'"

"Some new kind of salts, apparently," Weigand said, a little abstractedly. "Something just being introduced. And—" He stopped suddenly.

"That fits, anyway," Pam said. "Aunt Flora is always trying new things. She had to take something before breakfast every morning to wake up her stomach. That's what she says it does, anyway. This is probably about the same thing she usually takes—citrate salts, fruit salts. Anything that fizzes, because—" Then Pam stopped, because Weigand was looking so intent that the other two were looking at him and not, she thought, listening to her. She stopped and looked at Weigand.

"Professional sample," Weigand said. His voice was speculative. "Which means—something the manufacturers send to physicians, hoping that the physicians will try it out on patients. I knew a dentist once who had a whole cupboard filled with samples of dentifrice. He never gave them away but—" He stopped again, and looked pleased. "And," he pointed out, "we have a doctor in our midst. Dr. Wesley Buddie."

"Not in our midst," Pam corrected. "Not tonight."

"Near enough," Weigand told her. "Only—" He looked at his watch. The watch said ten minutes after two. Then he looked at the bottle. Mullins looked at it too, still a little resentfully.

"Perhaps not tonight," Weigand agreed. "Because it occurs to me that the bottle may really contain Mr. Folwell's fruit salts. And nothing else. Which would be a note."

Mullins glared at the bottle, as if he were now willing to suspect it of anything. He stood up when Weigand spoke to him.

"Send it down, Mullins," Weigand told him. "Have the prints photographed and have them run a test on the contents. For arsenic, first, obviously. Tell them we want a report first thing in the morning, and we don't have to know, to start with, how much arsenic. But tell them we'll want that, of course, as soon as they can run a quantitative."

"O.K., Loot," Mullins said, morosely. He carried the discredited bottle out again, still in the handkerchief. He left the Norths sitting in and on one chair, looking expectantly across at Weigand, alone in another.

"What do they all say?" Pam asked, when Weigand remained thoughtful. "Or haven't you asked them?"

"They all say they were fast asleep in trundle beds," Weigand told her. "No, I haven't asked them. Except your Aunt Flora. But now—" He shrugged. "However," he said, "they may as well have a chance to say it. All together. Come along."

He led them down to the drawing room and stepped ahead of them through the door. The major was pacing the floor in a dressing gown of appropriately military cut; the girls were sitting on a sofa and Bruce McClelland was standing near them, and nearest—Pam noted with interest—Judy Buddie. Chris Buddie sat by himself, reading. Ben Craig merely sat. Sand hovered. Weigand stopped inside the door and the Norths, entering around him, stood nearby. Weigand stared at the family, which stared back, except for Chris, who continued to read.

"Well," Weigand said, "one of you killed Harry Perkins. Right?"

His tone was conversational. The major whirled and glared at him.

"Nonsense!" the major said. "Damn foolishness!"

Judy Buddie made a little sound that was half "no!" and half mere startled sound, and Bruce bent to put a hand on her shoulder and turned his head to look indignantly at Weigand. Chris put down his book and stood up and Clem Buddie leaned forward and stared at the detective. Sand hovered more nervously. Ben Craig looked at Weigand, with no apparent hostility, and did not move.

"I had men outside," Weigand told them. "They didn't see anybody come in." There was a sound of movement from Pam North and what looked like the beginning of speech. Then Pam said "ouch!" and looked at Jerry and said, "Oh!"

"Also," Weigand told them, "I had a man inside. But he thought it would be a fine thing to have a cup of coffee and a sandwich down in the kitchen. So all he knows was that nobody came up from the kitchen. So one of you had a clear field to kill Perkins." He paused to let it sink in. Nobody said anything.

"Now," he said, and his voice had edge, "there's no use asking whether any of you was up and about, because you're all going to tell me you were sound asleep. Right?"

Nobody said anything.

"Right," Weigand said. "So we'll leave that until tomorrow. And none of you heard anything. And you all loved Harry Perkins devotedly and wouldn't have harmed a hair of his head. And none of you even knew he was in the house. Right?"

Somebody did say something. It was, unexpectedly, Sand.

"I'm sorry, sir," he said. "I knew he was in the house. I—I helped him hide. In the basement. He—he insisted on it, sir."

"Did he?" Weigand said. "And I suppose the police—" He stopped, apparently tired. "All right," he said. "You hid him. We'll go into that later, too, Sand. But I suppose it was natural. He said he was afraid, didn't he?"

"Something like that, sir," Sand told him. "I—I thought he was, sir."

"He was," Weigand said. "With cause. And he didn't come to us because he knew, or thought he knew, something which would incriminate a member of the family. He was very loyal." He let that sink in. "He is now very dead," he added. "Loyalty didn't work both ways. If I were one of you, and not the murderer, I'd remember that. However—"

They looked at him, restlessly, uneasily.

"I want to find out only one thing, now," he said. "Then I'll let you go back to bed, if you want to. And this time I'll have a man on each floor."

He looked at the major, and shook his head.

"You would," he said, cryptically. The major stared at him.

"Would what, eh?" the major demanded.

Weigand shook his head. He looked at the girls.

"Your grandmother has a ranch in the West you've both been to summers," he said. "Right? You rode and that sort of thing. Right?"

The girls looked puzzled, but Judy nodded.

"So what?" Clem demanded, conceding it. She stood up, now. Weigand paid no attention to her.

"You," he said to Bruce. "Were you a Boy Scout? Or you?" the last was to Christopher Buddie. Bruce shrugged and nodded. Chris looked rather embarrassed.

"In days of innocence," he said. "When I was young and helpless."

"Right," Weigand said. He looked at Craig and for a moment said nothing.

"Did you go to the ranch too?" he asked. Craig leaned back and looked up at Weigand and shook his head.

"Only once," he said. "It was—strenuous. Why?"

Weigand ignored the question.

"Were you in the last war?" he asked, instead.

"I don't get it," Craig told him. "But yes. I was in the Navy, for a while."

Weigand looked interested.

"As a yeoman," Craig went on, comfortably. "Yeoman's mate, first class."

"Right," Weigand said. He sounded dissatisfied. He looked around at them.

"That's all for tonight," he said, curtly. "I'll see you tomorrow." He turned and left them. Pam and Jerry followed him into the hall.

"There'll be men around," he told them. "Nothing more will happen tonight."

His voice sounded tired. As the Norths left him and climbed up toward the guest room, he was giving Mullins orders. Mullins no longer had the little green bottle. He looked disillusioned.

• 12 •

Lieutenant William Weigand, Acting Captain of the Homicide Squad, sat down at his scarred desk and regarded it with disfavor. He looked through the small, dirty gray window at the large, dirty gray world, and was disgruntled. It had stopped snowing, but it had not cleared and the wind still came out of the northeast. It was not a particularly good day to be alive, and 8:15 had not been a good morning hour to face it. And instead of staying in a small warm place and talking to Dorian after he was up, he had had to come to a grimy, drafty place and talk to Deputy Chief Inspector Artemus O'Malley, who wanted him to arrest somebody. Forthwith.

Weigand suspected that he had been spoiling O'Malley. There had been a time when O'Malley would, with only the grumbling natural to an inspector, let a week go by between discovery of murder and arrest for same. But recently Weigand had been lucky; once he had a solution and a suicide within twelve hours. O'Malley did not approve of the suicide, nor did Weigand himself. But O'Malley approved, perhaps inordinately, of the speed. He had almost told Weigand so; he had gone so far as to say that Weigand was beginning to show the stuff and that he him-

144

self, inspector in charge, could hardly have done better if he had been personally on the job instead of, as was naturally the case, the brains behind the job. Since O'Malley, at the race track for the afternoon and elsewhere for the evening, had not even heard of the job until it was finished, this seemed to Weigand even more than usually unfair.

But Weigand was used to the ways of inspectors and, in particular, the ways of O'Malley. They came worse than O'Malley, as a matter of fact. O'Malley, save for prodding and advice, to which it was unnecessary to listen with absorption, let him go his own way. Even now, Weigand was pleased to remember, O'Malley had no fixed idea as to who might better be arrested. He was a little inclined to favor Major Alden Buddie, but he had something to say, also, for Miss Clementine Buddie. His real preference, openly expressed, was Ross Brack, but he admitted he did not quite see how that could be managed, except on general principles. O'Malley felt general principles would be adequate, but was doubtful about the D.A.'s office.

"A funny bunch up there," O'Malley said, dourly. "What the hell do they want?"

The question was rhetorical, which did not stop O'Malley himself from answering it.

"Evidence," he said. "Something for the shysters to wrangle over. When I was your age—"

When O'Malley had been Weigand's age it appeared that evidence was not so much in use. They were good old days and O'Malley spent several minutes remembering them favorably. Then he told Weigand to quit wasting time and bring somebody in, and Weigand said he would do what he could and went to do it. He went back to his desk and stared at it and called for Mullins.

Mullins did not like the look on Weigand's face. The Loot was tired and—nervous looking. He seemed to be fighting himself, and the case; his face looked as if he were fighting the case, and as if the case had got in a low punch. He greeted Mullins with a "Well?"

"It just came in, Loot," Mullins said. "It's arsenic, all right. In the bottle. Only not very much. Not enough, they say."

"Not enough for what?" Weigand said. "Who says?"

Mullins was equable. The lab boys said. Not enough in the indicated dosage to kill the patient. The dosage advised on the label was a tablespoon in water. But in a tablespoon of the powder in the bottle, there would be less than half a grain of arsenic. Which would make anybody sick, but could hardly be expected to kill anybody who was not already half dead. Even if the dose were doubled, the quantity of arsenic would not be lethal. Mullins looked at Weigand doubtfully.

"Who," he enquired, "would want to poison somebody just a little? I don't get it."

Neither, Weigand admitted without enthusiasm, did he. Things got no better fast. It was much harder to think of a reason why somebody should half poison than to think of a reason for poisoning completely.

"Makes it look like a practical joke," Mullins said. "Only a guy who would joke with arsenic would be a sort of funny guy."

It would, Weigand admitted, show an odd sense of humor. But the whole thing was odd, from first to last. It was perhaps simplest to suppose that the poisoner had merely made a mistake; that he thought the amount of arsenic in the standard dose of the salts would be lethal. Perhaps he had even read of poisoners who defeated their own purpose by giving too much poison.

"It don't seem bright," Mullins said. He sat down.

Weigand let the remark lie, and after a moment Mullins went on. The fingerprint boys, with the bottle back in the office, had photographed and enlarged the prints on it and compared them, scientifically, with the prints of Ben Craig. They had thus succeeded in verifying what they already knew. They now, however, had it in proper form for trial, if it came into trial.

"I still don't see why we can't go ahead with them," Mullins said. He still sounded aggrieved. "Suppose there ain't any other prints. What's the matter with the prints we got? Why not pinch Craig and let his lawyer explain it?" He looked at Weigand hopefully. "We ain't working for the defense, Loot," he insisted. "Maybe they wouldn't wonder about other prints."

Weigand merely looked at him.

"Nope," Mullins said. "I guess you're right, Loot. Probably it wouldn't work. But it does show he gave her the salts, don't it?"

Weigand shrugged. That was, certainly, the inference to be drawn. And he had—or *had* he denied it? Mullins went back into his notes. He plodded, his lips moving. Then his face brightened.

"Yeh," he said, "he says she was drinking the stuff when he came in. And that the bottle was on the table, and it was a new bottle. But—wait a minute. *He didn't say it was a different bottle!*"

Weigand nodded. That, he said, was the way he remembered it. It was a point.

"But there's a chance that he wouldn't have noticed," he pointed out. "A good chance—he expected to see the usual bottle, and saw what he expected to see. As anybody might have."

Mullins looked doubtful.

"Yes," Weigand told him. "As anybody might have. We get into the habit of giving significance to such things, Sergeant; we get to seeing things too clearly and to expecting other people to see clearly too, and make logical deductions, at the time. But at the time—at any time— most people don't see clearly and make logical deductions. We don't, except when we're on a case. For example— could you identify any stranger you saw coming down this morning? Say the first man you met coming out of the house?"

"It was a woman," Mullins said. "At any rate—I think. No, I guess it was— oh, the hell with it. O.K., Loot."

Weigand nodded. That was the way it was. Looking back, you often wished, as a detective, that witnesses had had their wits about them. But it was a lot to ask. So possibly—even probably—Ben Craig would not have noticed that it was the wrong bottle. At least, it would be difficult to prove anything by the point. As to whether he had prepared the dose, and was now lying about it—well, that was confusing too.

"In the first place," Weigand pointed out, "she says she doesn't know. Which isn't reasonable, because when she began to suspect she had been poisoned, she would remember all she could about the circumstances, and probably remember who gave her the salts, even though she didn't know the salts had the poison in them. So, probably, she is shielding somebody."

"Somebody who tried to poison her?" Mullins asked. He seemed doubtful.

"Perhaps she had her own reasons," he said. "Now that we know where the poison came from, we'll have to try to get it out of her. Maybe she thought the person who gave her the poison was innocent— didn't know the poison was in the salts."

Weigand paused and drummed on the table and Mullins waited.

"And," Weigand pointed out after a moment, "she may have been right. If you were going to poison somebody would you put poison in medicine and then give the person you wanted to poison the medicine with your own hands? Or would you arrange to have somebody else give the poison?"

"Somebody else," Mullins agreed. "So Craig didn't do it, because that makes it too easy?"

Weigand smiled a little. There was something in that, he said. Supposing Craig had openly given the poison, openly leaving fingerprints on it, it was a better than fifty-fifty chance somebody else had put the arsenic in the salts. Mullins nodded and Weigand watched him nod.

"Then," Weigand said, "why did he lie about it, if he was so innocent as all that?"

Mullins thought it over. "Hell," Mullins said. "Maybe he *did* do it."

"Then why—?" Weigand began.

"Listen, Loot," Mullins said. His voice had a note of entreaty. "Let's take up something else, huh? You've got me going around."

Weigand thought a moment longer and then shrugged.

"Right," he said. "We'll let it go for the moment. But it's going to stay right there, Sergeant. We're going to have to think up some way Craig can be innocent and not innocent at the same time."

His fingers stopped drumming for a moment and he looked through Mullins.

"Or," he said, "maybe we don't. Maybe we don't after all, Mullins."

Mullins waited, but Weigand did not amplify. Instead, the lieutenant picked up the first of a sheaf of reports lying on his desk. It concerned the manner of Anthony's death, and added little to what they knew. It was formal, for the records. A .38 calibre bullet, fired from an automatic, had ended Anthony's life. (So the bullet had not come from the major's gun.) The bullet had entered the neck and ranged up and back, coming out the back of the skull—and taking part of the skull with it.

Death had supervened without an interval worth mentioning. Anthony had been in his late thirties or early forties and well nourished. He had been facing his murderer, who was below him, at the time of the shot, which had been fired at a distance greater than two feet, since there had been no powder marks around the wound. The distance, as indicated by the nature of the entrance wound, had probably been between four and five feet.

Weigand tossed the report into the proper basket, for proper filing. He took up another, which dealt with the body of Harry Perkins. It reported that Perkins had been hanged, with enough drop to break his neck; that he weighed 103 pounds and was undernourished; that there was a contusion on his jaw indicating that he might have been knocked unconscious before he was hanged. This report followed its predecessor into the basket.

There was a report from detectives who had searched Anthony's apartment after his body was found, and removed from it almost everything portable. The things removed were now in the possession of the property custodian, and were itemized. Weigand ran down the list. Anthony had had a good many clothes and a good deal of liquor in his apartment. He had also had marijuana cigarettes. Weigand said "well." He had had checkbooks and unpaid bills and receipts and very little correspondence. And he had had, with a rubber band around them, several letters which started, in most cases, "Darling" and ended, in all cases, "Clem." He showed Mullins this entry.

"Sometime," said Weigand bitterly, "we'll get a precinct man with a mind. Maybe. Get the letters, Mullins."

Mullins went. Weigand read on through the papers while he waited. Detective Stein, in charge at the Buddie house the night before, reported that all concerned had kept to their rooms and that there had been no disturbance. The girls, Clem and Judy, had doubled up in the former's room, and Bruce McClelland had been moved into Judy's. And as far as Detective Stein could report, everybody had slept well. If a guilty conscience had induced wakefulness, that fact did not come within the purview of the Police Department.

There had been a checkup, also, on Stephen Anthony's past, which had, from time to time, come within the Police Department's purview.

There was an arrest some years previous, for example, on the complaint of a wealthy woman—also, as Mrs. Buddie had been, appreciably older than Anthony. She had alleged that he had sold for his own benefit securities entrusted to him for purposes which remained a little vague. Then, without explanation, she had withdrawn her allegations, leaving the case, and the police, at loose ends. And another time he had been picked up on suspicion that he knew more than an innocent man should about the recovery of some jewels which had been stolen—or had they ever actually been stolen?—and had been returned mysteriously, with money changing hands. They had got as far as magistrate's court with that one, and the magistrate had, lugubriously, dismissed the charge. And Anthony had been born of Greek parents, whose name was not Anthony; he had appeared in New York some fifteen years previously, being then in his early twenties, and he was suspected of doing odd jobs for Ross Brack. After Mrs. Buddie had dismissed him he had several times, after a few drinks, complained to associates and made vague promises of getting his own back. His associates, who did not regard Mr. Anthony as dangerous, had been unimpressed. He had hinted of a new angle which was to bring him unprecedented affluence, but for fifteen years he had been dropping equally murky hints and remaining, on the whole, no more affluent than the next hanger-on of rackets.

There was, Weigand thought, tossing aside the papers which dealt with Mr. Anthony, formerly Anaragagnos, nothing conclusive in that. There was not, on the whole, even anything suggestive. He drummed the table.

The trouble was not, he reflected, that he lacked a hunch. He had a very good hunch. And usually good hunches could be proved or disproved, and there you were. You matured an hypothesis, on the basis of observed details—of events, fabrications, personalities. If too much showed against the first hypothesis, you matured a second, and perhaps after it a third. But if you knew your job, the first hypothesis was usually correct in essentials. You knew who had acted and what he had done and you could guess why. The rest could be filled in.

But here the method seemed to be breaking down. He thought he knew who, but the hunch was almost wholly speculative. If necessary, he could postulate a "why," although he was not certain it would be the right "why." What he did not know was, peculiarly, what. He knew somebody had killed Stephen Anthony, because Stephen Anthony was dead. He knew somebody, and presumably the same person—although that, again, was "hunch"—had hanged Harry Perkins. But these things were subsidiary. What he did not know was whether somebody had tried to kill Pam North's Aunt Flora. That was where the peculiarity lay.

Somebody had gone to the trouble of getting white arsenic—presumably picking a pharmacy which was not too scrupulous, putting up a good story (a desire to sprinkle the poison as an insecticide on some favorite plant, perhaps? Or a desire to use it in disposing of some loved, but ailing pet?) and had further gone to the considerable trouble of mixing the poison with the fruit salts. But it appeared that he had not done it to kill, because it would be easy to discover the lethal dose and not too hard to insure that the amount of the salts recommended would include ample arsenic.

"He only does it to annoy, because he knows it teases," Weigand quoted to himself. Which was silly, because who would tease with arsenic? He considered possibilities.

It was a possibility, for example, that the purpose *had* been merely to annoy, in a somewhat extreme sense; that it had been an unpleasant practical joke, played by somebody with an unpleasant mind and an active grudge. Somebody might merely have wanted, for reasons which did not appear, to make Aunt Flora extremely uncomfortable. This argued the presence, somewhere in the circle, of a malicious monster. Weigand shook his head, not believing in monsters and having noticed no psychopathic tendencies among those around Aunt Flora. Nor was it easy to imagine a chain of circumstances which would lead from such a malicious joke to a double murder; if somebody had been "teasing" Aunt Flora with arsenic, then the subsequent murders were unconnected. You came back then to coincidence, which got you nowhere. Or nowhere you wanted to get.

If not to kill and not to tease, then why arsenic in Aunt Flora's

medicine? A mistake? It seemed improbable; it was difficult to imagine so prodigious a mistake. Nobody had mistaken Aunt Flora for a
plant, and sprinkled her with arsenic. Nobody had mistaken her
medicine for weed killer, and reinforced it. Nobody had supposed that
a person not Aunt Flora would be more likely than she to take fruit
salts from a bottle carefully, as it appeared, insinuated among her
medicines. Reluctantly, Weigand returned to his first conviction—for
some reason, some person had given Aunt Flora enough arsenic to
make her ill and not enough to kill her, and so had achieved precisely
what he intended. Which did not make sense. Or—

Weigand stopped drumming on the desk for a second and then
began again, at a faster tempo.

Or perhaps somebody had intended the incapacitating, but not
lethal, dose as a warning of worse to come. It might have been somebody's way of telling Aunt Flora to watch her step, to abandon a course
she was following which was injurious to the poisoner. That would
make sense. But it would not fit in with the murders—unless. Unless
Anthony, also, had got in the way and had not been warned, but had
merely been stopped. It indicated a new forthrightness on the part of
the murderer, and a drastic change of method. But that might be
explained by the relationship between the murderer and his victims. He
might have been fond of Aunt Flora and wanted to give her a chance to
mend her ways; he might have disliked Anthony for other reasons, and
seen no cause to temporize. He might have killed Harry Perkins
because Perkins knew his identity, having discovered it either during
the attempt to poison Aunt Flora or during the murder of Anthony. Presumably, since he had come up with the arsenic bottle, Perkins's information pertained to the poison attempt.

This tied things together, but the pattern did not fit the hunch.
Weigand shook his head, dissatisfied. Then he had a new, and rather
startling notion. It occurred to him that he was getting things too complicated, because there was a much simpler pattern.

Suppose Stephen Anthony, possibly thinking he had an inheritance
coming and wanting to hasten it, had decided to dispose of Aunt Flora.
(This fitted with Anthony's vague hints about affluence to come.) Sup-

pose he had given her the arsenic, and had either miscalculated the dose—which was not out of his character—or had planned on one of those slow, methodical poisonings so popular, if criminal history was to be credited, among the British. And suppose Aunt Flora had realized what was going on and put a stop to it, partly out of pure annoyance with a man who was trying to kill her; partly to see that he didn't, in the future, succeed. That was in character, too. Aunt Flora might be expected to be drastic, if she moved. She might be expected to use a gun. And she would, as a former ranch-woman, know how to tie a bowline.

But there Weigand shook his head. This did not only fail to conform to the hunch; this was definitely anti-hunch. Because, while willing to believe that Aunt Flora might have killed Anthony, given so good a reason, he could not imagine any circumstances under which she would kill Perkins, of whom she had evidently been fond. And of whom, Weigand added to himself, she could have been sure. Because if what he had heard of Perkins's devotion to Aunt Flora was true, Perkins would never have dreamed of reporting one of her murders. He would, Weigand thought, have been more apt to applaud.

"Damn," Weigand said, aloud. Mullins was right; this was a screwy one. He found himself wishing that Pamela North would have a brainstorm. He went back to checking over reports, marveling at the completeness, and on the whole the uselessness, of information collected by the toiling detectives of various squads and bureaus. What advantage was there in knowing, for example, that the bullet showed six rifling grooves, spiraling to the left, and was therefore presumably fired from a Colt automatic? Weigand sighed. Of course, he thought in fairness, it may be useful later. He went on with reports, and Mullins came in.

Mullins tossed a packet of letters to the desk and Weigand pulled off the rubber band holding them. He ran through them, hurrying here and hesitating there. They were about what he expected—they were young and indiscreet and, reading them, the most resolute looker on the brighter side of things could not doubt that Clem Buddie and Ross Brack had been more than casual acquaintances—and more, for that matter, than close friends. The letters were, in the grimy league of Stephen Anthony, saleable, given a special market. But they had not been sold; Anthony had died with this financial anchor still to wind-ward. And did that prove, since the letters had not been recovered, that Anthony had not been killed for the letters?

Weigand decided that it did not, necessarily. Anthony might have been killed on the assumption he was carrying the letters and the mur-derer might have had no opportunity to search the apartment immedi-ately afterward. (But he had had most of that night, hadn't he? He may not have known where Anthony's apartment was. Or he may have decided that the letters were in themselves harmless, a tool rendered useless by the extinction of the artisan. And he was right; the letters were, now, harmless for their original purpose, since the police had them and the police did not blackmail.) Weigand finished the letters and tossed them into the basket. Another piece of the puzzle had come to hand; in the final picture it might well have its place. But it did not, at the moment, in itself provide a key.

Weigand found he had worked down to the desk. He lighted a cigarette, watched the smoke for a moment and stood up. Mullins stood up too and Weigand nodded.

"Right," Weigand said. "Time to go calling, Sergeant. We'll go see Dr. Buddie. And talk about medicines. We'll take our little bottle with us."

· 13 ·

It had stopped snowing, but it was still heavily overcast, and below the solid gray of high clouds darker clouds scudded toward the southwest. The northeaster held. Weigand, watching the people on the avenues buffeting their way uptown against it, skidding downtown with it at their backs, wished the Weather Bureau could afford to be less secretive. Presumably, German submarine commanders off the coast would have noticed, by now, that it had clouded up. But probably there was reason. Weigand liked to know what kind of weather was coming, but was willing to sacrifice the knowledge for the war effort. He was not, however, eager. Even last week's weather map, he decided, would be interesting to see. If weather maps interested you.

They went north and across town to Park, and up Park. They stopped in front of a large apartment building and went into a ground floor apartment which had its own entrance from the street, and an unassertive brass plate saying: "Wesley Buddie, M.D." A middle-aged woman in a white uniform met them among copies of the *National Geographic*. She looked expectant.

"No," Weigand said, "we haven't an appointment. But—"

"Then I'm afraid the doctor can't see you today," the doctor's protector told him, firmly. "He sees patients only by appointment."

That, Weigand told her, was natural. But they were not patients. They wanted to see Dr. Buddie on—another matter.

The woman looked at Mullins and came to the correct conclusion.

"If it's something about parking?" she said. "Or air raids? Or things like that? I could take care of it, probably."

"It ain't parking," Mullins told her. He was gruff; it always a little annoyed him that his occupation was so apparent. Mullins thought of himself, in moments of introspection, as a man who might be anything. But everybody else thought of him simply as a cop. It irked.

"No," Weigand said. "It isn't parking. Tell the doctor that Lieutenant Weigand would like a few minutes. He'll understand, I think."

The protector seemed to doubt it. She looked with determination at Weigand, who looked back mildly but otherwise did not respond. She waited for him to go away, and he did not go away. He was, her look told him, being exceedingly irregular. She should, his look replied, give his name to the doctor. She went from the reception room, displeased, and returned, still displeased. The doctor would see them, she reported. Her tone implied that it was most irregular of the doctor.

Dr. Wesley Buddie was sitting at a wide desk in the next room—a wide, orderly desk. He was a wide, orderly man. He nodded at Weigand and said, "Lieutenant." He nodded at Mullins and he nodded at chairs. The detective sat down and Dr. Buddie waited, politely. He took off his nose-glasses and held them in his hand, and tapped the desk top gently, indicating a receptive, dispassionate state of mind. Weigand laid the little green bottle on the desk. Dr. Buddie looked at it. Then he looked at Weigand and continued to wait.

"Have you ever seen it before?" Weigand said. Dr. Buddie did not seem surprised by the question, nor did he seem greatly interested.

"The preparation?" he enquired. "Or this particular bottle? Certainly I've seen the preparation."

"And the bottle?" Weigand was patient.

Dr. Buddie raised his eyebrows, Weigand nodded and he picked up the bottle. He turned it over, looking at it. He shook his head.

"Really," he said, "I have no way of knowing. I don't remember it, specifically. I may have seen it. Why?"

"Because," Weigand told him, "the arsenic came out of it. The arsenic that was given your mother."

Dr. Buddie looked at the bottle again, shook his head again and put the bottle down on the desk, pushing it toward the detective.

"I know nothing about that," he said. "If you are, in this very tactful manner, asking if I poisoned my mother—no, I didn't. If I wanted to poison anybody, I wouldn't use arsenic. I would use something better. But I haven't poisoned anyone." He paused and half smiled. "Except of course in the way of practice," he added. "And always with the best intentions."

Weigand picked up the bottle and made no response to the physician's professional jest. He turned it over in his hands, in turn, and pointed to the small, crescent-shaped label which read: "Professional Sample."

"You've seen that before, at any rate," he said. "Or labels like it."

"Naturally," Dr. Buddie told him. "I get 'em by the case. Samples of headache medicines and antacids and laxatives and nose drops and all the things that poor damn fools take. Apparently on the assumption that I will dish them out to patients."

"Do you?" Weigand asked.

Dr. Buddie smiled.

"Sometimes," he said. "When I know they won't do any harm, and if the patients haven't anything the matter with them. If they complain of headaches, for example, I tell them to take aspirin or, if they don't like aspirin, suggest something else—maybe even give them one of the samples. Supposing, naturally, that there is nothing really wrong. Most of the stuff I have thrown away."

Weigand nodded.

"Now, specifically, this," he said, pointing at the bottle. "Did the manufacturers send you this—not this particular bottle, necessarily, but bottles of this compound? You'll see why I wonder. Presumably it was sent to a doctor—passed through a doctor's hands, at some point. I have nothing to indicate that it passed through your hands. But you're a doctor and a member of the family."

"But not the family doctor," Dr. Buddie told him. "That goes without saying."

"Never?" Weigand wanted to know.

"Never," Dr. Buddie told him. "Physicians don't treat their own families, Lieutenant."

"Right," Weigand said. "To get back to the bottle—did you ever get samples of this stuff, whether you passed them on or not?"

"No," Dr. Buddie said. He said it flatly. Weigand wanted to know if he was sure.

"Yes," Dr. Buddie told him. "Quite sure. Because it's been on the market for years and they don't need to send out samples. The samples are to introduce a product, usually. This doesn't need introduction. But if I had got a sample, I might very well have passed it on—it's harmless; it may even be of some value. Chiefly mental, naturally."

"Mental?" Weigand repeated. Dr. Buddie nodded.

"Make them think they feel better in the mornings," he said. "Most people need something to make them think they feel better in the morning. Stuff like this has a nice, fresh taste. Makes you belch. Makes you think it's doing you a lot of good."

"And doesn't?"

Dr. Buddie shrugged. If you thought it did, it did, he said. Always assuming there wasn't anything really wrong, except eating too much and not exercising enough and having too much time to think about yourself. It was, further, mildly antacid.

"Looks more exciting than bicarb of soda," he explained. "Mumbo-jumbo of course. But that may be useful. Seems to help keep mother ticking, for example. Does her no harm, apparently."

"Then I gather," Weigand said, "that you don't try to discourage her from taking fruit salts, citrate salts—whatever it is? Right?"

"Why should I?" Dr. Buddie said. "Keeps her amused. She's got a mildly acid condition, anyway, as you would expect. Healthy old lady, however. Enjoys life. Enjoys her ailments. Likes to dose herself. I keep an eye on her, of course. Call it a semiprofessional eye. Now and then I send her something new to take." He smiled. "Always a great improvement for a few days," he added. "Typical case, my mother."

"Hypochondria?" Weigand wanted to know. The physician lifted his shoulders slightly.

"Technically, of course, hypochondria," he agreed. "But it's a big name for it. She merely makes the most of little aches and pains. Keeps her interested. Most people do that, in one degree or another. Real hypochondria is—well, an advanced degree. More like Ben. Although even he is reasonably mild about it. And of course he has got a sinus condition. Most people have."

"And takes things for it?" Weigand asked. Dr. Buddie nodded.

"Nose drops," he said. "That sort of thing. I send him things from time to time, too. Things that won't do any harm, and may soothe. Things to put in hot water and inhale, with very encouraging smells. And the steam vapor is a useful palliative. Doesn't matter what you put in it, as long as it amuses you."

Weigand found himself rather liking Dr. Buddie.

"You mean," he said, "that it is merely the steam which helps? And that the other stuff hasn't any real value?"

Dr. Buddie shrugged.

"'Real'?" he repeated. "How do I know—how does anybody know? Physically, no—it just makes a smell. But people like medicinal smells—makes them think they've got hold of something. So their minds get better, and they get better." He looked at Weigand, and smiled slowly. "Secrets of the profession, Lieutenant," he said. "Not to be quoted against me. There are few 'yes' or 'no' answers in medicine, Lieutenant. That's why doctors make bad witnesses."

"So," Weigand said, "to promote—well, call it mental health—you do sometimes send samples of proprietary medicines to your mother? And to Ben?"

"Yes," Dr. Buddie said. "Harmless things, to ward off hypochondria. Or enhance it. I don't know. Naturally, I use discretion. But most of these things"—he waved at the bottle—"are simple and harmless; most of them represent complicated ways of taking aspirin and bicarbonate."

"But you never sent this product?" Weigand asked again. The doctor shook his head.

"No," he said. "Neither with arsenic nor without it. As a matter of fact, mother used to use it until a year or so ago, when she decided she liked Wilson's Citrate Salts better." He really looked amused. "They're the same thing, chemically," he said. "Or so near as doesn't matter. Wilson's stuff is blue; this stuff is green. They taste about the same, however."

He tapped gently with his glasses on the desk.

"So there would have been no point in my sending her this, Lieutenant," he said. "She already knew it. And, as I said, it isn't a new product and samples aren't being sent out. That bottle came from a druggist's shelf, originally, I imagine. Without the arsenic. Is there much arsenic, by the way?"

Weigand hesitated a moment, decided it was not a secret, and shook his head.

"Not enough, apparently," he said. "That's what they tell me."

Dr. Buddie did not seem surprised.

"Obviously mother got a small dose," he said. His tone held no comment on this fact.

"Would you suppose," Weigand said, "that the size of the dose was an accident? Fortunate for your mother; unfortunate for the person who was trying to kill her?"

Dr. Buddie's shoulders rose and fell. He enquired how he would be supposed to know.

"Obviously," he said, "if it was an attempt to murder her, it was a mistake on the part of the poisoner. It seems a rather silly mistake, even for a layman. But laymen have peculiar ideas about drugs, often enough."

"About arsenic?" Weigand said, doubtfully. "With all the accounts of arsenical poisoning available? It seems—improbable."

Dr. Buddie looked at him. His eyes told nothing, and his tone told no more.

"Does it, Lieutenant?" he enquired. His tone dropped flat.

The two looked at each other for a moment. It was Dr. Buddie who resumed.

"As a physician," he said, "I would obviously know the dosage. If I were trying to kill somebody by poison, I would kill him. Possibly if I wanted to make it appear that a layman had done it, I would even use arsenic, counting on you to assume that a physician would use a better poison. I could have procured arsenic easily and put it into the bottle with Folwell's stuff and sent it to mother and she would, presumably, have taken it. Or put it in her medicine cabinet, where somebody else might have prepared a dose and given it to her. I see your point, Lieutenant."

"It isn't necessarily my point," Weigand told him. "Certainly it is a possibility. I take it that you didn't do any of these things?"

"No," Dr. Buddie said. "I certainly did not. A statement which is obviously without value, as you do not need to point out. Why should I have done any of those things?"

Weigand said he wouldn't know. Or wouldn't know if the doctor didn't.

"Money," Dr. Buddie said. "Naturally—it was so obvious that it did not occur to me for the moment. You think I tried to poison mother to get my share of her money. In that case, why didn't I make a job of it?"

"I don't know," Weigand said. "Why didn't you?"

"If I'd tried it, I would have," Dr. Buddie told him. Suddenly he stood up and stared down at Weigand.

"Damn it, man!" he said. "Surely you're not such a fool!"

Weigand told him to sit down, and Weigand's voice was easy and his words unhurried.

"Detectives have to ask questions and get answers," he said. "It's the way they have—the only way they have, doctor. I haven't said I think you poisoned your mother. I grant the weight of your arguments against it. So far as I know now you would have been a fool to use arsenic at all and know too much to use too little. Therefore, it would appear that you did not try to kill your mother with arsenic for her money."

His tone was quiet and reasonable; he seemed to be explaining the obvious.

"If new developments show that you may have given your mother poison without an intention of killing her," he went on, "we will consider the point when it comes up. If it appears that you tried to kill her, but not for her money, I'll ask you about that. When I want to know things, I'll ask people questions, doctor. You and your brother the major, and your nieces and your nephews and your aunts. And so polish up the handle on the big front door."

Dr. Buddie had sat down. He stared at Weigand.

"Don't tell me that you quote *Alice in Wonderland,* too," he said. He said it anxiously.

"Never," Weigand told him. "Well, almost never." He stood up and Mullins, who had tilted his chair against the wall, let it fall to the floor and stood up too.

"Thank you, Doctor," Weigand said. "Probably we'll be seeing you."

"Don't forget," Dr. Buddie advised him. "I wouldn't use arsenic—slow and uncertain. To say nothing of being needlessly painful for the patient. Keep you from running off at a tangent."

"It takes all the running I can do to stay in the same place," Weigand told him, gravely. He went out, with Mullins behind him, while Dr. Buddie recognized the paraphrase and made sounds of discontent. The receptionist looked at them with hostility and did not speak.

"'Bye, toots," Mullins said. She still did not speak. Weigand, leading the way to the car, decided that this was fortunate.

Driving the few blocks to the Buddie house, Weigand pulled into the curb in front of a cigar store. He left Mullins in the car, with the motor running, and went to a telephone booth. He deposited a nickel, dialed the operator, gave his number and got his nickel back. The sergeant on duty told him a message had just come through from Washington, and read it. Weigand said, "Yeh, I thought so. Thanks" and hung up. He went back to the car and drove on, over the rutted snow, to the Buddie house. Just as he stopped in front of it, snow began falling again.

Weigand, sitting in the library with Mullins, waited for Benjamin Craig, who sent word that he was just finishing breakfast. He was, Weigand decided, making the best of his enforced holiday from the bank. There was time while they waited for two visitors. Nemo honored them first, with long ears flopping as he advanced and an expres-

sion of beatific enjoyment as he sniffed Weigand's trousers. He found
them delicious and had no reticence in his approval; there was, clearly,
a fascinating odor which it was sheer, exciting happiness to investigate.
Weigand was slightly embarrassed; remembered Pam's cats and was
reassured. Nemo, it could be assumed—it was comforting to assume—
smelled nothing more outrageous than cats. Nemo went to Mullins and
was less rewarded. He turned, without comment, and trotted out.

"You don't smell good," Weigand told Mullins. "I smell very good."

Mullins was arranging his thoughts for an answer when Major Bud-
die came in. He came in bristling and he did not seem as pleased with
Weigand as had Nemo. His ears did not flap, but his eyebrows bristled.
He said: "Young man!"

"Yes," Weigand said, assuming that the major meant him, and mildly gratified. He didn't, he assumed, have many more years of being
called "young man," even as a reproach.

"Damned nonsense!" the major told him. "Some man of yours says I
can't leave. Eh? Got my duties, Lieutenant! Can't have this sort of nonsense, you know. War on. Eh?"

"Right," Weigand said. "I can't keep you, Major. You're perfectly
free to go, if you want to. I'll have to have a man go with you, of
course. Wherever you go. Just a matter of routine, but I have to be able
to get in touch with you if it becomes necessary."

"Eh?" the major said. He looked a little deflated. "Mean to say
you'd have a man following me all over the post? Look damned silly."

"Yes," Weigand said, "I suppose it would. But the alternative is for
you to stay here—I hope not for much longer."

"I could have him kept out, you know," the major said, thoughtfully.
"He'd be a civilian, of course. Eh? Couldn't wander all over the place,
you know—couldn't have that."

Weigand looked up at the major, who stood and bristled quietly.

"Yes, there's that," Weigand said. "You could try, anyway. You
could report that the police were following you, in connection with a
murder case, and that you found this annoying. That might hold us
up—until we got an order. But I'd think you'd find that rather embarrassing, too. Right?"

The major bristled down at Weigand, who continued to smile.

"Think you've got me, eh?" the major demanded. He stared at Weigand and then a smile broke fitfully on his face. "Maybe you have at that, Lieutenant. Won't be long, you say?"

Weigand said he hoped not. He couldn't promise, but he hoped not.

"On to something, eh?" the major said. He sounded interested. "Think you're getting somewhere?"

Weigand shook his head, still smiling. He said that, obviously, the major did not really expect him to answer that. The major thought it over a moment, and nodded.

"Well," he said. "Get on with it, eh? There's a war on."

Weigand nodded and the major, after another stare—but this time not a belligerent stare—turned in military formation and made for the door. In it he met his half-brother, Ben Craig, and made a sound which sounded like "Huh!" The major went on. Ben Craig came in and said "good morning" pleasantly, and sat where he was told to sit. Weigand stood up and half sat on the edge of a table and looked down at him.

"You told me, Mr. Craig, that you were a yeoman in the Navy," he said. "Didn't you?"

Ben Craig was comfortable. He began to make designs with his fingers, and to look at Weigand as if the detective were being considered for a loan. Then he nodded and said "yes."

"But you didn't tell me that you enlisted as a seaman," Weigand said, flatly. "You were transferred to yeoman at the end of three months. Right?"

Craig seemed faintly puzzled, but he remained polite.

"That is quite true, Lieutenant," he said. "I enlisted as a seaman in the U.S.N.R.F. 'Seaman for yeoman' they called it, or some such thing. After a few months—three is probably right—I was transferred. But why does it interest you?"

"I take it," Weigand told him, "that you're saying you don't know why it interests me?"

Craig made another design with his fingers, contemplated it, and shook his head.

"I'm not good at guessing, Lieutenant," he said. "It's a little hard to see what all this ancient history—" He broke off and folded his hands. It was as if he had snapped his fingers. "Of course," he said. "How obvious, when you think of it. Perkins was hanged. To hang him, somebody had to make a noose. Somebody made a noose expertly, or at least as if he had had training in tying knots. Now let's see—a bowline would be simplest, wouldn't it, Lieutenant? Somebody tied a bowline in the leash and hanged Perkins. And I was in the Navy."

He smiled up at the lieutenant and seemed pleased.

"But really, Lieutenant," he said. "How—how obvious. I was in the Navy and presumably learned something about knots when I was training; presumably learned how to tie a bowline. And so when a bowline shows up, I'm your man. Is detecting always so easy?"

He seemed honestly amused, and a little, politely, jeering.

"No," Weigand told him. "Only the easy things are easy, Mr. Craig. Like, for example—why did you let me infer that you had been only a yeoman—a clerk—and never learned anything about knots? The easy answer is: You thought the bowline would give you away and that you could get away by implying that you didn't know anything about knots. You thought the bowline would give you away *because you knew a bowline had been used.* You knew that, since nobody had told you, because you had tied it. See how simple detecting is, Mr. Craig?"

Weigand's voice was placid, as of a professor expounding an academic theory. Craig made steeples with his fingers and nodded over them.

"Precisely," he said. "And the alternative is equally simple. I did not tie the bowline and knew nothing about it. Your question meant nothing to me when you asked it, and I answered what first came into my mind. I said, yes, I had been in the Navy. I added—in order not to appear heroic—that I had been a yeoman. It didn't occur to me that you would try to make anything of it. If it had I would, assuming you would investigate, have been more detailed in my answer. Right? As you would say?"

Weigand nodded, pleasantly. He agreed that this version was equally probable. He smiled down at Craig, and seemed to appreciate him, and Craig looked at his fingers and appreciated himself.

"Now," Weigand said, "about the bottle—this bottle."

He took the little green bottle from his pocket and held it out, cupped in his hand. Craig glanced at it, and the glance seemed to be enough. His face sobered and he nodded slowly and his hands went out to grasp the arms of the chair. He did not shift his body, but after a moment he looked up at the lieutenant.

"So you found it," he said. "I expected you would. And so now— now you know. Or—" Then his face lightened up, as if he had suddenly thought of a pleasant possibility.

"Is the arsenic in it, Lieutenant?" he said. His voice was anxious. He read the answer, it seemed, before it was spoken, and his face fell.

"Yes," Weigand said. "There's arsenic in it, Craig."

Craig's body seemed to slump and his voice, when he spoke, was tired and hopeless.

"Then I poisoned her," he said. "I poisoned mother. I kept hoping—"

Mullins started up and came over to Craig.

"You admit it?" Mullins said. His voice was rough, but it held surprise. "So you tried to kill her?"

Mullins stood over Craig and stared down at him. Then he looked to Weigand, and his expression was one of triumph, but still tinged with puzzlement. He looked to Weigand for instructions. Weigand looked down at Craig and his expression was one of interest. He intercepted Mullins's enquiry and moved his head slightly, directing Mullins back to his chair.

"Are you confessing, Craig?" he asked. His voice was unexpectedly gentle and—wary. Mullins could hear the wariness in the lieutenant's tone.

"Yes," Craig said. "You can call it that. I gave her the poison."

"Why?" Weigand said. The question seemed not to pierce Craig's preoccupation. "Why?" Weigand repeated.

"What?" Craig asked. His mind seemed a long way off. Then it came back. "'Why'?" he repeated. Then the implication seemed to make itself felt. He shook his head, almost with animation.

"You've got it wrong," he said. "I didn't plan it—I didn't know I *was* poisoning her. But I gave her the poison. I poured it out of the bottle and mixed the dose and handed it to her. Isn't that enough?"

The question had the sound of an entreaty.

"You mean to say," Weigand asked, "that all you did was to prepare the salts for her? Innocently? Not knowing there was any poison in them?"

"Of course," Craig said. "Somebody else tried to poison her. But they *used* me. My God, man, isn't that enough?"

Weigand looked down at him, and he seemed to be studying him.

"Well," he said, "no. Not in our sense. If you administered poison unintentionally, you've done nothing illegal. And nothing wrong. You don't even have to reproach yourself."

"But my own mother," Craig insisted. He seemed to be seeking blame. "Think of it, Lieutenant! My own mother—and I gave her poison. How would you feel?"

"Unhappy, certainly," Weigand said. "But not—guilty. If it is as you say, you had no way of knowing. If it's as you say."

The repetition arrested Craig's attention, distracting him from his own unhappy thoughts. But he did not seem surprised.

"Naturally," he said. "You don't believe me. I gave the poison. I wouldn't expect you to go back of that. I suppose—fingerprints?"

"Yes," Weigand said. "Your prints are on the bottle, Mr. Craig. We knew you had given the salts—as you might have guessed we would."

"Yes," Craig said. "Of course they would be on it—I handled it. But I didn't fill it. Why should I?"

Weigand shrugged.

"Why try to kill your mother, you mean?" he asked. "Well—for her money, Mr. Craig. To get your share. Perhaps you were in a hurry for it."

Craig did not seem horrified at the suggestion; he seemed to have been expecting it. He nodded.

"Of course," he said. "It's all there—opportunity, motive—everything you need. And I didn't do it. I swear I didn't. Somebody—but what's the use? Everybody says that, I suppose."

Weigand nodded slowly.

"That they were framed," he amplified. "Right—they do, often. Is that your story?"

Craig's shoulders dropped, hopelessly.

"That's what happened," he said. "That's what must have happened. But you won't believe it. Unless—" He broke off, and seemed to be thinking. Thought apparently brought a ray of hope.

"Listen," he said. "Just my fingerprints. Doesn't that prove it? Wouldn't there have been mine—and somebody else's? If I'd known what was in the bottle, wouldn't I have rubbed my prints off? If there were any prints, wouldn't there have been a lot?"

Weigand looked down at Craig, curiously. The detective's fingers, reaching out to rest on the table top, began a slow, rhythmic patting of the surface. Finally he nodded.

"You have a point there, Craig," he said. "I wondered if you'd think of it. You suggest that the real poisoner—the one who put the arsenic in the bottle—wiped off his own prints, and any others which might have been there, and left the bottle clean for your prints?"

"Yes," Craig said. He sounded eager, now. "He did that—before he sent it to me. And then nobody touched it but me. That's what happened, Lieutenant." He searched the lieutenant's face, and his own fell. "But you don't believe me," he said. "I knew you wouldn't. I hoped the bottle would never be found. Then I could have lied and—fooled him. Because mother didn't remember!"

Weigand was interested. What didn't she remember?

She didn't, Craig explained, remember who had prepared the dose of salts that morning. To be sure of that, Craig had tried to help her remember—or pretended to—meanwhile denying by implication that he had prepared the dose himself. He was convinced that she now would never remember. But, meanwhile, the bottle had disappeared. Craig was terrified by this. Convinced that the bottle with his prints upon it would point straight to him as the poisoner, that his previous silence would count against him, that the police would never believe his story of a frame-up—he had searched desperately for the bottle for days. He had begun to hope that it had been thrown away, and that he was wrong in thinking the real murderer had taken it, to be used against him if it became necessary. And now—here it was.

"Who gave it to you?" he demanded. "The man who gave it to you planned to kill mother. And to make you believe I had done it. Who gave it to you?"

Weigand shook his head. It wasn't, he said, as simple as that. Assuming Craig was telling the truth, it wasn't that simple.

"We found the bottle," he said. "Nobody gave it to us. But—I may as well tell you this—we think that Perkins had it for a while. Probably until shortly before he was killed."

Craig seemed utterly astonished. His eyes opened and his hands again parted company and sought the security of the chair's arms.

"Perkins?" he repeated. "*Perkins?* But that can't be. It—it doesn't fit."

"Why?" Weigand wanted to know.

Craig seemed to be fighting a point out in his mind. His fingers formed a bridge over nothing and he studied them, as if for guidance. Then he made a decision and looked at Weigand for a moment and seemed to stiffen.

"All right," he said. "I don't know why I should protect him. Wesley. Wesley sent me the bottle. So it must have been Wesley. For the money." The idea seemed to grow upon him, as he expressed it. "That's it!" Craig said. His voice was stronger, more confident. "He wanted to kill mother and get his share of the money. He wanted me convicted, and then he would have got his share of the part *I* inherited. Two birds with one stone. That's it, Lieutenant. And then I suppose Anthony found out about it and he killed Anthony, and Perkins knew something and he got Perkins, too. And now, *now he'll have another try at mother!*"

Craig sounded excited, almost triumphant.

"*That's it!*" He repeated. "After this is all over, he'll try again. And now—now he'll have to get me, too, because I know. You'll have to stop him, Lieutenant!"

Weigand looked down at the round, excited man, whose fingers now were lacing and unlacing convulsively. Weigand looked across at Mullins, who was nodding slowly in agreement.

"We'll be careful," Weigand promised. "There'll be no more murders. You say he sent you the bottle?"

Craig did say so. Often, he said, Dr. Wesley Buddie sent him sample bottles of remedies, some for his own use and some to be passed on to Mrs. Buddie. The little green bottle of Folwell's Fruit Salts had been sent so, along with a sample of a new brand of nose drops. The salts were, the accompanying note said, for their mother. When he went to his mother's room that morning to visit her, as he did every morning, Ben had taken the bottle with him and prepared a dose from it. He had said nothing about the change, wanting to see whether his mother would notice the difference, or find the new compound more effica-cious than that she had been taking. She had apparently noticed no dif-ference. Naturally, since she had shortly developed symptoms of poi-soning, there had never been any question of the efficacy. Craig had left the bottle on the bed table; later, when he began to suspect that he had been used as an instrument of attempted murder, he had tried to find it and failed. It had disappeared.

"That's how it was," Craig insisted. "Of course, he'll deny it."

"Naturally," Weigand agreed. "You say it came by mail?"

The bottle had come by mail, in a corrugated mailing box. Craig had, after the lapse of time—he had thrown the wrappings away when he opened the package—some difficulty in remembering the details, Weigand thought. He believed the package was addressed on the type-writer; he was certain that it had Dr. Buddie's return address typed in the corner. The note—folded and tucked into the package—had also been typed. It was, however, initialed—"W.B." Craig had seen no rea-son to doubt that the initials had actually been written by his half-brother, although he admitted he had not examined them closely. They might, he agreed, have been forged—he had only glanced at the note, observed the initials, thrown the paper away with the box wrappings. Personally, he insisted, he had no doubt then, or now, that Dr. Buddie had actually sent the medicine. He agreed that his evidence might not be conclusive in court, if it came to proving that the note had not been forged.

"I've only a moral certainty," he admitted.

"Why didn't you bring this story to us at once?" Weigand wanted to know. Craig looked sorrowful and embarrassed; he agreed that he should have done so. But he had not wanted to accuse his half-brother, particularly since he had no evidence, not even the bottle. He had been afraid that his story would not be believed and that he would himself be arrested.

"After all," he said. "I did administer the poison. You would have had only my word; even now you have only my word, and an argument. Even now, I can't be sure you believe me."

"It's a reasonable explanation," Weigand said. "I don't know that I blame you for holding off. It has made things harder for us, of course. But I see your point."

"Then you believe me?" Craig asked. There was hope in his voice again.

Weigand lifted his shoulders.

"Part of it is theory," he reminded Craig. "You don't 'believe' in theory. But you've made a very interesting case, Mr. Craig. Very interesting."

"Then," Craig said, and hesitated. "Is there anything else? Or are you through with me?"

"For now, at any rate," Weigand said. "You can go, Mr. Craig."

Weigand and Mullins watched Craig go. Mullins turned and looked at Weigand, enquiringly.

"*Do* you believe him, Loot?" Mullins wanted to know. "It sounds O.K."

Weigand smiled.

"I don't think he tried to poison his mother," Weigand said. "I never did think so. I think he was framed, as he says."

· 14 ·

THURSDAY
11:35 A.M. TO 12:08 P.M.

Sergeant Mullins waited for Bill Weigand to continue, but Weigand did not continue. He had returned to a chair, and the fingers of his right hand beat a gentle tattoo on the chair arm. Mullins waited and as the minutes passed he became restless.

"Now what, Loot?" he enquired, and was startled at the sound of his own voice. Weigand returned from a distance and looked at him, at first without seeming to see him. Then Weigand saw Mullins, without favor.

"Now," he said, "we think. Or I think."

Mullins looked doubtful.

"No more questions?" he said. "We don't ask anybody about things?"

"Who?" Weigand said. "About what?"

Mullins thought it over.

"I dunno, Loot," he said, at length. "You think we know everything?"

Weigand drummed on the chair arm for a moment before he answered. Then he nodded.

"We ought to," he said. "We know a lot. And can guess a lot. And where are we?"

172

Mullins thought it over.

"I think Craig," he said. "He says he's framed. Guys that say they're framed—" The sentence ended because it did not need to continue.

"Nevertheless," Weigand said, "people have been framed. For what it is worth—I think Craig was framed. Don't you? On the merits, regardless of precedent."

"You mean paying no attention to guys being lying when they say they're framed?" Mullins enquired. "Just the way the story sounds?" He waited and Weigand answered "yes," without saying it.

"Yeh," Mullins said, "his story sounds all right. So it's the doc."

"What's the doc?" Pam North said from the door. She was holding Ruffy. Jerry was behind her and he was wearing a fur piece around his neck. The fur piece was Toughy, with bright eyes that looked like buttons and a tail which twisted up in a question mark.

"The guy who did it," Mullins said. "Only he got Craig to do it for him. What do you think, Mrs. North?"

"The cats got tired up there," Pam said. "All by themselves so much, and nothing new to smell. Did he?" This last was to Weigand. Weigand looked at her and then at Jerry. To the latter he said, "Close the door, will you?" Jerry closed the door.

"Council?" Mrs. North said. She seemed pleased. "Is this when we count the votes? Did he? I want to know before I vote."

"Did your cousin Wesley put arsenic into the bottle so your cousin Ben would put it into your Aunt Flora?" Weigand amplified. "That's what Ben says. Or he says that's what he thinks."

Jerry leaned over and Toughy dropped off on a table. He found a small vase, built like a baseball on a stem and filled with short-stemmed tulips. He batted the nearest tulip and then decided to eat the leaves. He made a crunching sound.

"Give," Jerry said. "Sit down, Pam."

Weigand gave. He gave in summary, but here and there he left in a detail. The Norths listened, Pam scratching Ruffy's ears. Ruffy began to purr and, apparently out of sheer good will, Toughy joined her. The room vibrated slightly and Mullins looked interested.

"They're awful little to make so much noise, ain't they?" he enquired, pleased. "Makes me think of the old 'L'—if you was on the other side of town, that is."

"Please," Pam said. "But it is funny. They do it inside, somehow. And sometimes when you can't hear it, you can feel it. They just sit still and vibrate."

"Meanwhile," Jerry said, "we sit still and vibrate. Don't we, Bill? Do you know?"

Weigand did not answer directly.

"He does," Pam informed them all. She looked at Weigand without favor. "It seems to me," she said, "that you just call us in to *tell* us, like Watson."

"Sherlock," Weigand said.

"I was thinking of us," Pam told him. "*We're* like Watson. You're self-centered, Bill. Only you don't seem terribly sure, somehow."

Weigand looked at her and smiled faintly.

"Elementary, my dear Watson," he said. "I'm not very sure. And I can't prove it."

Pamela North lifted Ruffy to the table with her brother, who decided he would rather bat her than the tulip. Ruffy ignored him and began to smell the tulips, one by one. They seemed to please her.

"Well," Pam said. "Where are we? Or don't we know? As to motives and things, and alibis."

"There aren't any alibis," Weigand told her. "No real alibis. That makes a nice start. No clocks, no where-was-who-when. Which ought to make it simpler." He stared abstractedly at the cats. "And which doesn't," he added. They waited. He continued abstracted.

"I think," Pam said, "it was somebody from outside—I mean from outside the house. Probably somebody inside the family from outside the house. Because the door wasn't locked."

Weigand returned to her, regarded her theory—which he seemed to find hanging in the air between them—and said, "Oh, when Jerry came, you mean?" Pam nodded.

"Somebody came in from outside to kill poor Harry," she said. "And so the door had to be unlocked." She thought it over. "I don't get that," she said, frankly. "What am I talking about?"

"The door was unlocked when Jerry came last night," Bill Weigand reminded her. "Somebody had tripped the catch, so it didn't lock when the door closed. Therefore, somebody came in, either with the aid of somebody or because he had tripped the lock himself when he went out earlier. Which does indicate that he had no key. But—"

"I've been thinking about that," Jerry cut in. "It doesn't have to be last night. It could be left over from the night before. And so it could have been tripped to let Anthony in, so he could be killed."

Weigand nodded and said, "Precisely." Pam looked doubtful.

"Somebody would have noticed," she objected. The three men shook their heads at her, in unison.

"No, baby," Jerry told her. "Not necessarily—not unless somebody tried it from outside, on the assumption it might be unlocked. Anybody who assumed it was locked would merely use a key, which would let him in just as well as if it were locked."

Pam looked at them and, after a moment, said: "All right."

"Then," she said, "it was somebody inside the family *inside* the house. Which could be anybody." She paused. "Except me," she added. "And Jerry, because he was in Kansas City. When I thought the telephone company had been so bright. Which is just as well, because we had motives, too."

Jerry looked at her and shook his head.

"If you mean your inheritance," he told her, "the answer is no. Because that applies only to Aunt Flora, and we weren't here then. It didn't make any difference to us if Stephen Anthony lived." He looked at Weigand. "What *is* the sequence?" he asked. "Or isn't there any?"

That, Weigand admitted, was the question.

"Suppose," he said, "we lay it out and look at it, starting with Aunt Flora. See what we know."

"All right," Pam said. She reached to the table, just as Roughy was about to push the ball-shaped vase over the edge. She removed Roughy to her lap and replaced the vase. "Where are we?"

This, Weigand told them, was what they knew:

Mrs. Flora Buddie, who had shortly before ejected her fourth husband, Stephen Anthony, had been given a small dose of arsenic in a digestive powder about two weeks previously. She suspected poison, although her physician was willing to diagnose merely a violent digestive upset. Her suspicions had been proved correct. The poison apparently was administered in something she ate or drank that morning, and since no analysis was made of unconsumed food or drink, it might have been in anything. The finding of the bottle, however, had proved that the dose, too small to cause more than acute discomfort, had been given in Folwell's Fruit Salts.

Mrs. Buddie apparently did not remember who had given her the salts. Weigand paused and looked at Pam. "Wouldn't she?" he asked. "You know her?"

Pam thought it over.

"Maybe not," she said. "She expects things just to—appear. As long as they do, she doesn't bother. Only sometimes she does. It might be either way, but she might forget."

"Right," Weigand said. "We'll assume for the moment she did forget, particularly since at that time she didn't know where the poison came from. She didn't have anything to focus on, I mean—maybe she thought it was the orange juice, or the coffee. Anyway, we'll assume she didn't. And the bottle disappeared."

To group the things they knew by the events to which they related, instead of chronologically, they knew that the salts containing the poison had been administered by Craig. The bottle bore only his fingerprints, a fact which he insisted showed that he had been framed. He told a story, which could neither be proved nor disproved, that he had received the bottle through the mail and that it purported to come from his half-brother, Wesley Buddie. This Dr. Buddie denied. Either might be lying; both might be lying or each might be telling the truth as he saw it. Because it was always possible that some third person had sent the bottle to Craig, making it appear—with the aid of a little easy forgery—that Dr. Buddie had sent it. All they knew about this was what they had been told; the stories diverged but were susceptible to reconciliation.

The bottle had disappeared, without anyone, except Ben, noticing its absence. Mrs. Buddie had kept her own counsel for almost two weeks, but she had invited Pam North, apparently planning to use her as an amateur detective. On the night of Pam's arrival, she had told the other members of the family of the attempt to poison her.

On that same night, her estranged husband had been shot and killed in the breakfast room.

The following night, Harry Perkins, who had been hiding out—with the help of Sand—had come to Pam's bedroom door, given her a package—"which you promptly lost," Bill Weigand interjected, disapprovingly—and promised to give information. He had been hanged before he gave it. Later Pam's room had been searched; still later, with the help of the cats, the bottle had been found. Presumably, it was the package which Perkins had given to Pam.

"And which I lost," Pam said. "Don't forget that—Lieutenant. Also, I heard a sort of bump—like a door slamming—the first night I was here. And didn't know what time it was."

"Also," Jerry said, "you hit me on the head with a vase. Because you thought I was the murderer."

"You two," Pam said, "sometimes make me so *mad!* I could—I could—." She looked down at Toughy, still in her lap. "They pick on me, darling," she said. "Scratch them!" Toughy looked up at her with languishing eyes and resumed his purring, which he had absent-mindedly interrupted.

"And hit you with a vase," Bill Weigand repeated, very gravely. "We also know that the murderer can tie a bowline; that he had an opportunity to take and secrete Nemo's leash; that he still has the gun he used to kill Anthony; that he does not repeat his method, which is an old wives' tale anyway; that he fired up at Anthony, who presumably was standing over him and that—although this is merely a deduction— he killed Harry Perkins because Perkins knew who he was and was going to tell. We don't know how Perkins knew."

They digested that. Mullins shook his head.

"Me," he said, "I don't get it. Any of it. I think we ought to ask some more questions. We don't even know why."

"Why what, sergeant?" Pam enquired.

"Why anything," Mullins said, succinctly.

Weigand shook his head. He said that, on the other hand, they knew too many "whys." They knew "whys" for practically everybody.

"Assuming the most probable," he said, "we assume that somebody did try to kill your aunt, Pam, and failed because they knew too little about arsenic. Then the motive for any member of the family is the commonest motive in the world—money. Your aunt has it; her potential murderer inherits from her; her potential murderer wants the money now. So he kills Mrs. Buddie. So—Now for Anthony, there are two possibilities: Either his murder had a connection with the attempt on your aunt, Pam, or it didn't. If it did, probably he was killed because he knew who had given your aunt arsenic. Because, even though the attempt failed, the fact that it had been made would—well, enrage Mrs. Buddie."

"Make her mad as hops," Pam agreed. "It would me."

"Right," Weigand said. "Which presumably would mean, at the least, that the person who had poisoned her could expect to get no money from her, now or in the future. It might mean that he would be arrested for attempted murder, to boot. But with Anthony out of the way, there was nothing to stop him—or her—from making another attempt on Mrs. Buddie."

"Try, try again," Pam agreed.

"On the other hand," Weigand went on, "Anthony was a candidate for murder on his own account. He was a blackmailer—he was blackmailing the major, almost certainly. He may have been blackmailing Clem or her sister, Judy. Bruce McClelland—by the way, which one of the girls *is* he after? He said Clem but—"

"I know," Pam said. "It's been puzzling me, because now he acts as if it were Judy. I think he found out too much about Clem and then met Judy that night and decided she was the one, really. And anyway, finding out—so he really knew—about Clem and Brack would—well, sort of dash him. So now I think it is Judy. Does it matter? I mean to them it does, I guess, but to the murder?"

It depended, Weigand said, on when Bruce McClelland had made the shift, if he had made it. Supposing he was still in love with Clem, or thought he was, at the time of Anthony's murder, he had a motive—

protecting her from a blackmailer. Otherwise, he shared the motive that everybody else had—a desire to silence Anthony before Anthony had a chance to expose him. "Even your aunt has a motive for Anthony," Weigand pointed out, and explained the possibility he had already outlined to himself. Pam and Jerry looked doubtful, but Jerry finally nodded.

"She might, at that," he said. "She's quite an old girl."

Pamela was silent. She was stroking the cat abstractedly and staring off into space.

"As for Perkins, to round it off," Weigand said, "the motive is obvious. He knew who had attempted one murder or accomplished the other, or who had done both."

"How did he know?" Pam asked. She was still staring across the room, seeking advice, it seemed, from the panels of the closed door.

"Oh," Jerry said. "Saw or heard something suspicious. Perhaps he was around somewhere when—"

"Not *Perkins*," Pam said. "It doesn't matter about that. That wasn't what I was wondering about. I knew something was wrong and it kept going around in my head and that's it. How did he *know?* Because nobody had told him, and he couldn't *see.*"

They all looked at her, now. She turned toward Jerry.

"The fingerprints," she said. "He couldn't have just seen how many there were because Bill says he only glanced at it. And nobody had told him. And yet he knew. But if it was the way he said, he couldn't know they were the *only* ones. Because you can't see them until they're developed, can you, Bill?"

She turned to Bill.

"Not usually," he said. "Not on the bottle, Pam."

"Then he must have known somehow before," Pam said, "and that means—*Jerry! You didn't really close the door!*"

"But I did, Pam," Jerry said, and then, with the others, he half turned to stare at the door. It was not entirely closed, and now it was opening wider.

There was a frozen moment while they stared. And then Benjamin Craig stood in the door. He still looked unaccountably placid, but now he had a gun in his hand. It was pointed at the two detectives and the Norths, and it was moving slowly from side to side. It occurred to Pam North, rather horrifyingly, that Benjamin Craig looked like a suburban gardener with a hose, abstractedly spraying water on the lawn. And she felt—and this was more horrifying still—that Benjamin Craig would, if it suited him, spray bullets from the automatic in his hand as casually as the gardener he so grotesquely represented would spray water from a hose.

Craig spoke, and his voice was unhurried and almost friendly—and the friendliness of the voice was most horrible of all. He nodded at Pam, and then the gun, pointing at her, hesitated in its regular movement.

"I made a mistake, Cousin Pamela," Benjamin Craig admitted. "I shouldn't have known about the fingerprints. You are quite right about that, cousin; sometimes you are really rather bright. He told me that before I shot him—just before. It was the last thing he said, as I remember. He said: 'Now yours are the only prints—' and I shot him before he finished."

He broke off and looked down at the gun.

"This goes off so easily," he said, pleasantly. "So very easily. You hardly realize that you have pulled the trigger. Because really it was an argument for not shooting him, wasn't it? But the gun had gone off before I thought of that." He let the gun move on, covering Jerry North, covering Mullins, covering Bill Weigand. "Not that it matters," he said. "Probably I would have shot him anyway."

It was unreal; it was, to Pam, like something seen on the stage, beyond the footlights; something safe and far away, on the little lighted platform of illusion. Ben Craig spoke the words as if someone else had written them for him to say; you felt that the automatic must hold blanks; that if Ben Craig pulled the trigger it would make a loud, harmless noise; that if one of them pretended to be hit and to die, he would afterward get up and walk away and go back to a dressing room and take makeup off with cold-cream and tissue. But Stephen Anthony had not got up and walked away.

"If only because he made me poison mother," Craig said. "I think I

would have shot him for that, finally. I—" He broke off, and after a
moment began again.

"But now I must get away, of course," he said. "I must bother you to
arrange that, Lieutenant. Because your men are very stubborn. They
say I can't go for a walk without your permission, Lieutenant. And of
course I must go for a walk." He smiled at them. "A long walk," he
said. "I came up to arrange it with you, really. I brought this along—in
case." He moved the gun up and down to indicate the identity of "this."
"It makes it a little awkward, so many of you," he admitted. "I had not
planned on that—or on Cousin Pamela's brightness." He looked at
Pamela closely. "I really hadn't realized, cousin," he said. "I really
hadn't."

Weigand spoke for the first time.

"It wouldn't have mattered," he said. "We knew anyway. You can't
get away with it."

Craig nodded. He seemed to take the remark as a reasonable statement in a debate.

"I can try," he said. "I can take you all with me—make it a little
party. You can tell your men downstairs that it's quite all right, Lieutenant—that we're all going for a little walk." He smiled at them and
waggled the automatic. "Think how easily it goes off, Lieutenant," he
said. "Starting with Cousin Pamela, for example. And—" Suddenly the
gun moved stiffly and held.

"*No!*" Craig said. His voice was no longer friendly. "I wouldn't try
it, Sergeant. There wouldn't be time!"

The others did not look at Mullins. They felt, rather than saw, the
small movement of a hand which had been creeping toward a shoulder
holster, and now dropped back again. They could see Mullins's movement of defeat reflected in Craig's face, even before he spoke.

"I'll want your guns, of course," he said. "My cousin will get them
for me, won't you, Pamela? The sergeant's? The lieutenant's? To
avoid—disturbance?"

"No," said Pam. "I won't, Ben. You can't get away with it."

"Get them!" Ben commanded. His voice had changed now. He was
out of character, now; he was speaking his own words—speaking them

in a voice no longer soft and friendly. The gun fixed on Pam and then Bill Weigand spoke.

"Get them, Pam," he said. "He'll shoot."

There was an instant, then, when Ben Craig's eyes flickered toward Weigand, following the voice—a moment when the gun was no longer rigid; when for an instant intent was broken. And it was then that Pam, who had half risen at Bill Weigand's words and put her hand out toward the table, felt her fingers touch the smoothness of the vase which was shaped like a baseball and was cool to the touch and held nodding tulips.

Craig's eyes had come back toward her and intent was hardening in them, when Pam threw the vase. She picked it up and threw it in one movement and tulips and water showered from it. And, his body moved by nerves older and wiser than the mind, Ben Craig ducked.

The vase hit the door frame and shattered two feet from Ben Craig's head. Shards flew out from it harmlessly. They were clattering on the floor when the room filled with sound and Weigand's gun was jumping in his hand. Ben Craig's gun jumped too, but it was pointed at the floor. It jumped again, with a roar, as Ben fell—rather slowly—among the fragments of the broken vase. One hand came down on a yellow tulip, crushing it against the floor.

Weigand was over him, then. And Weigand's right foot shot out, kicking the automatic out of Craig's right hand. It clattered across the floor and stopped silently on the rug. Weigand stood over the man on the floor and stared down at him. Craig stared back, and his eyes were filled with wonderment and question.

"Your legs," Weigand told him, knowing that as yet the pain had not started, that Craig didn't know. "But you weren't going anywhere, Craig."

Lieutenant Weigand's voice was hard and uninflected.

Craig looked down at the blood on his legs.

"No," he said. "No. Not anywhere."

Mullins was standing beside Weigand, now, and staring down at Craig.

"And this is the guy that was framed," he said. His tone was mocking, harsh. "So you was framed, fella!"

Bill Weigand looked at Mullins then, and there was an odd smile on his lips.

"Yes, sergeant," Weigand said. "This is the guy who was framed. Sure enough framed, sergeant—framed right into murder. Weren't you, Craig?"

The pain had begun, now. Craig's lips were moving, and the words that came out of them were words you would not have thought a middle-aged banker of peculiarly sedentary habit would have ever heard. Most of them were directed toward Pamela North, who listened with interest.

"You can tell he's been in the Navy," Pam said. Her words were casual, but her voice shook a little. Then she turned to Jerry.

"You see," she said. "The idea was right all the time. The vase, I mean. I just had to get the direction—oh, Jerry!"

And suddenly Pam was in Jerry North's arms, hiding her head against his shoulder. He patted her on the back and said, "All right, baby. There, baby." He looked down at the top of her head, reflectively. "It's all right, Pam," he told her. "Only if you were going to miss some-one—" He appeared to ponder it. Then he nodded. "It was a fine idea, Pam," he said. "There's nothing like a vase."

Abstractedly, in a familiar gesture, he ran his free hand through his hair. The bump was still there, but it seemed to be receding.

· 15 ·

Thursday
5:15 P.M. TO 6:35 P.M.

"Up to then," Pam said, "I thought it was the major, although it was hard to see him poisoning Aunt Flora. But then I thought—how does Ben know that there weren't any prints on the bottle but his? He couldn't know unless he wiped it off himself, and if he did that why would he leave his own prints on? Except that he'd know if somebody told him—and that meant somebody had told him between the time the bottle disappeared and the time the kitties found it. And so somebody must have been threatening him, because whoever it was didn't come to the police, and that sounded more like Anthony than anybody, because Anthony was a blackmailer anyway. And so it had to be Ben."

Pam paused, fished the olive from the bottom of her glass, and nibbled briskly around it. She pushed her empty glass across the bar to Adam, who beamed on her and took it away.

"We've had a hard day, Jerry," Pam told him, when he looked at her doubtfully. "Solving murders and everything. Two will be all right." She watched Adam stirring a new martini. "Or three," she added hopefully.

"As far as I'm concerned," Jerry said. "It isn't solved. Not very, anyway. All I know is who." He finished his own drink and pushed the glass across the bar. Adam welcomed it. "Of course," Jerry added, "I came in late. Probably that's it. But I can't say I get it."

"It was complicated," a new voice said. Bill Weigand, who looked extremely tired, but with a relaxed tiredness, had taken the bar stool next Pam North's. "Chiefly because the people were complicated. Particularly Anthony. A devious man, Anthony."

"The death of a devious man," another new voice said. This came from beside Jerry, who turned and smiled and said, "Hello, Dorian." Dorian Weigand said, "Hello, you" and then, to Pam, "Is it your fault I get left out of things?"

Weigand smiled across the Norths at her and shook his head gently.

"My fault, Dorrie," he said. "I can't have you being shot at. You're too new."

Pam sounded indignant.

"And for me it's all right," she said. "What am I? Second-hand?"

That, Bill told her, was Jerry's problem. Jerry frowned at him.

"I was in Houston," he said. "Reading another 'Gone With the Wind.' And she was visiting a nice, elderly aunt. And we look to the police for protection. And you are police."

Adam set martinis in a row along the edge of the bar. The glasses were too full to lift. The four bent in unison and sipped from the standing glasses. They sighed in approval.

"Good," Pam said. Then she turned to Weigand. "Well," she said. "Do we have to read it in the paper? After saving your life, probably?"

Weigand lifted his glass and sipped again. He said, all right, what did they want to know?

"Everything," Jerry told him, and Dorian, beyond him, said "Right." Weigand nodded. But it was not, he pointed out, a story to shout along a bar. Reluctantly, they moved to Charles's cocktail corner, taking their drinks with them.

"First," Pam said, "about Ben." Excitement went out of her voice, suddenly. She sounded a little frightened. "Will he live?"

"Live?" Weigand repeated, apparently honestly surprised. "Why yes he'll live—for a while. And he won't die from bullets in his legs." He looked at Pamela North and understood. "You needn't worry, Pam," he said. "You haven't a hand in it. Not that sort of hand. If he dies, it won't be your responsibility—not because of the vase, anyway." He smiled at her. "Or because of anything, actually," he added. "I don't mean the point about the fingerprints wasn't important, or that I hadn't missed it. For the moment. But that part of it was never too difficult. I always thought it was Ben."

It was, Pam told him, easy to say that. And, how, for example, had he come always to think it was Ben?

Weigand was not discomfited.

"Because he didn't like to stand up," he told them. "Even when he was startled, he kept on sitting down. Even when he was frightened, or angry. And everybody else in the family jumps up. Except the major, who never seems to sit down. And the person who killed Anthony was a sitter." He broke off. "The difficulty there was that it might almost as well be your aunt," he added. "Because she *couldn't* get up very fast. But it wasn't in character that she'd kill Perkins. She wouldn't need to. That left Ben—and no evidence."

Jerry said that, so far as he could see, there had never been much. Weigand nodded, seriously. That had always been the point, he said. Not who so much as how and why, and how did they prove it. You had to guess at how and why.

"Deduce," Dorian corrected. "Work it out, like a problem. Beginning chiefly with character."

Weigand smiled at her and said that he would, if she preferred, call it deduction. Now, however, Ben had saved them from further speculation. Because, in a hospital prison ward, Ben had decided to make things easy. Ben had, half an hour before, finished telling everything. It was, Weigand thought, a rather odd story, and it began with Anthony.

"The devious man," Pam said. "The blackmailer. It would—He—he was made to be the center of plots."

Weigand looked a little surprised, and nodded approvingly. Pam's remark was, he told her, more apropos than she could imagine. He looked at her again.

"Or is it?" he said. He had learned not to put arbitrary limits on the things Pamela North could imagine. Pam now merely smiled at him. Then she said that, anyway, he could tell the others. All she had was a notion.

Weigand left it for the future.

"Right," he said. He would summarize it. It began, as Pam thought, with Stephen Anthony and his deviousness: his restless search for fresh "angles" and his need of them after Aunt Flora had dismissed him, and he was on his own. The simplest angle—and here they really had to guess, knowing approximately as much as Ben Craig—was that offered by Clem's letters and the opportunity they gave to blackmail Major Buddie and, potentially at any rate, Clem herself and through her others. How far that had gone was, however, unimportant; the letters themselves were unimportant, except for what they proved about Anthony's method of making a living. What turned his method of making a living into a method of dying was, except for his character, entirely separate.

Anthony had been greedy; whatever he might have got through the letters wasn't enough. He looked around for new victims and decided on Craig, who was in a vulnerable position as a banker, since his repute and his profession were tied together. The only difficulty was that he had nothing on Craig. He decided to remedy that and he had to be given credit for the notion; his course might not be unexampled in the art of blackmail, but it was certainly uncommon. Anthony decided to provide by his own efforts the grounds on which he could subsequently extort the money to repay himself for his trouble.

He knew, of course, what it was necessary to know—that Aunt Flora took medicines freely for her partly imagined ill health; that Dr. Wesley Buddie occasionally sent sample products both to her and to Craig. He took advantage of these facts. He steamed a crescent label reading: "Professional Sample" from one of the bottles in his wife's collection. He bought a small bottle of Folwell's Fruit Salts. He got arsenic and added a little—*but not enough to kill.* He avoided as unnecessary the faintest risk of murder. He wrapped this bottle, forged a note with Dr. Buddie's initials, and sent it along to Craig. He waited to see what would happen.

What happened was what he hoped would happen: Craig took the bottle to his mother's room, mixed a dose from it and gave it to her. She became ill.

"Then," Weigand said, "Anthony went to see her and abstracted the bottle. He handled it carefully by the cork. And now you see what he had—he had a case of attempted murder on the part of Ben Craig."

Pam started to say something, and Weigand interrupted.

"Right," he said. "It wasn't a perfect case. But it was good enough to put Craig on trial, if not to convict him. It was good enough to convince Craig's mother that he had tried to poison her, even if it did not convince a jury. Craig stood to lose his reputation, if nothing else, from legal action. He stood to lose his inheritance, if his mother believed what the evidence showed. Either way, he was in a spot—and he had a pretty flimsy story."

Craig had found this out some days later when Stephen Anthony called him up. Anthony had been careful on the telephone, but he had been clear enough, too. He said he had a little bottle and that he had had a little of the contents analyzed and that they contained arsenic. He said he had reason to believe that Craig might be interested in the bottle and would like to talk to him about it. He said it looked to him as if there were fingerprints on it.

"But how," Jerry wanted to know, "could Anthony have known that they were *Craig's* fingerprints, unless he had them brought up, and knew enough to compare. And he hadn't had them brought up."

Weigand nodded. Anthony couldn't have known. But he knew that Craig had got the bottle and had handled it, and so that his prints would almost certainly be on it. *And Craig knew the same thing.* He had been wondering about the bottle and trying to find it, because he had begun to suspect the trick played on him. Anthony might only suspect that Craig had handled the bottle and left prints on it. Craig *knew* he had. So he had to agree to see Anthony, and he fixed a time when everybody in the house might be expected to be in bed and left the door unlocked. And he also, which was something Anthony hadn't counted on, got out his automatic.

"For which, incidentally, he had a permit," Weigand said. "On the chance it might be useful in the bank."

Anthony appeared and Craig led him to the breakfast room, saying they wouldn't be interrupted there. And then an odd thing happened, because Anthony had been thinking, too, about fingerprints and had realized that, for all he knew, there might be so many other prints beside Craig's that the evidence would be valueless. And so, before going to meet Craig, Anthony wiped off all the prints, being careful to handle the bottle by the projecting cork, so that his own prints would not get on the glass. He was being very devious, as became him.

Craig pretended, at first, that he didn't know what Anthony meant by the bottle, or by the suggestions he made or the hints—to start with—that money would take care of things. So Anthony, who had planned it very much that way, took the bottle out and handed it to Craig. And Craig took it and looked at it and handed it back, still pretending innocence—and still sitting comfortably in his chair. Anthony was standing up, and smiling and very sure of himself. He took the bottle by the cork and then he said:

"It's no use, Craig. You got the bottle in the mail—sure. But you can't prove it. You gave the poison to your mother—sure you didn't know it was poison. But you can't prove it. All that anybody can prove is what I can prove—that you gave your mother poison out of this bottle. Because, Craig, it's got your fingerprints on it—you just put them there. I cleaned the bottle up just before I handed it to you. Now yours are the only prints—"

He was leaning close to Craig, holding the bottle, gloating over his own cleverness, probably getting ready to fix a price on the bottle which linked Craig with attempted murder. But he had said all he was ever going to say.

"Because," Weigand said, "he had underestimated Craig. Craig hadn't much money—and he hadn't much respect for life. He was in danger of being charged with attempted murder, on evidence which seemed pretty convincing. And—"

"And I think," Pam said, her voice coming from thoughts a long way off, "that Ben must have hated Anthony anyway and—oh, been glad to kill him. Glad for a *reason* to kill him. Because Anthony was what he was and had married Aunt Flora and because that was—oh, humiliating. It made them all ridiculous. Like a practical joke, in a way. And Ben can't bear to be ridiculous. It does something to him."

Weigand nodded and said that, probably, there was something in that; that Ben didn't mind killing Anthony. And, whether that was true or not, Ben was in a spot; framed into a spot. Then—

"Well," Weigand said, "probably he decided he'd as soon be hanged for a sheep as a lamb. If it came to that. So he shot Anthony—maybe enjoying it—as Anthony stood there, gloating. Craig didn't even get up. He shot from where he was, sitting down in the chair."

And then, Craig admitted in his confession, he had forgotten two things. First, that the absence of other prints would be in his favor, rather than against him. He remembered that later, when he made his "confession" to Weigand, and tried to make the most of the point.

"He must have been surprised when he gathered that we had already thought of it," Weigand said. "One other mistake he made was in underestimating the police."

But that was not the mistake Craig had realized, and set down in his final confession. He had forgotten when he fired that Anthony still held the bottle.

"Obviously, I should have seen that I got the bottle before I shot him," Craig had written in his confession. "It was a mistake."

It was a mistake because, when Anthony fell, he dropped the bottle and because, since it was a round bottle, it rolled. And even that might not have been fatal for Craig if, in the silence which followed the shot, he had not heard somebody at the front door, entering the house.

"That was Clem," Weigand reminded them. "She got in in time to smell the cordite smoke, which she didn't recognize."

Alone with the body and with the gun in his hand, Craig couldn't risk being discovered. He put out the light, dodged into the drawing room and hid. He waited for a few minutes after Clem had gone upstairs, wanting to be sure the shot hadn't wakened anyone—it was a thick-walled old house, he had closed the door of the breakfast room behind him, everybody was sleeping on the upper floors. He had guessed the shot wouldn't be heard, but he couldn't be sure; he had to be in a position to appear, as innocently as possible, if the shot had been heard. Probably as if he had just been coming in, since he was fully dressed.

When he decided the coast was clear, he went back. His first thought was to conceal the body, chiefly to gain time. The opportunities for concealment weren't good, but Craig used what there were, propping the body on a chair behind the table, where it was not, at any rate, instantly visible to anybody who might happen to enter the room. He did this without turning on the light; his eyes had grown accustomed to the darkness, which was not complete because windows in the break-fast room let in a little of the light of the city, and he could see to move the body. The less light the better, for his purposes.

But he was just finishing with the body when he heard movement in the pantry which adjoined the breakfast room. And that frightened him—he still couldn't explain himself if he was found; he didn't know who was behind the door. He decided to go up to his room, make himself innocent in pajamas and robe, and then come down and find the bottle. He could do it innocently then—if anybody found him, he had come down for an early morning snack. And apparently, as it was, the person in the pantry had no suspicion of what had hap-pened. Presumably, Craig decided, whoever was there had come down while he was in the drawing room, gone from the hall into the pantry and was probably pouring himself a drink. Craig decided not to investigate.

"Let sleeping dogs lie," Pam said. Weigand agreed.

So Craig did as he planned. He changed to pajamas and robe and came back down openly, went into the pantry—he didn't care then whether it was occupied—found it empty, got himself some crackers and cheese for protective coloring and went back into the breakfast room. Since the body was not in plain sight and—

"But the carpet," Pam said. "It would have—have showed where Anthony fell."

It did, Weigand agreed. It showed the next morning. But it was a dark red carpet and the light was not strong. Even by daylight, Pam herself had not immediately noticed it. And if somebody came and saw the marks, Craig could always help them discover it. So Craig, feeling reasonably safe, turned on the lights, expecting to have little trouble in finding the bottle.

But the bottle was gone! Craig looked everywhere, in growing desperation, but it was gone.

"And then I realized," Craig wrote in his confession, "that I had made another mistake. I should have taken the chance, turned on the lights and looked for the bottle at once. But I don't blame myself for that; I made the best decision I could at the time, and that is all any man can do. The chances were that the bottle wouldn't be found until I found it. In the same circumstances, I would do the same thing again."

That was all very well, Weigand pointed out, but all the same it was a mistake. Because, venturing out of the pantry to which he had gone for a drink, in which he had stayed while he listened to voices on the other side of the door, in which he had cowered when he heard the shot, little Harry Perkins had stepped into the breakfast room, in fascinated fear of what he would find. (This was reconstruction, but it must be very near the truth.) He had found Anthony's body. And he had stepped on the little bottle, perhaps almost fallen and caught himself, certainly picked the bottle up. By the cork, since he heard of fingerprints.

And then, Harry, terrified by the enormity and danger of what he knew, had hidden while he thought it over, decided to tell Pamela North and to give her the bottle—which he wrapped up to protect the prints—and had made the fatal mistake of standing in the hall outside her room while he told her. And then Craig, coming up the steps behind him, and coming only by chance, had overheard—had heard the first whispers and had stopped on the stairs with his head below the hallway, and had heard enough to know who had been in the pantry and to guess that Harry was a danger.

"And that did for Perkins," Weigand said. "Craig had been looking for the person in the pantry, anyway, and had realized he might have to murder again. He had picked up Nemo's leash, idly at first, and then thought of it as a weapon, in case circumstances required a quiet killing. Well, after he had followed Harry Perkins upstairs, circumstances did require a quiet killing."

Weigand stopped and looked at his empty glass. He pulled out the olive and nibbled at it and nobody said anything.

"And that's all of it," he said, after a moment. "Was that the way you thought it was, Pam?"

"Yes," Pamela North said. "Just about. After I thought that Anthony was the logical person to send Ben arsenic, but not enough. Because all it did was look bad—I mean, it wasn't real. It was just—embarrassing. And then I thought of blackmail. And then it was easy. Only I didn't see how we'd ever prove it. And if Craig hadn't confessed, I still don't see."

Weigand nodded and said it would have been hard.

"But we had the outline," he said. "When you have the outline, you know what you need to fill in. And you can get it; you can always find what you want. It's always somewhere."

"That's because New York is such a big city," Pamela North said.

They were still staring at her in a kind of wonder, when the waiter brought the next round of drinks. Bill and Dorian Weigand and Jerry sipped hurriedly, as if they were grasping at reality.

Then Jerry ran a hand through his hair and spoke.

"What gets you," he said, "is that it sounds so damn logical. That's what's frightening about it. Sometimes I—"

But he took a deep drink instead of trying to go on. You could never tell where words might lead.